Independence Day's Search

A Larry Macklin Mystery-Book 20

A. E. Howe

This book is a work of fiction. Names, characters, places and incidents are the product of the author's imagination or are used fictitiously. Any resemblance to actual events, locales, business establishments, persons or animals, living or dead, is entirely coincidental.

CHAPTER ONE

Adams County was sweltering in the humid summer on a Monday at the end of June as I drove toward my dad's house. I was running late for an invitation to lunch, as I'd been sidetracked by a call from one of our deputies. He'd responded to a report of a prowler, but the incident had escalated when the prowler turned out to be a man, under a restraining order after assaulting his wife, who was trying to sneak back into the house to get some of his clothes. As I'd taken the original report and seen the bruises the man had left on his wife, I was more than happy to help the deputy write up the new charges and escort the man to jail.

Finally, I pulled into Dad's driveway and parked behind his marked SUV. I got out of the car without my normal hesitation, knowing I was safe from Mauser, Dad's one-hundred-and-ninety-pound Great Dane. The big black-and-white oaf wouldn't be running merrily down the driveway in the ninety-five-degree heat.

Dad came around from the back of the house and called to me. "Larry, over here!"

"What's this about?" I asked. Dad wasn't normally secretive, but he'd given me no indication of why he'd asked me out to his house in the middle of the day.

"Let's take a walk," he said evasively. "I'll get Mauser. He can use a little exercise." Dad turned toward the kitchen door, where the dog's anvil-sized head was visible through the cottage window.

"Isn't it too hot for him?" I didn't want Mauser distracting us from whatever Dad wanted to talk about. I was already considering any number of worst-case scenarios: Was he sick? Or had he finally decided that my promotion to sergeant had been a huge mistake?

"We'll be in the woods most of the time."

Five minutes later, we were walking toward Dad's barn with a reluctant Mauser moving quickly from shady spot to shady spot.

"What's the big secret?" I asked.

"Not a secret. Not really." Dad pointed toward his property line, which was fifty yards from the other side of his barn. "Marge Moseley wants to sell her property and I'm thinking about buying it."

"Okay…"

I was confused. Dad seldom asked for my opinion on anything. My mind was telling me that it had to be some kind of trick.

He looked over at me.

"I just want your opinion," he said, like it was the most natural thing in the world for him to be seeking advice from me.

"I'm not used to you caring what I think," I responded, my surprise making the words come out more harshly than I'd intended.

We had crossed over onto the Moseley property and were in the shade of the tree line. Dad turned and gave me an exasperated look, putting the conversation back on more familiar ground for me.

"Is it hard to understand that I want to bounce the idea off of you?"

"No." I shook my head. "It's just… surprising."

"Buying it seems… a little frivolous… I guess."

Mauser came over and leaned against me as if he thought I could save him from this death march in the heat. I stroked the top of his head absentmindedly.

"I *am* wondering why you need the land. You have plenty of pasture for Finn and Mac," I said, referring to Dad's two Quarter Horses.

"Come on."

Dad started walking and, with an effort, Mauser pushed off of me to follow him. We wandered down a narrow trail through a thick stand of oak trees and sweetgums, until finally the trail opened onto a five-acre clearing. The bright summer sun sparkled on a large pond in the middle of the clearing that was surrounded by lush grass and wildflowers.

"It's beautiful," I whispered.

"Marge said her husband dug out the field and dammed up the creek to create this pond for her. There's a cabin over there." Dad pointed to a picturesque clapboard structure on the edge of the clearing.

"How much does she want for this?"

"It's twenty acres with fifty feet of road frontage. The cabin is one bedroom, one bath. Rustic, but it's in good shape. They just used the place when they wanted to get out of Tallahassee for a few days. Now that he's passed away and she's going up to live in North Carolina closer to her family, she wants to sell it. Thing is, she doesn't want it to go to someone who will mess it up. She's offered it to me at a very nice price."

"I think it's great, but there's still the question of *why* you want to buy it." I was trying to fulfill my role as advice-giver and not just tell him that I'd buy the place in a heartbeat if given the chance.

"You know Jimmy loves to fish. The pond is stocked with bluegill and catfish." Jimmy was the little brother I'd acquired when Dad had married his wife, Genie, earlier that year. Jimmy had Down Syndrome and often seemed to me to be the very embodiment of every positive human impulse.

"He would love it." I was finding it harder to contain my

own enthusiasm.

"I've talked to Genie about it, and she said she might want to turn the cabin into an Airbnb rental."

"I can see that."

Dad and I walked to the edge of the pond. Mauser hesitated to leave the shade of the woods, but he couldn't stand to let us get too far away. With his tongue hanging almost to his knees, he darted past us and splashed into the water. Five feet into the pond, he dropped to his belly so that only his head was sticking out of the water.

"Mauser likes it," I said.

Dad's phone buzzed. He took it out of his pocket and, after looking at the screen, held it to his ear and said, "What?" After a brief pause, he said, "Makes sense. He's here. You can tell him."

I didn't like the sound of that. Cautiously, I took the phone out of Dad's hand. "Yes?"

"We just got a call that I want you to take," Major Sam Parks told me.

I was surprised. Parks was essentially the assistant sheriff, and he usually did not get involved in assigning cases.

"What case?"

"I asked dispatch to notify me if there were any calls involving the TV show they're filming in the county. Someone from the production company just called to report a missing person."

"That show about Bigfoot? Sure, I'll ride out there and take the report." My wife, Cara, was a fan of *The Big Search* and she'd mentioned they were filming an episode in Adams County. She'd be terribly jealous when she found out I'd visited the set.

Major Parks thanked me and hung up, leaving me to get the location and other details from dispatch.

Dad lured Mauser out of the pond with a combination of baby talk and treats, and we left the idyllic little glade behind.

As I drove to the filming location, I kept one eye on the road and the other on my dash-mounted laptop. As a sergeant, I found my time was never my own. Even when I had an opportunity to work my own cases, I always had to monitor all the other investigators as they took cases, filed reports and put in requests for everything from search warrants and informant payments to equipment and time off. I found myself enjoying taking calls more than I ever did when they'd been my primary responsibility.

Missing person cases were almost always resolved in a day or two with a positive outcome. I hoped that this one would follow the usual pattern with nothing but a few interviews and some paperwork involved before the person was located.

The show was filming on fifteen acres north of Calhoun owned by an elderly couple, Riley and Edna Mahoney. Over the years, they had been responsible for a high volume of calls to 911, so much so that the Mahoneys had been warned about making too many non-emergency calls. I'd been to their house a couple of times myself when I was on patrol. The Mahoneys thought that the sheriff's office should come out and check their property every time they heard a noise they couldn't identify. I remembered that more than one of their calls had suggested they were having problems with Bigfoot or aliens, so it was no surprise that the team from *The Big Search* had wound up on their property.

The Mahoneys lived in a modest ranch-style home with a backyard that was crowded with a number of outbuildings filled with old furniture, lawnmowers and various non-working vehicles. Today the area was even more chaotic, with two white panel vans and a couple of other cars parked at random in the front yard. I found a spot to park and got out of the car.

A man wearing headphones and carrying a pole with a microphone directed me toward Arianne Bass, who had called in the missing person report. She was around forty years old, good-looking with dark hair pulled into a tail, piercing blue eyes and a take-no-prisoners posture. She was dressed for a long day on set in jeans and a white T-shirt with a utility vest over it.

"Miss Bass, I'm Sergeant Larry Macklin with the Adams County Sheriff's Office. You called and said you had a missing person?"

"A sergeant? I'm impressed. I figured they'd send whatever Barney Fife drew the short straw. Yeah, we have somebody missing. Let's go talk over here." She walked to one of the white vans and leaned against it.

"Let's start with the missing person's name and stats," I told her, pulling a small notebook and pen from my pocket. I could have taken her over to my car and entered the information directly onto my laptop, but I preferred to take notes the old-fashioned way. It made it easier to read the body language and facial expressions of suspects and witnesses as I questioned them.

"Scott Nicholl, thirty-eight years old. He's six feet tall and has dark hair that's probably a shade or two darker than it would be if he didn't dye it," she answered bluntly.

"And what is your job with the show?"

"I'm the line producer and, most of the time, the de facto director."

"Nicholl is one of the stars of the show, right?" Cara watched every new episode of *The Big Search* and it had been impossible for me not to get roped into watching a few of them with her.

"Scott would tell you that he is *the* star of the show. He's got the looks but lacks the charisma to carry the show by himself." She frowned and looked over to where the crew was setting up for a shot with the Mahoneys.

"Miss Bass, if you don't mind me saying so, you don't seem very concerned about Mr. Nicholl."

"Call me Arianne," she said quickly. "If you want my opinion, he shacked up with some local sl… woman last night and hasn't crawled out of bed yet."

"Is it normal for him to sleep in till…" I looked at my watch. "…Four-thirty in the afternoon?"

"Let's say it wouldn't be unusual. The man has enough ego for ten actors and he's a professional skirt-chaser."

"If that's the case, then why are you wasting my time?" I made a point of closing my notebook.

"I'm the producer. Every episode of this show is worth about a hundred thousand dollars. And I answer to the executive producers and the insurance company. There is a reason they call it show*business*. I've lost a commodity, and there are people who will want to be assured that I'm taking Mr. Nicholl's absence seriously. Even though I've told them more than once that the man is a liability and is expendable." She sighed. "You're right. I shouldn't downplay this. Okay, ask more of your questions."

"You've already screwed up by telling me that you don't think he's really missing. We don't run a location service for wayward actors," I told her.

"I'm sorry we got off on the wrong foot. I was trying to be honest with you." She sounded exasperated, though it was hard to tell if it was with me or the whole situation.

"Let's go at this from a different angle," I suggested, remembering that Major Parks had given me this case for a reason. "Is there anyone in your cast or crew who is genuinely worried about Scott Nicholl? I mean, is there anyone who thinks he could be in danger?"

"Kayla does. She's been making a fuss all day, claiming that he could be in trouble."

"Okay. I'll want to talk to her."

Arianne looked suddenly chastened. "Look, I know what I told you, but Scott usually isn't more than half an hour late to cast call."

I opened my notebook and started taking notes again.

"Let me get a few more facts before I talk to Kayla. Are you all staying at the motel by the interstate?" It was a safe bet, as it was the only motel in the county.

"No, never. Our scouts sent us pictures of that place. We have standards." Arianne sounded appalled at the very idea. "We rented three houses through Airbnb. Most of the crew in one and the cast and executives in the other two."

"I'll need addresses."

She pulled out her phone. "I'll text them to you. All three houses are on the same lake."

I gave her my number and with a few taps of her fingers, I had the addresses. I was very familiar with the area, having had an embarrassing swim in that lake a few months ago.

"When was the last time you saw Mr. Nicholl?"

"Last night when we finished shooting." Arianne scrolled through some data on her phone. "According to my production notes, we finished at seven-twenty."

"Where were you working?"

"I'm not sure of the exact location. It was off in the woods somewhere. I can get Dirk to show you on a map. We were filming a re-creation of a Bigfoot sighting."

"Did Nicholl leave by himself?"

"No, he was in the other production car with Eli, Kayla and Dirk. Dirk was driving."

"Did you notice anything odd about his behavior yesterday or in the last week?"

Arianne laughed. "No, he was his usual obnoxious self."

"In a good mood?"

"Always."

"Did anything unusual or unexpected happen yesterday?"

"No. There were the usual number of problems. It was miserably hot and buggy where we were shooting."

I asked a few more questions, then asked her to send for Kayla Alvarado.

She was a petite, purple-haired woman in her early twenties. She stared at me earnestly as she approached.

"I'm really, really worried about Scott," she blurted before I had a chance to say anything.

"That's what Miss Bass said," I told her. "I need to get some information from you before I can start looking for him."

"Sure, whatever I can tell you." Her hazel eyes danced around as she tried to contain her nervous energy.

"How well do you know Scott Nicholl?"

Her mouth fell open as if surprised that I had to ask the question. "We're in love," she said dreamily.

"And you also work with him. What is your position on the show?"

"I'm one of the sound engineers."

"How long have you known Scott?"

"Six months, but we only recently started dating."

"You left the location with him yesterday?"

"Yeah, I caught a ride with Dirk and Scott."

"Was anyone else in the car?"

"Sure, Eli. Dirk was driving."

"Caught a ride to…?"

"We went back to the rental."

"All of you?"

"No. I guess it was just Scott and me. Dirk and Eli were going to look for someplace to eat."

"You're staying at the same house as Scott?"

"No."

"So you went to your house and he went to his? Or did you both go to the same house?"

Kayla sighed dramatically. "We went to his house."

"Was anyone else there?"

"Eli came in and changed clothes, but he left again with Dirk."

"So who's staying at Scott's house? Eli, Scott and…?"

"Dirk."

"But he went with Eli to eat?"

"Yep."

"What did you and Scott do after everyone else was gone?"

Her answer was an eye roll and shuffling feet.

"We're adults here," I reminded her. "I need to know what was going on with Scott before he went missing."

"We had sex, okay. Look, don't tell Arianne." Kayla bit her lip as she waited for me to assure her that I wouldn't rat her out to the boss. I didn't mind disappointing her.

"I can't promise anything. I won't go out of my way to tell her, but if this turns into a major investigation, there are no guarantees."

"I mean, everyone knows we're in a relationship," Kayla said quickly. "Still… Arianne might be jealous. He… dated her for a while."

I made note of the drama and the fact that Arianne had neglected to mention it, but decided to move on to the matter at hand.

"Tell me exactly what happened last night and the last time you saw Scott."

"Like I said, we had sex, then we both spent time, you know, looking at our socials. Then we were starving, but there wasn't any food in the house and Dirk took the car. Scott didn't want to call Dirk and have him come back, so I suggested we go back over to my house where we had some food. Scott said okay. And we walked around the lake." The words poured out of Kayla as if someone had left her stream-of-consciousness spigot wide open. The speed of her words made it difficult to take notes and keep up with what she was saying at the same time.

"Did either of you drink alcohol or take any mind-altering substances?" Time was, I would have simply asked if they had taken drugs. But after a witness neglected to tell me that a suspect was higher than a kite on mushrooms because she didn't consider mushrooms a drug, I altered my language to be more inclusive.

Kayla gave me a look that told me she didn't like the question. "Like what?" She was clearly stalling for time and hoping that whatever they'd taken wouldn't be included in my definition of mind-altering.

"What did you take?" I asked, bypassing her attempt to play word games.

"Just some poppers. He likes to do them during sex. It's kind of weird, but they make him——"

My hand flew up to stop her. We might need all the graphic details later, but not right now.

"What time did you walk to your house?"

"I don't know…"

"Maybe you could look at your phone. Did you send a message to anyone? Post anything on one of your social media accounts?"

"Oh hey, yeah, I did text Koby because Scott wanted to know who was at the house." She took out her phone and looked at her messages. "It was just before nine when we left Scott's."

"And when did you get to your house?"

"I guess it took ten or fifteen minutes to walk there."

"Was Koby there? Or anyone else?"

"Koby had gone with Dirk and Eli into Tallahassee, but everyone else was at the house."

"So you got to your house and…" I prompted her. Kayla was either spewing out answers or holding them in.

"We made some sandwiches and got some chips and stuff. Oh yeah, Scott had a couple of beers. After that, we went to my room and watched some of Scott's best stuff from the show. He's got, like, a dozen compilations of scenes that he really likes. He wanted me to see them so I could, like, you know, push the crew to get good footage of him."

"How did you watch it?"

"On my laptop."

"Did he stay the night with you?"

"No. He left around eleven to go back to his house." She sounded disappointed.

"Was that the last time you heard from him?"

"No. He texted me when he got back to the house."

"Can I see the text?"

She found the text on her phone and showed it to me. It simply read: *Home* with a smiley face emoji.

"Does that sound like Scott?" I asked.

"Yeah, sort of. Though he isn't much of a texter," she admitted.

"Do you know if anyone else saw him after that?"

"No."

"When did people notice he was missing?"

"I didn't notice until I got here and he didn't show up."

"When was this?"

"Our call-time was eight. We get here before the cast does, so I didn't expect him before nine or ten."

"If Dirk was the driver, didn't he think it odd that Scott didn't ride with him?"

"He thought Scott had spent the night at my house."

"Did anyone go back to the house to look for Scott?"

"Eli did." She pointed to a tall black man in his mid-thirties who was standing near the Mahoneys as they were being interviewed outside their house. I recognized him as one of the three stars of the show.

"Did Scott seem concerned about anything last night or in the last couple of days?"

Kayla shrugged. "He's always worried about how he looks on camera and how much time he gets in front of it."

"He wasn't acting differently in any way?"

"No."

"Thanks. I think that's all I need from you right now."

"Please find him," she pleaded, then walked away with her head down.

CHAPTER TWO

I approached Eli Oliver, who was smiling and chatting with the Mahoneys as Arianne positioned them for a shot.

"Mr. Oliver? I'm sorry to interrupt, but—"

Before I could finish, Riley Mahoney spoke up. "Sergeant Macklin, I'd like to talk to you about the deputy that came out to our place last month. You know, we've always been great supporters of your father and—"

"Sorry, Mr. Mahoney, but I'm here on another matter. I'll be glad to sit down and talk with you and Mrs. Mahoney when we can arrange the time," I said as diplomatically as I could. "Mr. Oliver, could I have a few moments of your time?"

"Well… We're about to film a—"

"Go on. We'll do some background shots and close-ups on the Mahoneys instead," Arianne told him.

Eli shrugged and followed me over to my car.

"Kayla said you went to check on Scott this morning?"

"That's right. We're staying at the same house. After Kayla spent all morning kicking up a fuss, Arianne asked me to drive over there and check it out."

"What'd you find?"

"Nothing. Place looked the same as when we left it this morning. If you want my opinion, Scott didn't stay there last night 'cause he wasn't there when we left this morning."

"You checked?"

"Dirk checked. He's the driver and didn't want to have to come back to pick Scott up."

"What exactly is Dirk's job on the show?" I asked.

"He's like a step above a gopher. He works with our sound crew on set and does other odd jobs, as well as being the designated driver."

"Did Scott have access to any other car?"

"If he wanted to go somewhere without Dirk or another driver, he'd just call an Uber."

"I'd like to go over and look through the house, if we can."

"Let me check with Arianne." Eli walked back to the group by the house, and I watched him have a quick, earnest conversation with the producer before returning to me.

"Okay, let's go," he said.

"You can get in the front," I told him, gesturing toward my car.

"That's good, 'cause I don't ride in the back of police cars," Eli said with a crooked smile.

I cleared the front seat for him, and he squeezed his large frame into the vehicle. "Man, it's cramped in here with all this electronic stuff."

"We live and die by the phone and laptop," I said, checking my messages as I started the car.

I had to make a couple of calls before we pulled out and headed for the lake. I glanced at Eli as I turned onto the main road. He looked uncomfortable, and not just physically.

"You think something happened to Scott?" he asked me.

"That's supposed to be my question. It's way too early for me to give an opinion. What do you think?"

"I don't know. Scott is such a... dick, man. He messes around too much. That's his persona on the show, but it's him too. You know what I mean?"

"Not exactly," I hedged.

"He fools around with too many women. Messes with people's feelings. He'll even flirt with a guy he knows is gay. Just stupid. So I guess I'm sayin' I could see him going off and making people freak out that he's not around, but…" Eli shook his head. "That's how he is with people off the set. Thing is, I've never known him to be anything but completely professional when it comes time to shoot a scene. It's like he can separate himself into two people. On set he plays the jerk for the show, but he's always focused when it comes to the production."

"I get it." And I really did. I'd known deputies like that, who were total professionals on the job but couldn't manage their personal lives with the same integrity. "Kayla said that she and Scott are in a relationship?" I asked.

Eli gave me the side-eye. "I'm not throwing shade on anyone. I'll just say that I'd be floored if Scott took their relationship any more seriously than all the others he's had."

"You're the rational one on the show, right?"

"Precisely. I'm the voice of moderation."

"You and Scott seem to have been typecast for your characters on the show. Of course, I guess it *is* a reality show," I said, almost seriously.

"Are you kidding? There isn't much real on the show except for the crazy people we interview! Like that couple back at the house; they're completely looney. If this show wasn't scripted, I'd tell them what I really think about their story about having half a dozen sasquatches coming up to their house every night to eat the peanut butter sandwiches they leave out for them."

I chuckled. "I have to agree with you about the Mahoneys. They're harmless, but not quite right in the head."

"I'm used to those types of people. It just gets a little old, nodding my head at all the crazy."

"You don't believe in Bigfoot?"

Eli sighed. "Who knows? There have been a few times

when we've talked to people and I've thought: 'These people are smart, rational and sincere.' They tell me they saw a creature clear as day fifty feet away from them and I'm like…" He shrugged. "Who am I to tell them they didn't see what they saw?"

"What about the third member of the cast? Jackie King, right?"

"She's cool. Does her work, doesn't mess with anyone who doesn't mess with her."

"Has someone messed with her?"

Eli got quiet and looked out the window.

"Are we talking about Scott? Seems there's a little chemistry between them on the show. At least the few episodes I've seen," I admitted.

Eli nodded. "That's where I learned to respect her. Scott came on strong about a year ago. It was into our second season when I think he was feeling insecure over the attention she was getting from the fans and executive producers."

"Came on strong? You mean making advances?"

"He's a master at knowing how much he can get away with. Funny thing was, she turned it around on him. It took him about two months to figure out she was screwing with him. Now she flirts with him on the show, and I can see it gets under his skin, 'cause every time she does it the ratings spike."

"Has that caused any friction when they're not working?"

"If Scott makes a comment about almost anything, she twists it around and zings him. It took him a while, but Scott eventually learned that he's outmatched and ignores her most of the time. Of course, there's another twist. See, she's a producer too, so she has some say in what happens with the show."

"I thought Arianne was the producer?" I was a bit confused by the movie production hierarchy.

"Arianne is a line producer, which means she's the one who makes sure everything on set runs smoothly. Jackie is a producer. Producers put the show together—make decisions about the cast, script and those types of things. *The Big Search* has several producers. Sometimes producers are people who just bring something to the table, like the original script or some other important element."

"Like money?"

"No, the people who finance a production are executive producers."

I turned onto the road that ran around the lake. "Tell me which house."

Eli pointed to a two-story, modern-style house that would easily cost seven figures if it was for sale. There were no cars in the driveway. On the off chance that it was a crime scene, I parked a couple of car lengths from the garage.

"They have you living in style," I commented as we got out of the car.

"One of the perks, but I get tired of being on the road four months out of the year."

"Where are you from?"

"My family and I have a home just south of Atlanta."

"Did the cast and crew drive or fly down here?"

"Flew and rented cars. It's SOP for the show. We only drive if it's within sixty miles of Atlanta."

"The whole show is run out of Atlanta?"

Eli nodded while giving the house an odd look.

"What do you see?"

"I just got the willies, as my grandma would say. It's nothing. The house looks the same as it did this morning and when I came back to check on Scott."

"Did you lock the doors when you left this morning?"

"I checked all the doors and windows myself. My wife says I've got more than a little OCD. I tell her I've got a lot of don't-want-my-stuff-stolen."

"Was it locked when you came back?"

"Yeah, I used my key. Well, I'm pretty sure. Now that you mention it, I just turned the key in the lock. I can't tell you for sure that the bolt was engaged before I turned the key."

"I want to walk around the house," I said after checking the front door to confirm that it was locked.

The house was a concrete-and-glass cube painted light blue with white accents. Facing the street was a three-car garage, while the back of the house was all windows looking over the lake. The house sat on four acres with a thick line of trees on either side blocking the houses next door. The backyard sloped down to the lake where there was a dock with an attached boathouse.

The only door on the back side of the house was the sliding glass door out onto the deck, and it was locked tight. There was a hot tub on the deck, and I approached it cautiously, remembering the time I'd found a boiled body inside of one. I lifted the cover slowly and was very glad to see nothing but clear water.

On the side of the house was another door that Eli told me led into a laundry room.

"I think my key opens this door too, but I've always gone in and out the front door," he said.

"When did y'all arrive?"

"Friday."

"Try your key."

With a little jiggling, Eli was able to unlock the door. The laundry room was narrow, with a washer, dryer, utility sink and cabinets along one wall, and it led directly into the garage. We walked through the garage, which was empty except for some tools and lawn equipment. The door from the garage into the kitchen was unlocked.

Inside, the house smelled fresh and clean. There were half a dozen dishes in a rack beside the sink.

"Does a maid come by and clean?" I asked.

"We declined that service. Arianne had some jewelry disappear six months ago at a hotel we were staying at. Turned out it was one of the maids, so ever since we've agreed not to have our rooms cleaned." Eli shrugged.

"Have you had any problems while you've been here?" I asked as we walked out of the kitchen and into a small family room with a couple of couches and a huge flatscreen TV mounted on the wall.

"Did you see the big guy standing off by the woods at the shoot?" Eli answered my question with one of his own.

"Wearing jeans and a khaki shirt, looked like a forest ranger?"

"That's him. Guy's name is Cody Morgan, and he takes all this Bigfoot stuff real seriously. He's gotten in Arianne's face several times in the last couple of days. Yesterday, Scott told him to shut his mouth if he wanted to get paid."

"How did that go over?" We'd stopped in the hallway at the foot of the stairs.

"You could tell the guy was furious. Still, we haven't had any trouble with him since then."

"Who is he?"

"He's what we call a local expert. There's one on every episode. Our scout digs around and finds some Bigfoot expert in the area to come talk about the local sightings, and then we have them kind of introduce the witnesses. Even though most of the time they've never seen them before."

"I've never heard of him. Is he from around here?"

"I don't think so. I know they had to give him a travel per diem because Arianne reminded him of it yesterday."

Making a mental note to learn more about Cody Morgan, I started up the stairs.

"Everyone sleeps up here?"

"Yeah, though on Saturday night, Jake slept over on the couch in the den."

"Who's Jake?"

"Jake Nash. You might have seen him on the show. He's our cameraman, but they script him into episodes once in a while. He's kind of the cowardly comic relief. You know, we'll hear a sound out in the woods and the camera shakes and we look at Jake who's like: 'Let's get out of here.' That sort of thing. He's the one that the freaked-out viewers can identify with."

There were five doors at the top of the stairs. The bathroom door was open and so were two of the bedroom doors.

"Whose room is whose?" I asked.

"That one is Scott's." Eli pointed to an open door, then one of the closed ones. "That one is Dante's."

"Who's Dante?"

"One of the producers. He comes and goes. Keeps an eye on our budget. He was only here the first two nights, but we have to hold a room for him."

"He's a producer like Jackie or like Arianne?"

"Dante is a producer like Jackie. Sometimes one of the other producers, or an executive producer, will come to a location. Executive producers get put up in the nearest five-star hotel and get a chauffeured car out to the location."

"Right, because executive producers are the ones with the money." I was starting to get a handle on all the different positions.

"That's right. The other closed door is my room and that one's Dirk's."

I walked into Scott's room. The bed hadn't been made. There were two suitcases and a carry-on bag in the room, with one of the suitcases open and sitting across the arms of a chair. There was a shaving kit on the chest of drawers by the door and a few clothes strewn on the floor.

"He's still got more than a little teenager in him," Eli said.

"Does anything look unusual to you?"

"Nope. We've been traveling together for a couple of years now and this is what I've come to expect from him."

"Have you seen anything in the house that you would think he should have taken with him if he left the house?"

"Nope."

With nothing pointing to foul play or suggesting that Nicholl was going to run off or take his own life, I left his room and, with Eli's permission, looked in each of the other rooms.

"Has anyone contacted his family?" I asked.

"No. His relationship with his family is… complex. He had a violent falling out with his stepfather long before he joined the show, and his mother hasn't spoken with him since."

"Any other family?"

"Stepbrothers, but they side with their father. I've never heard him talk about anyone else."

"Friends?"

"I think he has some out in L.A., but they're more showbusiness connections than they are real friends. At least that's the impression I've always gotten. His social circle is comprised of whatever woman he's going after at the time and those of us who work with him."

"You don't paint a very nice picture of Scott," I pointed out as I looked in the bathroom.

"He's a type. Great looks, some talent and a desire to be the center of attention. If his type really bothered me, I couldn't be in showbusiness."

"Call him." I pointed at the phone sticking out of Eli's pocket.

"We've been calling him all day," he said, frowning as he reached for his phone.

"I want to see if it's in the house," I explained.

He smiled and nodded as he pulled up Scott's number on his phone. "It's ringing."

We listened and didn't hear anything—no ringing, musical tones or buzzing. We went back downstairs and I asked Eli to call again. Still nothing. After another quick look around the downstairs, I was starting to wonder where this was going to lead. There was a good chance Scott had just decided to go off on his own.

"So what do you think?" Eli asked as we stood in the backyard again.

"First, did Scott have any drug or alcohol issues?"

"No. That was the first thing I told Arianne when they offered me the job. I won't share a house or hotel room with anyone that has addiction problems. I had an ex who burned her life to the ground with drugs. She almost destroyed me, and I wasn't even a user. Just dealing with it was… chaos. I won't go through that again for anyone."

"Has he exhibited any signs of mental problems like severe depression, schizophrenia, bipolar disease… anything like that?"

"Nope."

"Okay. Well, if that's the case then he's less likely to have wandered off on his own. Still, there's a chance that he did since we haven't found his phone or wallet. On the other hand, he doesn't have a car. At least, we don't think he does. Did he ever mention knowing anyone in the area? Maybe in Tallahassee?"

Eli shook his head.

"Still, with Uber and Lyft, anyone can catch a ride to wherever they want to go," I mused and started walking toward the lake. "I'm just going to take a look around the dock, and then we can head back."

A warm, humid breeze sent ripples across the surface of the lake as I made my way down the pine-tree-shaded slope to the water. I didn't expect to find anything of interest. There were some flotsam and jetsam caught in the reeds at the edge of the water—a plastic bottle, a paper plate, but nothing that pointed toward our missing person. Still, whenever a disappearance was reported near a body of water, you had to check it out.

We'd been fortunate not to have too many drownings in the county. Dad always spent a week near the end of every schoolyear going around and talking to students about summer safety. A big part of it was encouraging every child to learn to swim. He even had the sheriff's office co-sponsor grants with the schools to run swimming classes. Even before he'd become sheriff, it had been a personal project for him. When I was a teenager, my mother had finally told me why. Early in his career as a deputy, Dad had responded to the drowning death of a child not much older than I was at the time. The memory had haunted him for years.

Eli joined me at the edge of the lake. "We came down here on Saturday. I remember Scott saying he wasn't much of a swimmer."

"I want to check out the dock and boathouse."

It didn't take me long to look in the boathouse, which was little more than a carport over the water. There was room for two small bass boats or one pontoon boat, but it was currently empty.

"That's odd," Eli said. "There was a jon boat in here this weekend."

"You're sure?"

"Oh yeah. Arianne had all of us sign the release that the homeowner insisted on. And it included a release from liability if we drowned in the lake, with a specific clause about using the boat. Dirk got all excited when he saw the boat. He insisted on giving it a try. It wasn't big enough for all of us to go out on the lake at once, so we took turns."

"Can you think of any reason someone might've taken it out now?"

"Like Scott? He seemed to get a kick out of the boat, but he was happy to let Dirk run it."

"What about the owner? Could they have come and gotten it?" I asked.

Eli just shrugged.

I looked out over the lake where I could see several boats with people fishing or swimming from them. It wasn't unusual for kids to "borrow" other people's boats. Every year we wrote up dozens of boat theft reports, most of them involving juveniles.

I made a note to check with the owner of the house and see what they knew about the boat. There was always a chance they had just come to take it out on the lake themselves.

I walked out to the end of the dock. Satisfied that I'd done a thorough search of the property, I turned and started back toward the shore. As I walked, something white in the reeds about ten feet from the shore to the left of the dock caught my eye. My mind dismissed it as a Styrofoam cup, and I kept walking.

But when I stepped back onto the grass, there was a tiny alarm ringing in the back of my brain. I turned back to look at the Styrofoam cup and felt myself being drawn to it. With every step, my heartbeat quickened until I realized exactly what I was looking at.

"Stop!" I ordered Eli, who was following me toward the cup. "I want you to retrace your steps back to the dock and stand there."

"Oh shit!" he shrieked as realization dawned on him too. "Oh no! Oh man, that can't be…"

Eli was beginning to hyperventilate. I turned to him and managed to get him to look at me.

"I want you to go back to the dock. Don't talk to anyone. I'm going to call a response team. Understand?"

He nodded slowly. I repeated my instructions and then pushed him back toward the grass.

CHAPTER THREE

I pulled out my phone and called Major Parks. Normally, he would not have been the first person I'd contact, but he'd kind of gotten me into this mess. Plus, this had all the makings of a public relations nightmare, and he needed to know about it sooner rather than later.

"Did you find anything?" he said by way of a greeting.

"On a positive note, I found part of the missing person. Probably." I shouldn't have gone straight for the black humor, but I was irritated to be stuck out in the heat and staring at someone's severed foot floating in the lake. I quickly explained the situation and told him I'd be calling in the coroner and our crime scene team.

"I'll take care of the media." Parks sounded as unhappy as I was with the situation.

Next, I called dispatch and asked for a couple of deputies to be sent out to help secure the scene. This time of day was tough. Rush hour, even in a rural county, was almost always busy. My request could cause the watch commander to call in an off-duty deputy or two, which never made Parks or Dad very happy. Once that was sorted, I called the coroner's office and asked that they send their A-team.

Then I thought about who I wanted to assign as the

primary investigator on the case. I'd already decided to stay involved, but I wanted someone else to take the lead. After I looked at all the angles, I pulled up Mick Klein's number.

"Sarge," he answered laconically.

"I want you to take the lead on a presumed homicide," I told him.

"Presumed? Do we have a body?"

"We have a foot," I answered and heard a derisive snort from the other end of the line.

"What's the gag?" he asked suspiciously. He'd been the department's go-to burglary investigator before I took over as supervisor of criminal investigations. We'd butted heads a couple of times until I'd realized that the issues I was having with him sprang from his frustration at not getting more challenging cases. Since then, he'd become an even bigger asset to the team.

"No gag. This has the potential to be a big case. I'll fill you in when you get here. As to why I picked you, Pete is still recovering from his surgery, Julio and Lieutenant Eccles are on vacation, and Lynn is tied up with that domestic battery trial."

"You're always honest. I'll give you that," Mick said.

I gave him the address, and he assured me that he'd be there within fifteen minutes.

As I hung up, I saw Eli fiddling with his phone.

"Please put that back in your pocket!" I yelled over to him. The last thing we needed was for him to start calling and texting people, and then have a herd of hysterical bystanders and the media show up.

"I was just..." he started to say, but instead he nodded and put the phone away.

I looked back at the foot. It was in about eighteen inches of water, bobbing gently in the waves lapping at the shore. Movement under the water a few feet from the foot caught my eye, and I watched as some sort of creature moved in toward it, stalking the severed appendage. When I realized that it was a large alligator snapping turtle the size of a trashcan lid, I cursed loudly and moved in closer. It was stretching its neck toward the tempting morsel, and I had no choice but to go splashing into the water to chase it off. The turtle backpedaled, though not as fast as I would have hoped.

Knee-deep in the lake and guarding the severed foot from aquatic predators, I felt like I'd fallen into a bizarre nightmare. Apparently, the tantalizing odors drifting out from the foot were hard to resist, as the turtle made two more attempts to come in and steal a bite.

I looked up at the late afternoon sunlight and realized there was no way I was making it home in time for dinner. I texted my wife, Cara: *Major incident. I'm fine. Home late if at all. Love you.* Within seconds, she'd texted back with a thumbs-up and a heart.

While I stood in the water, I looked closely at the foot. It didn't look like it had been in the water for more than a day. There were no tattoos, scars, birthmarks or moles visible on the side of the foot that I could see, and the nails looked neat but not manicured. I was also pretty sure it was a male's foot, as hair was visible around the toes and just above the ankle near the jagged site of amputation.

I jumped when my phone buzzed with a call from Matti Sanderson, one of the deputies sent out to help.

"I want you to put up a perimeter around the house, including the driveway. When crime scene gets here, tell Shantel to wait for me. I'm stuck in the lake with a body part until the coroner's van shows up. When they do arrive, have them call me before they do anything else." Sanderson was an excellent deputy, and I knew she'd follow my instructions to the letter.

Minutes later, Mick called to tell me he'd arrived. I gave him as many details as I could, then asked him to get ahold of whoever could run the department's boat.

"I want them to go around the lake before it gets dark and see if they can spot any more body parts, or anything else that looks unusual. Make sure they to do a thorough job."

"Understood. Kelly and Lucero should be available," Mick said.

"Perfect. It's going to be a while before we have time to examine the house and boathouse. When I walked through it all earlier, I didn't see any obvious signs of a crime, so right now we have no idea where the crime scene is. We can't even be sure that this is a part of our missing person. We'll have to wait for Dr. Darzi to determine whose foot this is and if it's a boating accident or a shark attack."

"You had to go there," he chided me.

"Standing here in the water fending off a snapping turtle hellbent on eating someone's foot hasn't helped my mood."

"I think you're in luck. The crime scene van just showed up. Your days of being a turtle wrangler might be coming to an end."

Marcus Brown from our crime scene division came down the hill from the house, carrying a camera to document the scene.

"I made sure to get some photos of you knee-deep in the water hunting turtles," he joked as he finished up.

"You're all heart. Glad everyone is getting a laugh from this. Shantel didn't want to gawk too?"

"She's still unloading stuff from the van. You know, you're lucky it wasn't a gator."

He wasn't wrong. The thought had crossed my mind more than once and had me watching the water around me closely. Marcus took his camera and went back up to the house, chuckling

Twenty minutes later, Linda from the coroner's office finally called me.

"Sorry. We had to unload a corpse before we could head down here, and then we ran into traffic coming out of Tallahassee."

"I'm just glad you made it." I couldn't have been more sincere. I explained the situation, and we discussed what they needed to bring down to the lake in order to retrieve the foot and as much of the water surrounding it as was practical.

"I guess I won't need to take the foot's temperature," Linda said once she was beside me and looking at the pale object bobbing up and down in the water. She was wearing her PPE under a pair of waders that I wished I'd had and carrying a plastic bin about the size of a wash tub.

"I won't expect you to give me a time of death either." I waded ashore, trying not to disturb the water.

"I'm going to let it flow into the bin and then we'll bring it ashore and place the foot in a body bag. We'll save the water for analysis. I guess y'all don't know where the rest of the body is?"

"No, and you better get the foot before the snapping turtle comes back."

"I love turtles." Linda sounded positively chipper at the thought of seeing the turtle I'd been battling for an hour.

Her assistant, an intern I didn't recognize and that she didn't bother to introduce, looked at Linda like she was crazy.

"Do we both need to go in the water?" he asked, looking at the lake warily.

"Come on. I'll protect you from the killer turtles," Linda promised.

As I walked up on the bank, I looked down at my shoes. They weren't anything fancy, but they were comfortable, and now they were bound for the trash bin. With a sigh, I sloshed over to the dock where Eli was sitting with his back against the boathouse.

"My phone's been blowing up. I'm sure it's Arianne wondering where we are." He frowned. "Is that Scott's foot?"

"I don't know."

"What am I going to tell Arianne and the rest of the crew?" Eli's voice was barely above a whisper as he stared off at the water.

"I would prefer to inform them myself," I told him.

"That's one of the reasons I didn't want you calling anyone."

He pulled his phone out and looked at the screen before turning it toward me. There was another call coming in from Arianne.

"Answer it and tell her we'll be back within the hour, and we'll tell her what we found when we see her."

"She won't like it," he groused but answered the call. It was clear from his side of the conversation that his comment had been an understatement.

"I'm going to walk you back up the hill," I said when he hung up.

Eli looked back at Linda and the intern as they carried the plastic bin out of the lake. For a moment, I thought he was going to be sick. Instead, he coughed a couple of times and stared down at the ground for the rest of the trip back to my car.

"Would you like some water?" I asked, and his face turned slightly green as he shook his head.

"I don't think I'm going to be able to eat tonight."

"Try not to think about the… you know. Or any of the implications of it. There will be time enough for that."

"I hate myself for thinking about the show and what's going to happen to it, assuming that's Scott's…" Eli frowned. "This was an accident, right?"

"We don't know anything yet. There is a slim, very slim, possibility that it isn't even Scott's foot."

"Do you find feet lying around a lot?" he asked.

I decided to ask him questions to help take his mind off of the foot and to begin filling in details. "Can you think of anyone who might have wanted to hurt Scott?"

"You said it might not be him."

"I'm just asking questions."

"I get it. My uncle's a cop in Atlanta." Eli nodded and looked thoughtful. "Want to hurt Scott? I think he annoyed a lot of people. I told you he screwed with people sometimes."

"Who did he mess with?"

"'Mess with' is right. Women mostly."

"You're dodging the question. Are you talking about Kayla? You said women. Who else?" I tried to sound like I was encouraging him, not badgering him.

"I don't like gossiping about people," Eli hedged.

I could tell that he liked to keep his distance from trouble and drama.

"Right now, I'm just trying to get a picture of what might be happening. I'll come back for a sworn statement if I need to. That's when you'll be on the record."

"It wasn't just Kayla. He and Arianne had a thing too. Which is the problem. On most productions, you'd expect the line producer to shut that type of thing down, but Scott managed to sleep with her using his frat-boy charm."

"She didn't seem too worried about him being missing."

"I don't think she took the... 'affair' is too strong a word... the casual sex seriously. I'm not even sure she really likes him that much." He quickly added, "And it's been over for at least four months."

"She didn't take it seriously. What about Scott?"

"My guess is that he saw it as a way to neutralize Arianne so he could pretty much do whatever he wanted on location."

"What about Kayla? Did Scott take his relationship with her seriously?"

"I don't think so." Eli shook his head.

"Was he having sex with anyone else?" I didn't see the sense in mincing words.

"I already told you he flirted with Jackie, but she wasn't going to go there. Besides those three, Scott would look for any woman hanging around the set that matched his criteria."

"What are his criteria?"

"Female between the ages of eighteen and fifty. Big, small, blonde, redhead, tall, short. I've seen him flirt with all types. He *did* avoid mean women. Sometimes they were only mean to him 'cause they knew that would deflect his pushy type of charm."

"Were any of the women mad about him flirting with other women?"

"Mad… no. We've had a couple of women come to locations and throw things and scream at him. The last time was about two months ago. That's when even Arianne had to recognize that Scott's behavior was a problem. I know she read him the riot act. Not that she could threaten to fire him, not without more cause. And, of course, he had a comeback for her."

"Because she'd been having sex with him?"

"And because he brings a lot to the show. There are investors to think about. That's one of Jackie's favorite lines."

"What about husbands, family, boyfriends? A guy who sleeps around like that is going to run afoul of a few men."

"Agreed, but none of them ever came around, and Scott never mentioned any trouble of that kind."

"Is Scott into anything else that might get him into trouble? Something like gambling, drugs…?" I suggested.

Eli shook his head. "No. It's like I already told you, his one vice is women. He wasn't interested in sports like a lot of guys, so he wouldn't even know how to bet on a game. We did some location work last year in Nevada, and when we went to Vegas, he was only interested in hooking up with women. I've never even seen him fool around with pot. The few times he's gotten hurt, the only drugs I saw him take for pain were Advil or Tylenol, over-the-counter stuff. A couple of times he had a cold, he complained when the drugs he took made him feel drowsy the next day on set."

Eli leaned back against my car and looked thoughtful. "You know, that's another reason we put up with him. We've all had to deal with stars that were messed up with drugs, mentally messed up, or up to their eyeballs in debt. Looking at Scott, his college-boy antics weren't that hard to deal with."

My phone buzzed, and a quick glance told me it was Dad.

I stepped away from the car and answered.

"Parks gave me the overview. Where are we now?"

I could tell that Dad wasn't happy as I gave him an update. He hated cases that drew media attention. There were police chiefs and sheriffs that loved to get in front of the cameras and ride the wave of a high-profile case, but Dad wasn't one of them. It wasn't even that he hated the media; he just found that when they shined their spotlight on one case, other cases lost out.

"I'll check with Leon County and see if we can get an hour or two of helicopter time to check out the lake before it gets dark," he said. "If we assume that the foot belongs to the missing actor, do we have any idea how it could have gotten severed?"

"Not really. As of right now, the last person known to have seen him is a young woman working for the production company. She says they spent the evening together, first at his place and then at hers, before he left to walk back to the house he was staying in. There's about a quarter mile between the two rental houses. I've seen a text from his phone that said he was home. I have another witness who says that the missing man had a way with women, including several on the production."

"You remember what I told you when you started high school?" Dad asked.

"Keep it in my pants or suffer the consequences." I remembered his turn of phrase because I'd known that he'd be the one to make sure I suffered.

"At least you never screwed *that* up," he said cheerfully, making sure the implication that I'd screwed up many other things was clear. "Is there a chance this is just a tragic accident?"

"One in fifty would be my odds."

"As long as we don't have to close the beaches for the Fourth of July." I'd come by my dark sense of humor honestly.

I told him about the alligator snapper I'd had to shoo

away from the severed limb.

"Killer turtle wouldn't be the most ridiculous plot that the SciFi channel ever used. You know, I joke, but I was out on the Apalachicola River a few years ago in a canoe and saw one that must have weighed over two hundred pounds. Easily as much as Mauser."

"The best case for an accident is that Scott, or whoever the foot belongs to, drowned in the lake, and the body was dismembered by alligators and turtles. Hopefully, we'll find the rest of the body soon. Otherwise, we'll have to count on Dr. Darzi being able to deduce a lot from the foot."

"Keep me updated. I'll call LCSO and see if they can do a flyby," Dad said and hung up.

I knew that the main reason he'd called was to get enough information so that when a news agency or politician contacted him about the case, he'd be able to give them enough information to satisfy them without jeopardizing the investigation.

I went to my trunk, where I kept a duffle bag with an extra set of clothes, just in case. I changed into fresh socks and tennis shoes, making a mental note not to leave the sodden pair of shoes in the trunk for very long in the summer heat.

Then I checked in with Sanderson. She reported that Shantel and Marcus were still documenting the scene around the house and boathouse, while Mick had started talking to neighbors and securing permission to walk through their yards.

With the situation on autopilot for a while, I told Eli to get in the car, and we headed back out to the filming location to face Arianne.

CHAPTER FOUR

The film crew was just returning from an early dinner break when we got back to the Mahoneys' property. Eli told me that a night-shoot was planned for that evening.

Arianne walked up to us, taking a big swig out of a Styrofoam cup.

"We need to talk," I told her.

"Did you find him?" she asked, picking up on the tone of my voice and glancing at Eli, whose expression was blank.

"Not yet. At least we hope not." I was trying to be honest and straightforward without giving her false hope.

"What does that mean?" She frowned.

"You might want to set the cup down and lean against my car," I suggested. I didn't think she was the type of person to go weak at the knees when receiving bad news, but there was a difference between bad news and a severed foot.

She didn't argue, setting the cup down on the hood and resting a hip against the fender. "So tell me?"

"We found a foot in the lake behind Scott's house."

The color left her face, and I was glad I'd had her lean against the car. She shook her head as if trying to get her ears to pick up better news. "A foot? Just a... foot?"

"We don't know if it's his foot or not," I clarified.

"Do you often find feet floating in the local lakes?" There was a tiny hint of hysteria in her tone.

"No," I said bluntly, "so we're going on the assumption that it's his foot for right now. The coroner's office will want a DNA profile to match with the foot. This will be even more important if we don't find the rest of the body."

Arianne laughed darkly, and I could tell she was trying hard to hold on to her composure. "Conveniently, we actually have a sample of his DNA. One of the first episodes this season, we did a thing involving Bigfoot DNA, and we had all the stars of the show submit their DNA for comparison and elimination… you know, just reality-show nonsense."

She stood and staggered a bit. "What a bunch of…" She shook herself and reached for her phone. "Okay. We'll do whatever's necessary to help you out. Right now, I need to call some people."

"Don't. I've got some questions I need to ask first."

Arianne looked like she was going to argue with me, but instead she nodded. "Bad news can always wait. Ask away. But… I may have to call a lawyer if this gets into areas that would be sensitive for the production company. You understand that?"

"I'm not formally questioning you. I'm just trying to get some background. But anytime you want a lawyer, it's your right to have one present."

"What I am going to need is a Xanax." She took a deep breath. "Okay, ask your questions." Her eyes looked over my left shoulder as though already seeing the freight train of trouble coming down the track toward her.

"What was your relationship with Scott?" I asked gently.

Arianne spat out an expletive and chewed on her nails. "Funny thing is, as soon as Kayla started making a fuss about him not showing up this morning, I knew the shit was going to hit the fan. Yes, I had a sexual relationship with Scott. And, for the record, I'm using the past tense because you did."

"Fair enough," I agreed. "Are you still having a relationship?"

"I don't know. It was just a friends-with-benefits thing." She sighed heavily. "I was being used. I knew that. He was only having sex with me because it meant I couldn't call him on any of the other quasi-professional relationships he had with co-workers. If I'm being honest, I was using him too. Really, that's why it worked.

"My husband of ten years dumped me last year. I came home from a location to find him gone and our joint accounts cleaned out. He sent me an email from France telling me that I'd abandoned him for my job and he needed a real relationship. His real relationship just happened to be with a twenty-two-year-old anorexic model with a brand-new set of breast implants. Thus, I arrived at the lowest point in my life."

"I'm sorry to dredge it all up. Investigations will do that." I nodded for her to continue.

"Scott was good medicine for me. He was willing to do what I needed and didn't ask for anything more than a little free rein when it came to his personal life on location. Was it professional of me? No. Did I have a choice? A *real* choice? No. I swear he saved me from a bottle of pills and the long sleep." Arianne wiped her eyes.

"What can you tell me about his other relationships?" I asked, shamelessly taking advantage of her vulnerability.

"Well, there was his relationship with Kayla, obviously. He wasn't technically her boss, but I still shouldn't have allowed it. Then, because of the show, he has his share of groupies. I know he keeps a running list of them on his phone and often sets up a meeting with one or two whenever we're going to be on a location near them."

"Did he meet anyone while he was here?"

"He borrowed the car Friday night. I didn't ask where he wanted to go, and he didn't tell me." She shrugged.

"Was taking the car another perk of his relationship with you?"

She gave me a hard look.

"No… and yes. Any of the above-the-line cast members and crew can borrow a car. We make sure everyone is listed on the rental agreement. I'll admit he did it more than anyone else."

"Besides Kayla and you, was there anyone else on the production that he had an unprofessional relationship with?"

"He tried with Jackie, but she's a match for anyone. I think she's the first person I've ever seen get under Scott's skin. He couldn't have her, and she made sure he knew it."

"There was tension?"

"That's a good word for it. He wanted her, and he wanted to rub her nose in it. But she's smarter and quicker than he is. The hitch was that he needed her on the show. Jackie is the real star. Anyone that looks at the show's social media can see who the fans love. Scott has his groupies and Eli has his own niche group of fans, but Jackie powers the show. She lifts it from the muck of most of the paranormal reality shows."

"Was he jealous of the attention she got?"

"I think that was part of the reason he wanted to sleep with her. Sex is a dominance thing for him." Arianne saw the look on my face. "No, not whips and chains and *Fifty-Shades-of-Grey*-type dominance. It's more of a mental, put-her-in-her-place kind of dominance."

"Is that what it was with you?"

"I'll admit it gave him an advantage over me. But we both knew that if he went too far, I'd pull the rug out from under him."

"How close did his relationship with Kayla come to crossing the line?"

"I told him two weeks ago when we were in Louisiana that if Kayla came to me and complained, I'd back her to the hilt no matter what it cost me. He knew I was serious."

"Can you think of anyone that would want to hurt Scott?"

"Hurt? Like really hurt? No… No." Arianne seemed

appalled by the idea. "If he was… killed, then it had to be a mugger or something."

"It's early days. We don't even know if it's Scott's foot," I said, trying to be reassuring but failing miserably. "There *is* an issue that I'll need your cooperation with. I'd like to seal off the house."

"I… Did something happen in the house?"

"I don't know. Since the foot wasn't found in the house, I don't have the legal right to seal it off. But by the time that we learn whose foot it is, it might be too late for the investigation. Valuable evidence could be lost."

"What about everyone's belongings?"

"I'd like to collect the clothes that everyone was wearing last night and all of Scott's possessions. As for everything else, I'd like to have a chance to see it, but everyone can take the rest of their stuff with them."

"I don't suppose the sheriff's office is going to pay for another house for them to live in while we're here?" Arianne groused.

"There are months I'm surprised the office can pay my salary." I smiled apologetically.

"I'll arrange for Eli and Dirk to stay somewhere else. It's up to them if they want to let you look through their stuff."

"That's all I'm asking."

Arianne nodded at Eli, and they headed over to the rest of the group to break the news. I watched them, very much wanting to follow and talk to the rest of the cast and crew. But the investigation at the lake was the priority right now.

Even though it was already evening, we still had a couple of hours of summer light left. I climbed back in my car and checked my messages. I'd been getting regular texts from everyone at the lake updating me on their progress. The most recent one from Dad informed me that the helicopter was on its way from Leon County.

I started the car and called Mick to tell him we had permission to close off the house where Scott had been staying.

"I've gone twenty houses in both directions around the lake from where the foot was found," he reported. "Less than half the houses had someone home. Lots of rentals. I found two earwitnesses. One seems pretty solid. An old guy who doesn't like his sleep disturbed. He heard a noise, tossed and turned for about thirty minutes, then heard a boat out on the lake. He was very precise about the times. His neighbors didn't hear anything, but they weren't surprised that *he* had. Seems he's complained about noise to them in the past."

"Sounds good. What about the lake? Did you get to look down by the water?"

"Everyone who was home let me check out their backyards after I told them there might be a body floating around. There were enough of them that I got a pretty good look. Didn't see anything."

"I want to go out on our boat," I told him.

"Lucero and Kelly are out on it now. He just told me that they're getting low on gas, so you might be able to catch them at the marina."

I thanked him and quickly called Deputy Tori Kelly.

"We can meet you at the Quayside Marina, which will work out well. We've got about half an hour of gas left," she shouted over the sound of the boat's outboard engines.

The Quayside Marina was an institution in Adams County. The Dennis family had been running it for the last fifty years, almost since the day the manmade lake was formed. Granny Dennis, the matriarch of the family, still worked in the kitchen of the restaurant and walked through the dining room regularly to make sure everyone was satisfied with the food. I was disappointed I wouldn't have time to enjoy any of it tonight.

When I got to the dock, Travis Lucero was at the helm of our military-grade Zodiac, waiting in line to fill up the gas tank. Dad had purchased the boat second-hand from St. John's County two years earlier. He'd balked at the price of the engines until Major Parks had found a federal grant that we could use to buy them and outfit the boat. Kelly and Lucero had practically begged Dad to send them to a patrol boat training class down in Fort Lauderdale, also paid for with grant money.

Tori Kelly came back from the marina store. At five-foot-two, she was the shortest deputy in the department and one of the toughest. She was tugging at her patrol belt as she approached.

"Hey, Sarge. Unlike some people, I can't just hang it over the side," she said, giving Lucero a good-natured frown.

"I can't help it if I come better equipped," he joked as he pulled up to the pumps.

"You wish," she shot back and helped tie the boat up to the cleats.

"Find anything?" I asked.

"Nope. We started down by the recovery site and have been working our way out from there," Kelly said. "We're going slow so we don't disturb any evidence if we find it."

"*We're* going slow, but all the other boats aren't," Lucero said, shaking his head.

"There were a lot of boaters out when we first got here," Kelly admitted.

"We even pulled over a ski boat for reckless driving," Lucero said. "We thought about mentioning what we were looking for to some of the other boaters, but Mick said to keep it on the DL for right now."

"We don't want people going crazy," I agreed. If you told one boater that there was a dead body in the lake, he'd call all his friends and there'd be another dozen boats adding to the chaos.

Once we were fueled up, I clambered into the boat while Lucero and Kelly argued over who got to drive.

"Kelly, you drive," I instructed, and Lucero scratched his ear with his middle finger in her direction.

"We're also looking for a jon boat," I reminded them.

"Yeah, Mick got the registration number from the owner, and we were able to pull up the description. I think he contacted the grouper troopers and let them know to be on the lookout for it." Lucero had to shout, even though Kelly was keeping the engines down to little more than an idle. "Normally, a body wouldn't float to the surface for a couple of days, but I'm not sure how being dismembered fits into the picture."

I didn't know either. Adams County didn't have quite as many lakes and rivers as other parts of the state, so I hadn't had to deal with as many drowning victims as some deputies. Still, we had our share. We'd been lucky and recovered most of them in a couple of days, though I couldn't remember any of the bodies being dismembered.

Even over the sound of the two outboard engines, I heard the distinctive thrumming of a helicopter rotor. Looking up, I saw LCSO One flying over us at about five hundred feet. As the helicopter circled, my phone rang.

"We've got an oil slick about a quarter mile north of you," the pilot informed me.

I relayed the information to Kelly, who gave me a thumbs-up as she pulled the throttle forward and wheeled the boat into deeper water. With guidance from the deputy in the helicopter, we found the oil slick that was drifting north from a point of origin not far from the west side of the lake. By land, it was probably about a mile from where the foot had been found.

"How deep is it here?" I asked once Kelly had idled the engines.

"About thirty feet. The deepest point in the lake is about forty feet."

We all looked over the side of the boat, but with the glare from the setting sun, we couldn't see anything below the surface.

"I'll go down," Lucero said, already taking off his shoes.

"I'm a better swimmer than you," Kelly said.

"Let Travis do this," I said, and she glared at me. "Hey, I let you drive."

Lucero showed her the finger again, and she stuck out

her tongue at him in a show of true law enforcement professionalism. I hid my smile, knowing the banter was evidence of the true camaraderie between them.

Lucero had come prepared with a pair of swim trunks on under his clothes. After digging out a mask, snorkel and flippers from under the front seat, he directed Kelly to where he thought the best spot would be to drop the anchor. He donned the mask and flippers while Kelly prepared a buoy for him if he found anything. I felt like a third wheel.

Kelly and I watched Lucero roll off the side of the boat into the tannin-colored water. He circled and got oriented before swimming over to the anchor and following the rope down to the bottom. He made five dives before swimming to the side of the boat.

"I need a light," he told Kelly. "I think we've found your jon boat."

Lucero made two more dives before he gave us a thumbs-up. Kelly helped him get the buoy and line set so he could tie it off to the sunken boat while I tried to figure out our next move. I knew we needed to get a good look at the boat where it was before we attempted to raise it. I didn't want to screw up any evidence, so I decided to call the Florida Department of Law Enforcement to see what sort of assistance they could give us. A part of me wanted answers now, but I consoled myself with the knowledge that patience was a virtue to be nurtured in law enforcement.

"We'll need you back out on the lake in the morning," I told Kelly and Lucero when we had docked at the marina.

"Oh, don't punish us," Kelly said, crying crocodile tears while Lucero tried to contain his glee.

CHAPTER FIVE

It was dark by the time I got back to the lake house. My stomach lurched when I saw the scene that greeted me. Besides Mick's car and Sanderson's patrol car, there were two news vans and a couple of other cars that I didn't recognize.

Before I could even get out of my car, a reporter came over and blocked me from opening my door.

"Have you found the rest of Scott Nicholl's body?" the man asked, sticking a microphone in my face. His cameraman was a dozen feet behind him, trying to get the camera's light to work. *A small mercy*, I thought.

"I can give you Major Parks's phone number if you'd like to talk with him." I had to make an effort not to intentionally hit the man with the car door as I climbed out. Unfortunately, the cameraman got the light working and blinded me with it as I tried to get past them.

"You're Larry Macklin, right?" the reporter asked, following me. "Your dad is the sheriff. Why isn't he here overseeing this investigation?"

It was a stupid question, and I should have ignored him. Instead, I turned around and faced him and the camera.

"We currently have two investigators, several deputies,

our boat patrol, our crime scene unit and the coroner's office all working on this case. In addition, we've received assistance from the Leon County Sheriff's Office's aviation unit. Sheriff Macklin is following the investigation, but…" I let a long, dramatic pause build. "…as you know, this is not the only investigation or operation that our office is currently working on."

I turned and almost ran smack into the other news station's camera, which was there to accompany Tina Knightly, a full-bodied blonde tornado who liked to ambush law enforcement officers and make them stumble over their own tongues. There was a sign in our break room at the office warning our deputies not to talk to her under *any* circumstances.

"Larry, you can do better than that," Tina admonished me. Using an officer's first name was one of her favorite tactics to throw them off their mark.

"No comment," I tossed out like a warrior's shield.

"How many body parts have been found?"

I raised my hand to fend off her cameraman, an Hispanic man who was looking as eager for the story as Tina.

"Five!" Tina shouted, looking at the hand I was holding up to block the light from the camera.

It was such a stupid attempt at a gotcha that I was almost suckered into saying something. With a strong force of will, I held my tongue and moved to the crime scene tape blocking the driveway to the house. Sanderson met me at the tape and stood stalwartly in front of the press, practically daring them to try to follow me.

Of course, that would be on the news with Tina saying that the sheriff's office was blocking the press's access.

"You survived the relentless Tinasaurus," Mick chuckled as I met him at the front door.

"Quiet! They have mics that can pick up a whisper at a hundred yards," I told him, hoping I was joking.

Mick put on his battle face and shot the two cameras a look that should have broken their lenses.

"We're lucky that she's a glory hound and usually won't lower herself to cover stories in our lowly little county," he grumbled.

"The lure of someone missing from a national TV show is going to bring out the flies." I frowned.

"I have good news, though. Judge Andrew issued us a warrant to search Nicholl's possessions." Mick handed me a bag containing gloves and protective clothing.

"How'd you manage that?" Without having yet identified the owner of the foot, I'd doubted we'd be able to get a warrant to search Scott's room.

"In the affidavit, I leaned on the need to locate Scott and used the argument that, even if it isn't his foot, it still suggests that something dangerous is going on in the area."

"Well played," I said, impressed. Judges took their responsibilities seriously and, rightfully, held our feet to the fire when we made warrant requests.

"I also got an expedited warrant for his phone data. I talked to Lionel and he contacted Scott's service provider. With luck, we might have ping data by noon tomorrow. Shantel is upstairs filming now. We're also clear to search the common areas of the house. The other two guys who were staying here, Eli and Dirk, have already been by to collect their stuff. Since the warrant didn't cover their possessions, I wasn't able to go through any of it."

We put on the protective clothing as Tina told her cameraman to stay focused on us. I resisted the urge to throw something at them.

I was eager to look through Scott's belongings. Whenever I searched someone's possessions, I always envisioned all the great clues I'd find that would help solve the mystery in less than an hour. I was like a gambler, always sure I'd walk away a winner. And, like a gambler, I was usually disappointed.

"You go out looking for a missing person and find a foot instead," Shantel chastised me as she met us at the stairs, sounding like a disappointed mother. When I'd first started at the department, she'd done more than anyone else to train me on how to conduct a forensic investigation. Because my father was the sheriff, some of the other deputies and investigators had given me the cold shoulder, but Shantel had always pointed out pitfalls at crime scenes that saved me from embarrassment and failure.

"I found what I could," I defended myself.

"Did you give Miss Tina a kiss when you came in?" Shantel asked with a wicked smile, and I heard Mick snort back a laugh.

"Don't even get me started," I told her.

"I hate every time I see her at a crime scene, because I know she's going to put your father and Major Parks in a bad mood for weeks."

"You aren't kidding. At least there isn't an election coming up."

"I'm done upstairs. Let me know if you need me to document anything you find *in situ*."

"Listen to you, throwing out Latin phrases," I joked.

"Don't get sassy with me." She wagged her finger in my face.

Mick and I went to Scott's room, where I headed straight for his luggage. I half expected to find drugs or something illicit. Instead, there were only clothes and men's health magazines. There was a MacBook Pro sitting on the dresser, but the warrant didn't give us the right to search it, leaving me feeling incomplete.

What wasn't in the room was more interesting than what was. There were no keys, no wallet and no phone.

I called Arianne.

"I need Kayla's number," I told her.

"She's right here." Before I could say anything, she handed the phone off to Kayla.

I heard dramatic sniffling before she said in a hoarse voice, "Yes?"

"Can you tell me what Scott was wearing last night?"

"He was wearing the same clothes he'd worn on location. He normally has, like, three sets of the same clothes in case one pair gets damaged… You know, for continuity. Wait! Gabby took pictures of us in our clothes on Sunday. I'll get her to send you his photos." I could hear her choking back tears as she talked.

"Would you put Miss Bass back on the phone?" I didn't want to burden Kayla with any more chores.

"Would you send me contact numbers for everyone in the production?" I asked Arianne when she came back on the phone.

"I'll text them to you. Kayla is pretty torn up." I could hear the woman crying in the background.

"Include anyone local who was involved, including…" I checked my notes. "Cody Morgan."

A few minutes later, my phone buzzed with a list of phone numbers, followed closely by the pictures Kayla had mentioned. I compared them with what was in Scott's suitcase and scattered around the room, finding only two complete outfits that looked just like what he was wearing in the photos.

I called Kayla back. "Are you sure he had three outfits like the one he wore yesterday?"

"I think." She sounded exhausted from crying.

"Were you all in his room last night?" I knew she'd said they'd had sex while at the house, but that didn't necessarily mean it was in his room.

"Yes." Her voice was small and distant.

"Did you notice anything that you wouldn't have expected among his belongings?" It was a long shot, but I couldn't drag her over to the house and have her look around the room tonight.

"I don't know what you mean…" Kayla's voice trailed off and I heard the phone change hands.

"She's taken a… sleeping aid," Arianne told me.

"Keep an eye on her."

"Of course. She's making it sound like her relationship with Scott was very serious." Arianne dropped her voice. "I didn't see that. It looked like every other frivolous fling he's ever had."

I thanked her and assured her I'd update her first thing in the morning. I wasn't going to tell anyone about finding the boat until we had more information, and I might even wait until we'd brought it to the surface. Visibility had only been about four feet that evening, so Lucero hadn't been able to see much on his free dives down to the boat. All we knew for sure was that the registration sticker matched the information the owner had given us.

It was frustrating having to walk past the other bedrooms, unable to search them without the residents being present. We moved downstairs and looked through the kitchen and living room. The rooms were neat and uncluttered. I got the impression that the film crew hadn't had much time to sit around the house.

The garage held various yard and household tools, including saws, hammers and wrenches. Against one wall were pieces of PVC pipe, boards and other items that could be used to make repairs around the house. The door on the east side of the garage opened into the narrow laundry room that Eli and I had come through earlier. The utility sink was dry, and nothing in the room looked like it could have anything to do with Scott's disappearance. If we had a different warrant, I would have been taking things off the shelf, pulling the washer and dryer out from the wall and having Shantel's crew take apart the drains.

"Nothing suggests anything happened in the house," Mick said.

"The text that Kayla got could mean several things. *Home* could mean that he was inside the house when he sent it, or it could just mean that he was within *sight* of the house. Another angle is that the text could have been sent by a third party who was trying to mislead Kayla… and us."

"Agreed. If that is Scott's foot, I don't think he made it inside the house," Mick said as we walked back through the house one final time.

"If he did make it to the house, then he went back out

again and something happened. We can't ignore the possibility that he took off and the foot belongs to someone else."

"Maybe *Scott* killed someone," Mick suggested. "That would be a nice twist."

"It would have been helpful if Scott had a tattoo or a birthmark on his foot."

"We can't be that lucky."

"We should be able to get Scott's DNA to the coroner's office in the morning, and hopefully they can do an expedited match."

"Doesn't it usually take longer?" Mick hadn't worked violent crimes in years. There weren't many burglary cases where anyone was going to pay to develop a DNA profile.

"If they have a DNA sequence to compare it to, they can just do a limited number of markers rather than a complete sequence. If it comes back as a one-in-a-million match, then we're good. They can always do a more complete analysis later. There's plenty of foot to work with. It's not like when you have a very small sample and, if you use it up in a simple comparison, you don't have any left for a more detailed one."

"Got it." Mick nodded "Hey…"

I heard him stop walking and his tone caused me to turn and face him. "This show, *Search for Bigfoot* or whatever. Have you ever seen it?"

"Cara's a fan, and I've watched it with her a few times," I admitted.

"I guess I'm going to have to watch a couple of episodes." Mick didn't sound too sure. "Where can I see it?"

I was a little surprised by the question. Mick was younger than Dad.

"It's on a couple of the streaming services. I can't remember which one we watch it on. It's free on that one, or you can probably pay if you want to watch it on whatever you have." As I talked, Mick looked at me like I was discussing advanced physics.

"I don't do any of that stuff. My last ex-wife was into all that, but I never understood sitting on the couch watching other people do things."

Mick wasn't being funny. I could tell that he'd just decided to opt out of TV. I knew how he felt. I was the same way with video games. My eyes always glazed over when a bunch of my peers started talking about the latest games. Dad had given me such a sour look the one Christmas I'd asked for a PlayStation that I'd never asked again. And I'd never had a chance to play at a friend's house growing up, as all of their parents had made us kids stay outside unless an actual hurricane had been passing overhead.

"You can watch on your laptop. I'll show you how to pull it up."

Mick nodded solemnly, looking as excited as if I'd told him I could help him take a plunge into an icy river.

To my relief, the news vans had left by the time we came out of the house. We checked the crime scene tape and got assurances from the watch commander that a deputy would be posted at the house all night.

I looked past the house, down to the lake, where the half moon was making the water sparkle. I wanted to go back out onto the lake and search for the rest of whoever's foot we'd found. The irony was that if it wasn't Scott's foot, then we were being seriously misdirected from the hunt for him. I'd need to expand the land search tomorrow on the off-chance that he wasn't in the lake.

Mick left, and I sat in my car for a while, answering texts and responding to emails and reports. I knew that if I went home, I wouldn't get them done tonight. Finally caught up and on the way to my place, I called Dad.

"Your favorite reporter was here tonight," I told him.

"She blew up my phone earlier this evening. There are reporters and then there are bloodsuckers. She's in the latter class."

I filled him in on the jon boat and the search of the

house.

"I'll get a dive team out there tomorrow morning," he promised. We didn't have our own dive team so, like the helicopter, it was something else that we had to outsource from larger counties with more resources. "You saw the foot. Do you think it belongs to Nicholl?"

"I don't have much experience at identifying people by their severed feet. All I can tell you is that it looked like it belonged to a male. Toenails looked neat. The skin was too wrinkled and waterlogged to tell what condition it'd been in before being in the lake for a day, but I'd say it didn't come off of a homeless man."

"What do you think about it being bare?"

"Maybe someone pulled the victim's clothes off when they dismembered him. Or if it was an animal attack, the shoe might have been pulled off during the act of predation."

"You were just a kid when Judge Gallagher got killed. He was fishing in Sander's Lake when a gator grabbed him. He was wearing a creel with half a dozen fish in it and was in waist-deep water. His son said he'd snagged his lure on a tree branch and went to retrieve it. Anyway, wearing a basket of bait on his hip, he was making his way further out into the water when a twelve-foot gator grabbed him. Everyone said the thing shook him for almost a minute before pulling him under the water."

I grimaced. "That's horrifying. I remember some kids in school talking about a guy getting eaten right in front of his family. I guess that's who they were talking about."

"Being a judge and a prominent person in the community, everyone demanded that the body be retrieved. It took divers a week to find him and get the body out of the hole the gator had stuffed it in. I was there the day they brought him to the surface. Not a pretty sight."

"I get it. No matter how Nicholl ended up in the water, there's a chance that a gator has taken him to its hole to soften him up and eat him over time. What a lovely thought." *How do you explain that to someone's friends and family?* I wondered.

"And Lake Loka is ten times the size of Sander's Lake."

"We saw half a dozen alligators when we were out there today."

"And with city people and vacationers around the lake, I can promise you there's been some idiot throwing marshmallows to the cute lake lizards," Dad said, and I didn't have to see him to sense his irritation. Dad didn't suffer fools lightly.

"I'll keep my fingers crossed that we aren't looking at a situation like that."

"Go home and get some sleep," he told me in a fatherly tone I wasn't used to, then hung up.

When I got home, Cara was already in bed. It was almost midnight and I did my best to assemble a sandwich from some bread and cheese without waking her. However, when I went to get the mayonnaise from the refrigerator, I saw her watching me from the doorway to the bedroom.

"Sorry I woke you." I told her, and smiled because she looked so cute in an oversized shirt with her red hair mussed and her eyes heavy with sleep.

"I was worried about you," she yawned.

"I can tell," I laughed.

"It's late." She smiled and came over to give me a hug. "I was worried."

"Are you sure you didn't just want the inside story about Scott Nicholl?"

"There were a dozen different rumors going around the clinic. Is he really dead?" she asked with true sadness in her voice.

"At this point I don't know. It doesn't look good. What were the rumors?" I was always fascinated by the veterinary clinic's central location on the Adams County grapevine. Cara spent part of her day at or near the reception desk and heard all the latest gossip the clients brought in along with their animals.

"Everything from the fact that Nicholl was dead and one of the other members of the cast killed him, to Bigfoot did it or it's all a big publicity hoax." Cara got a glass of water and sat down at the table with me.

Ghost, the young white cat I'd found while working another case the previous autumn, jumped into my lap and made eating my sandwich quite a bit harder. Ivy, our older tabby, just eyed us from the back of the couch in the living room, looking grumpy that we were making so much noise and disturbing her night's rest.

"All I can say is that Nicholl is definitely missing and that we found a body part that doesn't eliminate the possibility of Bigfoot being involved."

"What do you think?"

I shrugged. "We're going to do a DNA test that should give us the answer. Though even if the body part is from Nicholl, it would be possible to lose this particular item and still be alive."

"You're being coy about what body part," Cara said with arched eyebrows.

"Not that part. But for the moment we're keeping the details to ourselves." Even as I said it, I doubted the cast and crew would be as discreet with the information, even though they'd been warned about talking about the investigation.

"I just can't believe he could be dead."

"You've watched the show more than I have. Tell me your opinion of the hosts of the show."

"Scott is the funny guy and Eli is the calm and rational one. Jackie is the super-smart girl-power character. Jackie and Scott seem to have some chemistry. A little flirty with a twist. She does the flirting and then will kind of give him a saucy smile if he takes the bait. It's sort of like the game where you put your hand out to shake with someone, then take it back when they put their hand out."

"Does that leave Eli as the odd man out?"

"No. He seems to be playing his own game. I guess it's like he takes advantage of the other two facing off, and he'll sometimes steal the spotlight by doing the daring thing. You know, he'll be the one that goes in the cave where a sasquatch has been reported, or at night he'll be the one to run through the bushes after the animal they've seen on their night-vision camera."

"Hmmm…" I said. "It's hard to tell how much of that is scripted. Eli was rattled when we found the severed body part. Still, he came across like you said. A bit above all the interpersonal goings-on."

"I read an article online that talked about his background. He served in the Army straight out of high school. I think he tried out for one of the elite units but got hurt and couldn't finish. When he got out of the service, he ended up doing commercials in Atlanta, where he was hired to host a local news show."

"Any other reality shows on his resume?"

"I think he's done a couple of nature documentaries, but not a lot."

I looked at the clock and the small hand was approaching one.

"We better get some sleep." I stood up and took my plate to the sink.

Alvin, our Pug, was snoring loudly from my place on the bed.

"You'll need to tell him to make room when I get done taking a shower," I told Cara.

"He was just taking advantage of your work ethic. You'll have to be the bad guy and move him when you come back. I don't have the heart," she said, crawling into her side of the bed.

CHAPTER SIX

My phone was buzzing with a long list of texts before I even got out of bed. I grabbed another quick shower and was dressed and eating cereal by seven o'clock. I was wearing a department polo and BDUs, since I might be spending most of the day on or around the lake.

"We meet again." Cara shuffled over and gave me a kiss. "I'm still tired and I managed to get eight hours sleep, even with you coming in late from hobnobbing with TV personalities. I can only imagine how you feel."

"And I'm going to have another long day." I was looking through my texts as I tried to talk to Cara and eat my cereal at the same time. Dad had already put me in contact with two counties offering dive teams. I accepted the first offer and asked the second to hold their team on standby, just in case the first team had to pull out before we were done searching the lake.

"You aren't listening to me," Cara teased as she started boiling a pot of water for tea, and I realized that I'd completely missed her last few comments.

"Sorry," I said without taking my eyes off my phone.

She poked me on the arm and when I looked up, gave me a quick kiss.

"That's in case you're gone when I come out from my shower. Can I trust you to pour water in my cup?"

"Promise."

One of the texts was from Pete. *Are we having fun yet? Saw you for a hot second on the news with Tina the Spiderwoman.*

Call me when you get the chance, I texted back.

A minute later, the phone rang.

"My leg is aching this morning, so I was already up." Pete didn't sound happy, but he was doing much better than he'd been before his most recent operation. After the surgeon had finished rebreaking the leg and inserting enough metal to make a small car, he'd been very optimistic about Pete's chances to regain a full range of motion and strength in his leg.

"Good. I need you to cover some of my duties while I recover the boat and fish around in the lake for more body parts."

"I guess I can't argue since I'm pulling down sergeant's pay anyway."

"That's the can-do attitude I've come to expect. I need you to go through the latest reports and assign cases. Don't give Mick anything new unless it's tied to a case he's already got on his plate."

"With Julio and Phil on vacation, and you and Mick out of rotation, that doesn't leave many options," Pete groused.

"If you need to, you can take a few cases for yourself," I said, smiling. It was good to have the old, grumpy Pete back. We'd been partners for a long time, and he'd always been like a bear woken up from hibernation in the morning, until the crash that had almost crippled him. I was glad that it was finally looking like he'd soon be able to make his long-delayed lateral transfer to head of the tactical team.

"Up yours with a rubber hose. Fine, I'll solve all your cases while you float around the lake in a boat and bask in the limelight with Tina Oh-What-Big-Cameras-I-Have Knightly."

"You're a pal."

"I've got you covered," Pete said seriously and hung up.

I texted Mick and told him to meet me at the marina, then I called Dr. Darzi, our coroner. I hadn't expected him to answer his phone before eight, but I should have known better.

"My friend," he greeted me. Even with his light Indian accent, or maybe because of it, his enunciation was better than mine. "When will you be sending us the rest of the body?"

"We're looking for it. When can you tell me if the foot belongs to Scott Nicholl?"

"We got the DNA sequence that the show provided to us, but I will tell you that I'm not going to be able to make a positive ID with it. The sample was not taken or processed under rigorous standards of care."

"I understand. Still, if you tell me they match, then I can move forward with the presumption that Nicholl was the original owner of the foot. Even if it's his foot, he still might not be dead."

"This is true. People have their feet amputated all the time and live long lives afterward. However, not many have them cut off outside an operating room and survive without medical treatment."

"Our missing person alert went out to all hospitals within two hundred miles. What else can you tell me from the foot?" I asked.

"When we examine it, I should be able to make some observations about the owner's health prior to being separated from their limb. And I should be able to determine if it was removed before or after the subject died."

"What about toxicology?"

"There won't be a lot of blood left, and without the other organs, toxicology will only tell us so much. Toenails could show us certain types of long-term poisoning, but I don't think you suspect the victim was poisoned."

"If this isn't Nicholl, will you be able to make a guess at the victim's size?"

"Not really. The bones of the leg are more helpful when it comes to estimating a person's height and even weight. What I *can* tell you now, just based on my cursory exam when we extracted the DNA, is that whatever severed the foot from the leg was not a knife."

"Not a knife. Can you narrow that down?"

"Possibilities would include an alligator or another animal, a boat propellor or a chainsaw. I should be able to give you a better short list after a microscopic examination of the ends of the bone."

"How long before you can give me an answer on the DNA?"

"Tomorrow. I'm calling in a few favors to get it done for you, my friend." I could hear the smile in his voice.

"I appreciate it."

"Anything for my best customer." Darzi chuckled and told me he would get back to me as soon as he knew more.

Sunlight was coming in through the kitchen window, and I could hear Cara finishing up with her morning routine. I remembered to pour water over the teabag in her mug as promised, then headed out into the sultry summer morning.

Mick was on the phone and pacing up and down the dock when I got to the marina. He hadn't dressed down and was wearing the same outfit he always did—a button-down shirt, brown coat and brown trousers.

"I got the watch commander to give us two additional patrol deputies to help canvas the homes around the lake today," he told me as he put the phone back into his pocket.

"I'm impressed, especially since we already have Kelly and Lucero helping out with the boat."

"He wasn't happy. He called Parks and made sure he had authorization to bring in off-duty deputies if things get busy."

"The upside to working a priority case." The words were barely out of my mouth when I saw Tina Knightly pull into the marina's parking lot, with a different cameraman in tow this morning. "And then there's the downside," I growled. She was the last thing I needed to see first thing in the morning.

I looked at my watch. "I'm going to give Kelly and Lucero a hard time for not getting here early enough to avoid her."

"You want me to handle her?" Mick had an odd smile on his face.

"We aren't authorized to shoot the media," I reminded him.

His smile got bigger, and he pulled a red onion from his pocket. "After last night I came prepared."

He walked quickly over to the gangway that attached the floating dock to the porch that wrapped around the marina's office. I saw him take a large bite from the onion as Tina and the cameraman hurried toward me. The gangway was only four feet wide, so they couldn't get around Mick.

Tina slowed down as she approached him. Even from where I was standing, I could see that Mick was chewing the onion with his mouth open. I had to work to control my gag reflex as I saw him take another bite and spew bits of it a foot from his mouth.

Tina stopped four feet from him, obviously furious that he was blocking her way. I couldn't hear what they were saying to each other, but as Mick talked, he was slowly moving closer to her. At first, I thought she might try and stand her ground, but when he took yet another bite of onion and another step toward her, she backed up. The anger on her face was clear from fifty feet away.

I saw her order the cameraman to point his weapon at Mick, who just kept moving closer. Mick looked like he was talking to his best friend as he walked toward them. When the cameraman, no doubt captivated by Mick's performance, tripped while walking backward, Tina finally broke. She looked like she was going to hit Mick with the microphone she'd been carrying, but instead she shouted, "Go to hell!"

loudly enough for me and everyone who lived on the lake to hear her.

Reinforcements in the form of Tori Kelly and Travis Lucero showed up at just the right moment. I thought Tina might try to confront them, but by that point her hair and makeup were mussed and she must have decided to regroup. Grinning broadly, Mick came back down to the dock with the other deputies in tow.

"You're disgusting," I said in admiration.

"It's only fair," Mick said. "How many times have we had to deal with suspects and witnesses with halitosis and other hygiene challenges that have left us gagging?"

"Almost daily when I was on patrol," I admitted.

I got on the phone and called the dive team that was coming in to help with the search, and directed them to a public boat launch on the other side of the lake, where they wouldn't have to fight their way past Terrible Tina.

"Where did she come from anyway?" Kelly asked once we were all on the boat.

"Transferred from Miami," Lucero answered. "I heard she pissed off the news director at her old station."

"Why did WTHA hire her?" I asked.

"'Cause she gets ratings and WTHA had nowhere to go but up," Lucero said.

"How do you know so much?" Mick asked.

"I spent two years as a journalism major at FSU before I came to my senses. I've got friends at WTHA."

"I actually feel sorry for the cameraman. He didn't look as excited to be with her as the guy last night. At one point he locked eyes with me, and I thought he was going to mouth 'help me,'" Mick chuckled.

"He might have if you hadn't smelled like rotten onions," I told him and waved my hand in front of my nose. "Do you have any mouthwash with you?"

"That's the gratitude I get for saving you from another embarrassing encounter with the fourth estate." Mick grabbed a bottle of water from a duffle bag at his feet, took a swig and spat it overboard before pulling out a sampler-sized bottle of mouthwash. "I told you I came prepared."

We swung around to the other side of the lake to meet the dive team. I filled them in on the current situation and how we wanted to proceed.

"Bringing up a boat, even from just thirty feet, can be tough. Especially if you're trying to preserve evidence," Sergeant Meggs, the officer in charge of the four-person team, told us.

"We're hoping to get up as much evidence as we can before we attempt to raise the boat."

"Makes sense. You say it's a jon boat, so it's got an outboard engine. We could take that off and pull it up separately, which will take much of the weight off the boat. Still, everything we dismantle is a piece of your puzzle you can't put back together again," Meggs explained.

I understood what he was saying. If we could photograph the boat or study it in place, we'd know more about what happened before it sank. If we started taking the boat apart, there could be questions we'd never have the answers to. It was a dilemma without a good solution.

"I don't guess we could get any meaningful pictures of the boat on the bottom," I said.

All the divers shook their heads and Lucero answered for them, "Not with the current state of visibility down there."

"I wish I had a better answer," Meggs said.

"We'll just have to do the best we can. Do a thorough search of the craft before you attempt to bring anything up," I said and saw the smirks on the faces of the divers.

"We're on top of this. We'll be making multiple dives, fifteen or twenty minutes at a time. Each time we surface, we'll write notes on what we found and compare them before coming up with a plan and going down again," Meggs explained.

"Sorry. Y'all are the experts." I held up my hands in surrender.

"And we won't forget that y'all are the lead investigating

agency. Before we take any action, we'll confer with you." Meggs nodded to his team. "Let's get ready."

They spent the next twenty minutes talking with Lucero about what he'd seen the day before and coming up with their plan of attack.

After the first hour went by without finding a body, I decided I didn't need to be there. I left Mick in charge of the recovery of the boat and any other items they found, and asked Kelly to run me back to the marina. I stepped back onto land with caution, but there was no sign of Tina or her news van.

I decided to head out to do more interviews with the cast and crew of *The Big Search*. But first I called dispatch to make sure that the BOLO for Scott Nicholl was getting plenty of attention.

"Are you joking?" Marti in dispatch asked me. "We've spent half the morning answering calls from citizens and other departments that want to get in on the hunt. Lose your average Alzheimer's patient and you have to beg people to read the bulletin. Lose a celebrity and everyone and their sister wants to help."

Both amused and frustrated by his comment, I called Arianne to find out where they were shooting.

"I thought about cancelling today," she told me after giving me directions. "But then I thought about all of us sitting around in the two houses staring at each other and I decided it would be better to be working. Kayla is still in bad shape, so Jackie told her she could stay behind."

"She's at the house alone?" I asked, not liking the idea at all.

"No. Jackie thought someone should stay with her, so we're rotating. Anyone not needed at the shoot for a while is going back and staying with Kayla. I'm not so worried about someone else hurting her as much as I'm worried about her hurting herself."

When I arrived at the day's shooting location, I could see a significant difference in everyone's energy and attitude from the day before. When they weren't actively filming, they gathered in small groups, talking listlessly or looking off into the distance. I was sure that everyone was wondering not only about what had happened to their colleague, but what this was going to mean for the show and their futures.

"Who do you want to talk to first?" Arianne asked. She looked like she'd aged ten years overnight, and she knew that I noticed it. "I know I look like crap. Jackie and I were on the phone half the night, soothing the fears of our producers."

"Do you want to sit down? Can I get you some water?"

"A tumbler of whiskey might help." She shook her head. "I'm fine. Really. I just need some sleep."

"I can understand that. Okay, let's see. If he's here, I'd like to talk to Cody Morgan first."

"He's sitting over there in his truck. Good luck. He's not much of a talker."

I walked over to an old Dodge pickup where a man in his mid-fifties was sitting watching the crew set up the next shot.

"Are you Cody?" I asked once I was standing at the driver's door. He hadn't even turned his head to look at me as I walked up.

"Yep." He kept looking straight ahead. His profile would have matched an artist's sketch for Hemingway's *The Old Man and the Sea*, right down to the craggy face and grey beard.

"I'd like to ask you a few questions about Scott Nicholl's disappearance."

Cody turned his head and looked straight into my eyes.

"I don't know anything about it."

"You might be able to help fill in some of the timeline and, maybe, give me some insight into the cast and crew's personal interactions."

He guffawed and suddenly his mouth curved into a smile and his eyes lit up.

"You might be right." He nodded his head to the other side of the truck. "Get in and I'll tell you what I can."

I went to the other side of the truck, which would have been on the showroom floor sometime around the beginning of the new millennium. It had the crappy paint job of all Dodge trucks from that period, but looked like it would still be running long after all the new cars were on the scrap heap.

I climbed in and was hit with the smell of old fast-food bags and gun oil.

"This is the worst mistake I've made in years." Cody nodded through the windshield. "I should have known better. I guess it's true that there's no fool like an old fool."

"What is your role on the show?" I had a vague idea from what I'd been told by the others, but I wanted to hear it from him.

"I'm backdrop. Just some old set dressing is all. Not that I can't use the money. Still, feels like I've sold my soul." He tapped his chest.

"What do you mean?"

"I know what people say about me. *He's a true believer.* That's what they call folks like me. Why? Because I've seen one."

"A Bigfoot?" I tried not to sound too incredulous.

Cody turned his head and smiled at me.

"You can call me a nut, but be careful. Karma can bite you in the butt. There's a chance that one day you'll see something. Maybe it will be a UFO or a monster or a ghost. Who knows. But when you see it, there'll be no doubt in your mind about what you saw. You'll tell people and they'll look at you like you're Noah telling folks it's going to start raining and they need to put on their waders. When that happens, you'll know what it's like to be alone."

"I can see where that would be a hard pill to swallow," I said sympathetically.

"Know what's worse?"

I shook my head.

"You meet someone who believes you, and after talking to them for a while, you come to the conclusion that they're crazier than a bedbug. That's the day you really look in the mirror for the first time in your life and ask yourself, 'How crazy am I?'" Cody's face looked as though it was made of stone, hard and impervious.

"Is it true you had a run-in with Scott Nicholl?"

"I've had arguments with all of them. Nicholl isn't the worst of the lot. He's just part and parcel to this sham of a production. I thought they were going to at least try and do a real investigation into the cases here in North Florida."

"Haven't you ever seen the show?"

He looked embarrassed.

"I… kind of… I don't know, *believed* them. I thought Jackie, Eli and Scott were actually interested in Bigfoot." Cody sounded like a big kid who'd learned that Santa wasn't real.

"I can see how that would have made you mad." I was curious where this would go.

Cody looked me in the eyes.

"I know about murder inquiries. You're trying to get me to say I was angry enough that I could have killed someone."

"What do you know about murders?" I felt the hairs on the back of my neck stand up.

"I've been a part of a few murder investigations."

I couldn't stop my hand from reaching back and feeling for the butt of my gun. How awkward would it be for me to draw on him from inside the truck? My mind was doing a number of calculations. I took a deep breath to calm myself.

"How did that happen? Were you a law enforcement officer?"

"Nah, I haven't ever been a cop. I know a bunch of 'em though. I know the chief of police in Calhoun."

"You know Chief Marks?" My hand relaxed.

"Yep, she's good friends with a friend of mine."

"Who's that?"

"Kay Lamberton. She and her brother owned a funeral home that I worked at for a while."

I remembered Darlene introducing me to Kay shortly

before the ice storm last winter.

"That's good to know. Then I guess you wouldn't mind me asking Chief Marks about you?"

"Hell no. We had lunch together on Friday," he said. "Like I told you, I know how y'all have to go about clearing people."

This was going to put a different spin on how I continued my questioning.

"You know that Scott's missing. What I need from you is an insider's look at what happened the day before he disappeared. How long have you known them? The cast and crew?"

"I met up with them in Apalachicola about a week ago. We stayed at a hotel there and spent three days filming around Tate's Hell, and then two days at Sumatra on the Apalachicola River."

"Did you see any fighting among them?"

"You could tell that they'd worked together for a while. Smooth, you know. They didn't have to have long discussions about the shots or the interviews. The only fly in the ointment was me. The witnesses they dug up were the worst kind. The type that say crazy things. I know from watching the show that that's normal. But it was different when I knew the area and that there were real cases with trustworthy people who you could believe when they said they saw something. I tried to tell Jackie and Arianne that I could bring in some terrific reports from folks like cops, hunters and veterans who'd seen things they couldn't explain any other way than Bigfoot. But they weren't interested."

His passion boiled up from his soul. There was no doubt that Cody was a true believer, and that he was completely disgusted with the direction of the production.

"What about Scott? Since y'all got here, had he been acting differently?"

Cody put his hands on the steering wheel and leaned back in the seat.

"I'm trying to think back to Saturday," he said and closed

his eyes. "It was our first day shooting at the Mahoneys' property. We were supposed to be there at eleven, so I got there around ten-thirty. Arianne and the crew were already there. The cast showed up about ten after eleven. They had a hard time finding the house."

"What kind of mood was everyone in?"

"Most of them weren't happy with the heat and humidity. The cast especially were irritable when they were told that they couldn't film inside the house 'cause the light was bad and the house was too full of junk."

"Were they mad at anyone in particular?"

"Arianne took most of it, and she blamed the guy they had scouting witnesses and locations. Mostly, everyone was just tired of filming in the heat. The week before was tough on them."

"Not you?" I asked.

Cody smiled. "I've spent all my life out in the Florida woods. I won't say you get used to it, but you adapt. Their mistake was that they took every opportunity to sit in the air conditioning. If they'd just get out in the weather and stay in it, the heat wouldn't hit them so hard. Of course, the actors are worried about their looks, and Gabby, who does the makeup and clothes, was worried about what the heat and humidity would do."

"Tell me about your arguments with the cast and crew." I wasn't going to ignore him as a suspect, even if he did come with references.

"As soon as I met the Mahoneys, I knew the type of witnesses they were. According to them, they have a family of skunk apes living in the woods behind their house. The witnesses that Arianne had lined up the week before were better, but not by much. Anyway, I went to her and told her that I thought the Mahoneys were imagining things. That's when she told me I wasn't there to judge the show. She told me I could leave if I didn't like it. But if I did, she told me they'd still use the footage of me from the week before, but would expect me to pay back the per diem and advance I'd gotten for this week."

"Was anyone else around when you talked with her?"

"Nicholl must have been within earshot 'cause he came over and told me that this was a show for entertainment, not a documentary on some imaginary monster, and that I should get over myself, which was a laugh. I told him he was the one with the ego and that they were all just a bunch of clowns."

"How'd he take that?"

"Just laughed in my face. Said he was happy to be a very well-paid clown. He told Arianne to kick me off the production."

"But she didn't?"

"No. At first, I thought she was going to, but then Jackie came over and told us to cool off. Later, she asked me if I was willing to stick with the show." He looked over at me with a shamed look on his face. "I won't lie. I need the money, so I told her I'd stick with it if I could say what I wanted in front of the camera. She agreed as long as I didn't badmouth the witnesses, the stars or the show."

I was about to ask him why he thought Jackie intervened on his behalf when my phone rang.

"We've got a body, but not the one we were looking for," Mick told me. "You need to get over to the rental house, pronto. I've already called Shantel."

CHAPTER SEVEN

When I arrived at the lake house there were two patrol cars and Mick's unmarked already there, and the crime scene van pulled up right behind me. Mick was standing in the driveway with his phone to his ear and walked out to meet me.

"What have we got?" I asked, not sure I wanted to know.

I'd used my lights and siren to get there. On the drive over, I was trying to wrap my mind around the fact that a crime had been committed at a house where one of our deputies had been stationed overnight.

"Put on your stuff, and I'll walk you through and show you."

I suited up in protective gear while Mick put on a set of his own. Shantel had sent Marcus out to deal with this latest headache, and we told him that we'd have a plan after looking over the scene.

"I can't see anything out of place," Mick said as we walked in the front door and through the living areas toward the garage. "I cleared the house but didn't take the time to look for anything other than dead bodies or bad guys."

The door leading to the garage was open.

"Was this door open when you found the body?" I asked.

"No, it was closed. I decided not to touch it any more than I had to. I made notes and took pictures already."

"Bleach?" The odor hit me as soon as I stepped into the garage.

"And lots of it. This door was open." He pointed toward the laundry room.

As soon as we got within five feet of the room, I saw the body sprawled out in front of the washer and dryer. "Shit!" I muttered, then followed it with even more creative curse words. "Does she know yet?"

"Was there a news van out front?"

"Point taken."

Lying on the floor was the body of the cameraman who'd been with Tina Knightly the previous evening. There was a nasty-looking wound to the back of his head, and his clothes and body had been soaked in bleach. In fact, the whole room seemed to have been drenched in bleach. The odor was suffocating. The dead cameraman's jeans and T-shirt looked like he'd decided to do a home tie-dye job, with the bleach leaving odd, faded patterns across his clothes.

"Whoever it was used three bottles of bleach, probably from that cabinet."

Mick coughed and pointed to an open cabinet underneath the utility sink. I could see a couple of jugs of detergent still inside. The empty bleach bottles had been tossed in the garbage can between the washer and the door to the outside.

"Who found the body?"

"I did. I decided to do another turn around the house and yard when I got here, and as soon as I got close to the door, I smelled it," he said, pointing to the exterior door. "I looked through the window and saw our friend here, and when I looked closer at the door, I could see the pry marks where someone had cracked the door frame to get inside. I haven't touched the outside door. I came around the inside to get a better look at the victim, then started making phone calls."

I looked around but was feeling light-headed from the bleach fumes.

"Let's get out of here before we pass out," I suggested.

We retraced our steps through the house to the front door.

"Did the watch commander keep someone here all night?" I asked as I breathed in fresh air.

"Yep."

"Who?" I asked, feeling my teeth clenching in anger. If it was up to me, whoever it was would have a very bad morning.

"Greer. Karter with a K," Mick said with a disdainful smirk, nodding toward one of the patrol cars at the street. "He's over there. He was working a twelve-hour shift. I got here just before he was scheduled to go off-duty."

I looked over and saw Karter Greer sitting in his patrol car, tapping at his laptop. *No doubt writing a report to try and frame this in a way that puts him in the most positive light*, I thought.

Greer was a young deputy who had only been with the sheriff's office for a couple of years. His work was adequate at best. He was part of a clique in the department that made me sound like a grumpy old man when I talked about them. All in their early twenties, they spent more time grousing about work than actually doing any of it. I knew that there'd been a passive effort by the watch commanders to break them up by arranging their shifts so that they didn't work together, but sometimes it wasn't practical. And they seemed to have formed a bond that wasn't easily broken.

"Marcus should start with that cottage door into the laundry room. Have him photograph it, process it for prints and DNA, then open it up so the place can air out," I told Mick, then headed for Greer's car, grinding my teeth all the way.

He'd apparently seen me coming through his rearview mirror, because he quickly got out of the car and stood beside it, looking at me like a twelve-year-old who'd spilled the milk.

"What time did you come on duty last night?" I asked.

"I had a twelve-hour shift. I guess I checked in about ten-fifty. That's when the watch commander called me in and told me that I'd be here all night."

"Did he explain what you were supposed to do?"

"Watch the house." Greer's voice was barely audible.

"Would you interpret that as not letting anyone into the house?"

"I guess." He looked down at the ground.

"What if I told you that at least two people were in the house while you were on duty?"

"Maybe they got in before I took over," Greer said, his tone slowly changing to a more defiant and defensive one.

"Wouldn't you know that? Didn't you walk around the house when you got here and look at everything to make sure it was secure?"

"Maybe I should have, but Sanderson said it was secure so I… you know."

"You didn't check it when you arrived. So when did you check the house for the first time?"

Greer's face was now an ugly shade of red. "I walked around the house several times," he muttered.

"I want to see your notes."

"I… I don't have my notebook." He was looking everywhere but at my face.

I nodded toward the open door of his patrol car. "You don't make notes on your laptop?"

Greer stared off over my right shoulder, the muscles in his face twitching.

"Answer me," I demanded.

"You're not my su—" He was going to say "supervisor" until he remembered that I'd been promoted to sergeant earlier that year. I might not have been his direct supervisor, but I still outranked him.

"Mick!" I called out.

"I'm here," Mick said from beside my left elbow. My attention had been so focused on Greer that I hadn't noticed him come up.

"I want you to watch Greer. Don't let him access his phone or his laptop."

"No way! You can't do that!" Greer shouted angrily. All his passive resistance changed into resentment and, unless I was mistaken, fear.

"While you were out here… doing whatever it was you were doing in your patrol car… a man was murdered inside the house that you were being paid a decent salary to keep an eye on. While you were sitting in a county-owned car sucking down air conditioning made possible by county-bought gasoline, wearing clothes paid for by the county and wearing a star given to you after you took an oath to serve and protect the residents of that county… while you were doing that, a murder was committed almost literally under your nose!"

"You can't accuse—" Greer started to defend himself, but I cut him off.

"Stay right there or you'll find out what I can do." I was furious to think that one of our deputies had failed so miserably in his duty.

"Watch him," I told Mick again.

"He'll be right here when you get back." Mick was wearing a vicious smile that suggested he'd like nothing better than to kick the feet out from under Greer and handcuff his hands behind his back.

I went out of earshot and called Major Parks, who included internal affairs in his long list of responsibilities. He answered on the second ring, and I explained the situation.

"His file is too thick already," Parks said, and I could hear the frustration in his voice. "I should have recommended his termination six months ago, but we've been having a tough time filing our current vacancies."

"Any minute now, Tina Knightly is going to show up, and I can just imagine the shit show she's going to make of all this. Which is going to make it difficult to interview her about why her cameraman was on private property, and the fact that he probably crossed crime scene tape to end up where he was found."

"You think he broke in?"

"More likely, he was just lurking around outside hoping to get footage of… who knows. My point is, if we go ahead and take action against the deputy who was supposed to be watching the house, we'll help cut off some of the criticism."

"Yeah, we should be on solid ground. We'll need to check the activity on Greer's personal phone during that time. Hell, for all we know, he committed the murder," Parks said darkly.

"You have a point." I didn't honestly think Greer had anything to do with the murder. He was just an incompetent boob, but we would still need a warrant to seize and search his personal phone, as well as any other electronics he might have had with him. He was the only person we knew who was present when the murder took place, which would give us probable cause to think he was involved. "I'll write up the affidavit for the warrant myself."

"You may tell Greer that he is suspended without pay with his employment status dependent on the outcome of an internal investigation. And if he has any questions about what rules he violated to get the unpaid suspension, tell him to see me and I'll quote the rules verbatim. I wrote most of 'em. Get the affidavit done. I'll bring Ted up to speed." Dad and Parks had been friends as well as colleagues for decades, but hearing about this from Parks wasn't going to make Dad any less furious about it.

I walked past Mick, who was still watching a fidgeting Greer.

"I'll be right back," I told them and headed to my car. I didn't want Greer to know how much trouble he was in until I'd filled out the affidavit and gotten the warrant.

As I was typing, I got a text from Dad that read: *Take the SOB's star, ID, gun and car keys.* Parks had obviously spoken him.

It took the judge less than fifteen minutes to issue the

warrant. I walked back over to Greer's car with a smile on my face.

"I want your phone and any other electronic devices that might show what you were doing during the commission of the murder. This includes, but is not limited to, your personal phone, a Fitbit, smart watch, tablet and laptop."

"You can't do this!" Greer exclaimed.

"Oh, laddie, I think he can. See, he has the warrant right there to prove it," Mick said in his best faux Irish accent.

Greer was starting to hyperventilate and look around. Usually, that was a sign that a suspect was getting ready to bolt. I didn't think Greer was stupid enough to run off, especially since I didn't have a reason to arrest him… yet.

Slowly, like his internal gears had been switched to half speed, Greer reached into his pocket and pulled out his department cell phone, then took off the Fitbit he was wearing. He handed them to me, but I shook my head, telling him he wasn't done. Grudgingly, he pulled out his personal phone and placed it in my hand.

"Anything else?" Mick asked like a waiter at a five-star restaurant.

Greer looked like he wanted to spit in both of our faces, but then I saw him relax just a bit as he tried to mentally adjust and figure out his current status. I thought I would help him out.

"Major Parks wanted me to tell you that you're suspended without pay pending a full investigation. If you have any questions, he would be glad to discuss the matter with you."

"I'll sue!"

"A lawyer! The last resort of a desperate man," Mick said cheerily.

"There's one more thing…" I paused for dramatic effect. "The sheriff asked me to get your star, ID, gun and keys."

I held out my hand, giving Greer the opportunity to hit me, or at least knock my hand away, and dig his hole even deeper. Instead, he reluctantly placed the items into my waiting hand.

"This isn't over," Greer muttered angrily.

"You're free to go," I told him and made shooing motions toward him.

Greer automatically reached into his pocket for his phone, then his hand froze in place. He looked around as it suddenly dawned on him that he had no car and no phone to call for someone to pick him up. His inner turmoil was writ large across his face as he tried to decide which was worse: asking one of us to call someone to pick him up; or walking off and figuring out how to get home on his own. He decided that asking for our help was the lesser of the two evils.

"You want me to call your mom?" Mick asked mockingly.

"Call Deon," Greer said through gritted teeth.

Mick dialed Deon Gonzalez's number. Deon worked dispatch, and I'd seen him hanging out with Greer and his patrol clique. Deon had flunked out of the academy and never quite accepted the fact that he wasn't going to be a law enforcement officer.

As Mick dialed, Greer reached out for the phone, but Mick shook his head.

"I'll talk to him," Mick said, then turned his attention to the voice that answered. "Deon, your friend Karter with a K has found himself in a spot of trouble. He'd like you to give him a ride home." Mick listened for a second. "He's in it up to his ears, my friend." He listened some more, then said, "Okay, I'll text you the address."

"Is he going to pick me up?" Greer asked.

"He'll be here in about thirty minutes," Mick said as he texted the address to Deon.

"You can wait out at the curb," I said.

I walked away from them and smiled thinly as I passed Deputy Andy Martel, who Mick had called in to help secure the scene. He had been careful to stay within earshot of our conversation but not to make eye contact with any of us.

Martel was a solid deputy who didn't spend much time socializing with the other officers.

My next responsibility wasn't going to be pleasant. I needed to notify the deceased's next of kin, but the only thing I knew about him was that he worked with Tina Knightly. Apart from getting the dead man's name and relatives, I would need to interview Tina about what she knew. I was assuming that she had sent him there, but why? With great reluctance, I called the TV station and asked to speak with her.

"I have bad news," I said after identifying myself to her.

There was a long silence, and I could almost hear the wheels turning in her head. She had to know that this had something to do with her cameraman. "What news?" she finally managed to say.

"The cameraman who was with you yesterday has been found dead." My words were straightforward and dispassionate.

Whatever Tina had been expecting me to say, that wasn't it. There was no response for several seconds, so I said, "I need his name and next of kin for a formal notification and identification."

"Where was he killed?" she asked, sliding into reporter mode.

"First, tell me his name and next of kin."

She sighed. "His name is Saint Mendoza. I don't know who his next of kin is. Maybe his mother? She lives down in Tampa. When was he killed?"

"Sometime last night," I said, throwing her a bone. "Your station must have an HR department. Contact them, find out who his next of kin is and call me back or text me," I told her and hung up.

Five minutes later, I got a text with Mendoza's mother's name and number, then Tina immediately called me back.

"Where was he killed?" she asked.

"I'll be glad to talk with you in person," I answered.

I could sense her hesitation. I knew that *she* knew I was

talking about an interview where I was the one asking questions, not her.

"Where do you want to meet?" she finally asked, apparently having calculated that she could still get enough out of me to make the conversation worthwhile.

"I'm at the lake house. Meet me here." She was used to institutional spaces, so I knew I wouldn't get much of an advantage by making her come to the sheriff's office. Besides, I wanted to talk to her as soon as possible.

"I'll be there in thirty minutes."

As I hung up, I wondered if Tina would tell her bosses about her involvement in Mendoza's death, because I had no doubt that she *was* somehow involved.

CHAPTER EIGHT

I looked over at Karter Greer, who was standing out by the mailbox looking like a lost Cub Scout in his uniform without the star.

My phone buzzed. It was Dad.

"This is a godawful mess. I mean, what the hell was the stupid…" Dad ranted for a while, using language he normally reserved for the worst of highway traffic to cast aspersions on Greer and his ancestors. Finally, he finished with, "I'd like to kick Greer in the ass."

"I wish I'd been wearing a body cam when I told him you wanted his star, gun and ID," I said.

"Now we've got to clean up the mess his dereliction of duty has left us with. With Tina on the warpath, you'd better step lightly."

"She's in the middle of this. There's no way that her cameraman was here without her having ordered it," I pointed out.

"Still, you have to be careful or she'll flip it on us." Dad sounded weary. I was surprised that he would let Tina's oafish approach to journalism make him want to treat her differently than any other suspect.

"I've got this. She wasn't too cocky on the phone." I

wasn't concerned.

"Larry, I'm serious. I don't want you kicking this hornet's nest," Dad cautioned. "She's already filed a complaint against Mick for his juvenile onion stunt." Dad didn't sound amused.

"I understand," I said, thinking he was worrying too much about Tina Knightly.

"Keep Parks and me up to date. We're already getting a steady stream of calls from the media."

I promised I would and then we hung up. I'd go over that phone call again and again in my mind during the next couple of days.

What I needed to do now was call Mendoza's mother. The disappearance of Scott Nicholl was already a national story, and another death connected with it was going to have the news channels blaring all the details. No one in law enforcement wanted a victim's family to get the news via TV or a website.

Not knowing if Mendoza's mother would speak fluent English, I called dispatch and asked one of our dispatchers who spoke Spanish to join me on the call.

"I'm trying to reach Maria Mendoza," I told the man who answered the phone.

"I'm her husband. What do you want her for?" The man's accent was heavy, but not hard to understand.

"I'm Sergent Larry Macklin with the Adams County Sheriff's Office. I'm afraid I have some bad news about your son Saint Mendoza."

"He's my stepson. Has he been in an accident?" Concern replaced curiosity in his voice.

I could hear a woman asking questions in the background. She had heard enough that her voice was becoming increasingly panicky.

"I'm sorry, but he was found dead at a residence here in Adams County. We haven't yet established the cause of death."

I heard loud screams from the woman and a string of

Spanish from the man. Later, when I asked the dispatcher to give me an idea what they'd said, he told me it was mainly prayer and denial. The horror of losing a child was the same for everyone, regardless of culture.

I managed to get back some control of the conversation and told the stepfather that I would be in touch with them when we knew more. He assured me that they would make preparations to come up as soon as they could.

I found Mick watching Marcus taking prints from the back door of the house.

"What's the word on the coroner?" I asked.

"ETA is half an hour. I told them there wasn't a hurry."

I turned to Marcus. "Find anything?"

"A couple of partials, but I wouldn't count on them being related to the crime. I found two that were blood smears. Looked like they came from latex or vinyl gloves. The good news is, if we can find the gloves then we'll almost certainly have DNA on the inside from the killer and on the outside from the victim."

"Wouldn't that be sweet? Everything all tied up in a neat little package," I said wistfully, knowing there wasn't a chance in hell of it happening that way.

With the door open, the worst of the bleach smell had wafted out of the utility room. I walked back inside and stared at the corpse.

"What do you think happened?" Mick asked. I'd been asking myself the same question.

"Best guess is that Mendoza here stumbled upon someone, maybe the person who disappeared Nicholl."

"Or maybe Nicholl himself," Mick said, echoing a thought I'd had earlier.

"It wouldn't be the first time someone had a psychotic break. The main problem with that theory is that Nicholl has no history of mental instability, and he's a bit old for the first onset of symptoms of schizophrenia or something similar."

"Unless drugs or alcohol were involved."

"Everyone says he was clean. Normally, I wouldn't put

too much stock in what friends know or don't know, but with them traveling together like they do, he'd have had a hard time hiding a serious habit."

"Take the wrong drug and it's one and you're done. Or a medical event that loosens your bolts," Mick suggested.

"What about the foot?" I asked.

"*If* that's Nicholl's foot. Maybe Mendoza wasn't Nicholl's first victim."

"Don't even suggest such a thing. Anyway, we should have that nailed down shortly." I glanced at my watch. Tina would be there any minute. "There's my least favorite option, which is that we have three separate events. Nicholl going missing is one. The foot belonging to someone other than Nicholl is two. And, finally, this mess here is unrelated to the others. Mendoza pissed off a jealous husband and they stalked him here and killed him. Or better yet, Tina killed him."

"That's the perfect solution. Mad Tina killed all of them," Mick said. "Wouldn't it be lovely to lock her up and throw away the key?"

"I've never seen anyone who hates law enforcement quite as much as she does." Marcus shook his head. "She's even done hit pieces on the support units like us. She smeared a friend of mine who works in Tallahassee by dragging up all kinds of personal issues and making them sound worse than they were. Almost got my friend fired."

"Tina's a real sweetheart. The question I've got is: How much did she have to do with this?" I pointed at Mendoza's body, then looked at my watch again. "I guess I'll go find out what she has to say for herself."

"You can let Linda, or whoever the coroner sends, come down whenever they get here and do their thing with the body." Marcus looked at the scene. "We've got photos and video of this area and have processed most of the surfaces. Hard to tell if we've got anything useful. The bleach is going to complicate things."

I went around to the front of the house and saw Deputy

Martel body-blocking Tina Knightly, who was pointing a small camera in his face. I walked over to them, and the camera immediately changed focus from Martel to me.

"Miss Knightly, let's step over to my car," I suggested.

"That disgusting stunt your goon Mick Klein played on us this morning was pathetic. You should know that I've filed a report."

I thought about pointing out to her that Mick's "stunt" had worked, but I thought a little honey might work better.

"Sorry about that. Mick can get carried away sometimes. Besides, you have to admit that you haven't made a lot of friends in law enforcement."

"My job as a reporter isn't to make friends."

"And you'll understand that making friends isn't what the county pays Mick and me to do either."

Tina seemed to think about this for a moment before demanding, "I want to see Mendoza."

"So you can film his dead body for the nightly news?" I said into the camera, which she quickly switched off.

"How dare you! Mendoza was a… colleague."

"I guess it's hard to call him a friend when you can't even remember his first name." I had to make an effort not to smirk.

"Get off your high horse. I'm a reporter and he was one of the best cameramen I've ever worked with. I respected him and his work." Her pert little nose rose higher as she spoke.

"This interview will go better if you drop the bullshit." I turned and started toward my car, confident that she would follow me. I wasn't disappointed. She was so hungry for information that she probably would have followed me off a cliff.

Once I got to the car, I placed my notebook on the hood and looked at her.

"So who's interviewing who?" Tina asked.

"We can take turns. However, I have a few rules."

"Of course you do." She didn't repress a frustrated

frown.

"First, no recording the interview. Second, and this is going to be the tough one for you, everything stays off the record unless you have my express permission."

"Talk about bullshit. I write what I want," she said petulantly.

"Fine. Then this conversation is over, and you can get your butt on the other side of the crime scene tape." I picked up my notebook and stared at her.

"Everything is off the record unless you give me permission to publish it." The words came out of her mouth like she was spitting out jagged glass.

"Human to human here." I pointed back and forth between us. "That man is dead. He has a family. We need to find who did this. I don't believe you all were besties, but can you at least try and help us by subverting your personal agenda long enough for us to find the person who killed him?"

"I gave you my word," Tina said, acting like that meant something. But I knew from listening to my father, Major Parks and Darlene Marks, Calhoun's current chief of police and my former partner, that Tina couldn't be trusted. Still, I wanted to talk to her, and this was the only way to do it without trying to drag her into the office for a formal interview. She might refuse or, even worse, she could insist on having a lawyer at her elbow who would shut down every line of inquiry.

"Then let's talk. First, why did you send Mendoza here last night?"

Her eyes blazed. "How dare you accuse me of—"

I shook my head. "Uh uh! If you're going to pretend to be offended and act like you're an angel of virtue, we might as well stop now. I don't care about you sending Mendoza here to trespass. That's old business. What's important now is *why* he came here, when he got here and if there was any communication between the two of you after he got here and before he was killed."

I watched her chew on this for a while.

"You told me I have to keep this off the record. What about you? Is everything I tell you off the record?"

Now it was my turn to chew things over.

"Here's the deal. As long as it doesn't involve a felony, I'll won't push any charges. I can even make you look like a good citizen when I write my reports. 'Knightly came forward with…' That sort of thing," I told her, and she nodded.

"Okay, I told Mendoza that it would be great to have some footage of the house at night. If he could catch anyone on camera, it would mean a little extra in his pocket."

"When did he get here? For that matter, *how* did he get here? There's no car."

Tina shrugged. "After dark. He keeps his own schedule after work. Maybe he got a ride with one of the guys he shares an apartment with. They were all from the same area of Central America." She saw my expression. "Don't go there. He has a Green Card all neat and tidy. The station wouldn't have an employee off the books."

"Go on. So he goes home and…"

"Has a few beers, takes a nap, then goes out and does any night work we might have discussed."

"Did you get a call or text from him last night?"

"I usually do. He doesn't always understand the significance of what he's seeing. Like last night, he asked if I'd be interested in the fact that the deputy out in front of the house was snoring away in his patrol car."

I felt my gut roll over. "And you told him…"

"He took about ten minutes worth of footage of the deputy and sent it to me."

"I'll give you a news flash that's on the record. Deputy Karter Greer has been suspended without pay pending a full investigation into his possible dereliction of duty."

"Way to get in front of my story. 'Deputy Sleeps While Man Murdered Less Than a Hundred Yards Away' is a killer headline."

"Every organization has bad actors," I said pointedly.

"Which is what every crappy organization says when they get their names in the paper," she shot back.

I wanted to zing her with a good comeback, but I didn't want to start sparring with her. Besides, she was right.

"So you told him to film the deputy. What did he do after that?"

"I didn't hear from him again." I thought I detected a hint of regret in Tina's voice.

"What time did you talk to him?"

"Around one o'clock."

"Did he have a habit of calling you in the middle of the night?"

"If it gets a story, I'll take a call anytime. I've been on some rough locations where you learn to catnap. I seldom sleep more than an hour or two at a time."

That's probably one of the reasons you're so crazy, I thought, then asked, "What were you really hoping he'd find last night?"

"Macklin, this was a fishing expedition, nothing more. I thought there was a chance this missing person deal was all a hoax to gain publicity for the show, so maybe we'd catch Nicholl sneaking back into the house, or one of the other members of the production company doing something stupid. Who knows. Some of my best stories started from nothing."

"You thought it might be a hoax, even though we found a body part?"

"Ha! First off, you don't have to play coy. I know it was a foot you found. Second, I don't even have to go on the dark web to buy a human foot. Did you know that the selling and trading of human body parts is legal in most states?"

"However, Florida *is* one of the states where it's illegal to buy, sell or possess human body parts for any reason other than research or education," I told her.

Tina rolled her eyes. "A minor technicality. My point is still valid. It's possible to obtain a foot easily enough. Make a missing person report, toss a body part into the lake and next thing you know, your show's ratings are up ten, fifteen or maybe even twenty percent."

"Just because you don't have any scruples doesn't mean everyone else is without them."

"In the entertainment business? Aren't you the naïve junior detective?"

"Aren't you the cynical journalist?" I responded.

"That's redundant. If you aren't cynical, you aren't a journalist. So, junior, who do you think killed Mendoza?"

I decided to stop the verbal jousting and ask a serious question. "Did he ever mention having any enemies, or issues with anyone?"

She looked thoughtful. "No, he never mentioned anyone who wanted to hurt him."

"What else did he talk about?"

"Family. He sent a lot of his paycheck down to his mom. That's why he shared a house with those other guys."

"Who are they?"

"I asked him once. He said they're mostly construction workers, or at least that's what they're doing here. I got the feeling there was a lot of turnover in the house. But he never complained about them."

"I'll need Mendoza's address."

"I'll get HR to send it to you." The talk about Mendoza's family and way of life had caused a small glimmer of humanity to show in Tina's eyes. A *very* small glimmer.

"Was there anyone at work that didn't get along with him?"

"No. Mendoza was an easygoing guy. I've worked with some real pricks, and if he'd been like that, I'd tell you. Hell, if he was as big a jerk as some cameramen, I wouldn't even care that he was dead. How was he killed?" she asked, hoping to catch me by surprise with the question.

I considered my answer. I wanted to give her enough to keep her talking, but I didn't want to reveal any information we might need to use later.

"There are signs of a physical altercation. We'll know more when Dr. Darzi completes his report."

"Signs of a physical altercation, huh? Was he hit? Strangled? Kicked?"

"There was blood." I tossed her another bone to keep her talking. "What have you found out about Scott Nicholl and the other cast and crew?"

"Nothing worth my time. Like I said, if you'd asked me yesterday, I would have put money down on the whole disappearance shtick being a hoax."

"Where were you last night?" I asked.

"At home. Where do you think I was?"

"Maybe you were here with Mendoza. After all, he *was* working for you at the time."

"What kind of ambush is this?" she asked angrily.

I was surprised at how fast she got her back up. *Does she have something to hide?* I wondered.

"You aren't stupid. I have to eliminate you as a suspect. You knew him. You say you sent him here. If you had a reason to kill him, it would be the perfect setup."

"Don't you pull that 'I'm just doing my duty' crap with me."

"Let me see your phone." I held out my hand and, for a second, I thought she was going to slap it away. She didn't, but she also didn't pull out her phone.

"Forget it. You want my phone? Get a warrant." Tina was in full pugnacious reporter mode now.

"Just show me your last dozen texts from Mendoza, and the phone calls you made and received last night," I requested reasonably.

"Go to hell!"

"So you *are* hiding something," I said with a smile.

"We'll see who's got secrets." Tina had an ugly expression on her face, like a bully who'd been told they wouldn't be getting the nerdy kid's lunch money anymore.

"And we were playing together so nicely." I shook my head in mock sadness.

"I was being nice. Now you're going to see what it's like when I'm not nice," she threatened.

"All I asked was that you provide proof of what you told me. Now why would you get all worked up about that?" I asked, not bothering to point out that she was exhibiting the classic behavior of crooks when called on a lie: become all self-righteous and try to bluff your way through it. "The only way I could get a warrant for your phone is to tell the judge that you admitted sending Mendoza over here with the express purpose of breaking the law by trespassing and possibly interfering with a criminal investigation."

"You said you wouldn't use it against me," she growled, clearly madder than a cat in a rainstorm. But I wanted to know if she was really trying to bluff me out of pressing the issue, and I temporarily forgot my earlier conversation with Dad.

"I said I wouldn't use anything if it wasn't a felony. All I'm asking you to do now is show me your phone so I know that you were home like you said. If you weren't and you were here… well, the odds go up that there is at least one felony involved and all bets are off."

"I promise you all bets are off," she spat. "I'll show the world what a bunch of amateur bumpkins run the Adams County Sheriff's Office," Tina promised, sweat beading on her brow.

"We'll talk again," I warned her.

"I'll have a couple of lawyers next time, junior." She was already walking away as she yelled out this last warning.

I wanted to feel good about getting under her skin, but a wee voice in the back of my mind wondered if I hadn't kicked the very hornet's nest that Dad had warned me about.

CHAPTER NINE

"That woman is dangerous," Deputy Martel observed, interrupting my thoughts as I walked back to the house. I was surprised because he usually leaned into his Midwest stoicism. There had been days when I'd worked with him and he had literally never initiated a conversation.

"There's a limit to how much she can hurt me," I said in a cavalier manner that I would soon regret.

"You haven't watched any of her opinion pieces. I saw her do a hit piece on a police department up in Georgia. Nice guys. She made them look like Satan's playmates."

"Thanks for the heads-up," I told him, starting to second guess my tactics with her.

I had made it sound like I could easily get a warrant for her phone, but the truth was that a judge would be leery of any warrant for the phone of a reporter. Most judges didn't want the trouble that could be caused when a news organization's lawyers started talking about Constitutional rights.

The coroner's van pulled up, interrupting my thoughts. Linda got out with yet another new assistant.

"This is Avery. He's coming on full time," Linda introduced the young man. He was easily six-foot-five and over two-hundred-and-fifty pounds, with brown hair and soft eyes that made his size less intimidating.

"You ought to be able to do the heavy lifting for Linda," I said, reaching out and shaking his hand.

"Glad to get the job." He wore a shy, genuine smile. Everything about him was disarming. I decided that it was the opposite of a Napolean complex. With his size, he'd never have to prove himself to anyone.

"Rumor has it you found a whole body this time," Linda joked. "It would make things easier if it was missing the foot you found."

"You got that right. Marcus is done. You can come on down and take stock of the deceased. We're as sure as we can be without a formal identification that this is a cameraman named Saint Mendoza. He worked for WTHA TV. Our current timeline places his death between eleven o'clock last night and eleven o'clock this morning. Obviously, anything you find that contradicts that timeline would be interesting."

"We'll use the usual, temperature and the body's stage of rigor mortis, to give you a window. If you could tell us when he last ate, that could be helpful, but as you know, that's a tricky science at best."

"I had a professor who showed us all the variables that could affect the speed of digestion to show us how unreliable it is as a predictor of time of death," Avery said as we walked around the back of the house.

"He wasn't wrong, Kong," Linda told him.

"You know, you don't have to put up with her supposed sense of humor," I told him.

"I made the mistake of telling her that Kong had been my nickname since I went through a growth spurt at sixteen." He laughed as he moved easily along, carrying two duffle bags of supplies that I knew weighed close to fifty pounds each. Normally Linda would have been carrying one of them, but he seemed happy to play the part of her sherpa.

"We're getting along fine," Linda said with a grin.

As soon as Mendoza's body was in sight, she had eyes for nothing else. It was that intense focus which she could turn on and off as needed that made her so good at her job.

"Sorry about the smell. It's actually a lot better than it was," I said as Linda and Avery got suited up for the examination and removal of the body.

"The bleach is going to cause some damage to any evidence we find on the exterior of the body." Linda was turning her head this way and that, examining the corpse from several feet away while Avery took pictures for the coroner's own documentation.

"The powers that be are talking about having us wear body cams when we go out to examine and collect bodies," Linda said. "I'm not opposed, but it's one more thing to get in the way or break down. I'd hate to have to postpone an examination because our body cams didn't work."

"If they use the same ones we do, they're reliable," I said.

Linda stepped awkwardly around Mendoza's body so she could get to the head and mouth. "This area is so narrow, I may have to move the body to do some of my examination."

Once in position, she carefully attempted to flex the body's hands and arms to test the amount of rigor mortis. Next, she looked at the eyes and opened the mouth, shining her flashlight inside to look for any obstruction. Then her gloved hands went to the head and gently palpated the skull.

"There is a significant soft area at the back of his skull corresponding to the blood that is caking his hair. No external signs of any type of toxin, though the odor of bleach makes it difficult to smell anything else."

"Is it possible that he fell backward and hit his head on the counters?" I asked.

Linda felt the skull again.

"We'll have to wait until we can shave his head and take X-rays to be sure of the shape of the injury, but I'd say it was a rounded object, not the sharp edge of a counter." She looked around. "I don't see anything else, except possibly the rounded edge of the utility sink, that would be compatible with what I'm feeling."

I looked at the sink and quickly determined that it was in the wrong position. If Mendoza had hit the back of his head on the sink, he would have had to get back to his feet and stumble a few steps, then fall to the floor to get to his body's current position. It was possible, but we already knew from the bleach that someone else had been present. It seemed much more likely that this person had hit him over the head with a fatal blow and then poured bleach all over the body.

"How long has the door been open?" Linda asked.

"About an hour."

"Do you know what the thermostat is set at?"

I looked around the room for any vents. "I don't think this room is air conditioned. It's part of the garage."

Linda got up and let Avery bag Mendoza's hands and feet.

I left them to finish their examination. I didn't need to see any more of the indignities they would have to put the corpse through. Things like taking the body's temperature were a necessary part of Linda's job, but I didn't have to stand around and watch.

I called Pete to see how all the other cases in CID were progressing.

"I got this," he said cheerily. "Maybe I'll just take your job."

"Maybe I'll let you have it. I had to deal with Miss Knightly. Not a pleasant person."

"She's a snake in the grass," Pete assured me. "I hope you didn't make her mad."

For the second time, I got the uncomfortable feeling that I might have made a mistake when I accused her of withholding information. Still, I was sure she hadn't wanted me to see something on her phone.

"I'll be in at some point today, but I don't know when," I told him.

"Good luck getting past the news vans. Your dad and Major Parks have already given a couple of interviews. Lot of interest when a TV personality drops off the radar and a cameraman turns up dead. Not to mention finding body parts in the lake."

"I know. There were a couple of vans out at the lake. We had to designate a spot for them to do their location shots."

"How's Mick doing? I was surprised you put him on the disappearance."

"He's fine. I wouldn't be looking over his shoulder if this wasn't such a high-profile case. He's getting the Mendoza case too since it's almost certainly linked to Nicholl's disappearance."

Next, I called Dr. Darzi's office to see if the DNA comparison between the foot and Nicholl's sample had been completed.

"Not our fault," he began. "Not even the fault of the lab. The information that the production company sent over was incorrect. I've got the lab talking with the production company, and they've assured me that the problem has been worked out. Tomorrow. Maybe even in the morning, assuming everything is transferred correctly this time."

"So the check is in the mail," I said.

"Precisely. My friend, I promise I will stay on it."

"Thanks," I said and started to hang up.

"Not so fast. What is this about another body?"

I explained about Mendoza.

"Bleach. With you there is always a complication. How do you like our new technician, by the way? I wanted someone who could handle the bigger bodies. Sadly, Americans aren't getting smaller."

"You're not wrong," I agreed. "We had a suspect recently that we couldn't get in the back of a patrol car. Had to get a van to take him to jail."

"We will get to your newest victim's autopsy, maybe tomorrow afternoon or Thursday morning."

After hanging up with Darzi, I decided to leave Mick at the crime scene and headed back to interview more of the cast and crew of *The Big Search*. We still had to find Nicholl, and now I had a new question: Where was everyone last night? I also wanted to see how they reacted to the news that a man had been killed in the house they'd rented.

When I arrived at the spot where I'd left the production company that morning, they were still setting up shots. For a minute, I thought they'd hit paranormal TV gold when I saw Bigfoot walking through the woods, but I quickly figured out that it was a guy in a suit as they filmed a reenactment of a sighting.

As I approached them, I wondered who they'd found to play Bigfoot.

"Good thing you aren't filming in the fall," I said when Arianne walked over to me.

She looked back at her Bigfoot. "You aren't kidding. We've had some run-ins with hunters at other locations. We're getting ready to break for a late lunch."

"Going somewhere?"

"No. We had a caterer bring out lunch. Pro-tip: Never let your cast and crew leave the set for a meal. It'll take you half a day to get them all back, and then a portion of them will be half-lit. We've got enough food for you if you want to join us."

"Sounds good. If some of them don't mind talking while they eat, then I certainly don't."

"Sure. Any news on Scott?"

"We're bringing in a dog team this afternoon."

"I notice you aren't personally coordinating the search. Does that mean you don't think he's lost in the woods?"

"I thought we had a better chance of finding him in the lake yesterday. I still think that's where he is." I paused. "Having said that, I wouldn't be surprised if we find him in the woods, or if he walks into the sheriff's office this afternoon."

"What about that… foot?" She lowered her voice when she asked as though it was a taboo subject.

"We don't know whose foot it is yet. There was a mix-up in the data that your production company sent to the pathologist."

"Sorry. Our agreement with the actors was that those results were to be kept confidential, so they had numbers rather than names attached to them. It's silly 'cause anyone who knows the cast could look at them and figure out whose were whose. We also allowed each member of the cast to see the results first and redact anything they didn't want shared. Anyway, long story to say that an assistant mismatched the numbers with the names. Honestly, you can't get good help these days, and it seems like you can't fire bad help."

"Even if it *is* Scott's foot, that won't stop our search for him. Right now, we're looking at it as a recovery effort."

"My phone is blowing up with calls from national news organizations," Arianne groused.

"And you're still filming," I pointed out.

"We have contracts. I don't decide whether we pull the plug on the show. That's someone else's call. Money people. I'll give you a little cynical insight—the money people are rubbing their hands together right now. All this publicity is going to keep the show in the spotlight for days or weeks. Maybe even months depending on what happens."

"Isn't Jackie a producer?"

"She supports the show moving forward. I talked to her about it earlier. I can't say I'm sorry about it. I like Scott. I hope he's found alive and unhurt, but it's our jobs on the line. You don't shut down a factory because someone falls into the machinery. I guess that makes me sound as greedy as the show's executive producers." She shrugged.

"I can appreciate your honesty," I said, thinking that it was more than a little callous and spoke to how she really felt about Scott. *Or*, I thought, *how badly she needs the job*. "How's Kayla holding up?"

"She's sedated. Jackie talked to the other producers, and they've agreed to keep paying her, even though she's not working, and to pick up her medical expenses." Arianne gave a sardonic chuckle. "More of my cynicism, but I'm sure they're worried about her suing the production company for her pain and suffering. In this day and age, she might even claim that Scott sexually harassed her into a relationship. Nothing surprises me anymore." She shook herself. "Enough of my Debbie Downer routine. Come on over and get some lunch."

"Before lunch, I want to go over everyone's movements last night," I said, taking out my notebook.

"Last night? Why?"

"Just routine," I said with as much nonchalance as I could manage. I stood there with my pen hovering over the paper, hoping that the thought of lunch would keep her from considering my answer.

"Nothing much to say. With Scott going missing, I asked everyone to stay in and not go wandering off to Tallahassee or wherever to get drunk. That brought up a request to bring in some liquor. Normally I wouldn't allow it, but under the circumstances I thought it was the better option."

"We're talking about at the house you're staying in?"

"Both houses. I had a talk with everyone, and it was agreed that they could do some controlled drinking in-house. I put a heavy emphasis on *controlled*. Their part of the bargain was not to get sloppy drunk and not to leave their house after dinner. Everyone agreed to the rules. And, as far as I know, everyone abided by the rules."

"I'm still a bit confused by the hierarchy between you and Jackie. She's one of the stars and she's a producer, but you seem to make a lot of the decisions?" I asked.

"My dad was in the Navy, so I look at it like Jackie is an admiral and I'm the captain of the ship. She outranks me, but unless she *wants* to take over, she lets me be in charge of all the day-to-day operations."

"Going back to last night." I flipped through my notes and read off who was originally staying in which house. "Which house did Dirk and Eli move to?"

"Eli is in my house. We gave him Dani's room and she

moved to the other house with Dirk."

"Kind of doubling up in the working man's house," I observed.

"Privilege of being above the line. Eli has a contract that stipulates a private room. Worker bees have no such guarantees."

"Sucks to be them."

"Truth is, they could be replaced this afternoon, and they know it. For every crew member, there are a hundred qualified people that would give their right arm for a chance at steady work on a TV show."

"Or right foot?"

Arianne grimaced. "Guess that was a bad choice of words."

"Was everyone up and ready to work this morning?" I asked.

She gave me a suspicious look.

"What's going on?" She clearly wasn't going to be waved off again.

"This morning, we found a man dead in the other house."

Her eyes bugged. "Scott?"

"No. A cameraman who works for a Tallahassee TV station."

"What happened to him?"

"That's what we're trying to figure out."

"But it wasn't an accident or you wouldn't be asking these questions." I could see her making the connection. "You can't think that one of us…"

"We don't think anything right now. We're just gathering facts. And one of the facts I'm gathering is where anyone connected to the house was last night when this man died."

"I don't like it," she muttered, more to herself than to me.

"Someone being killed in a house you were renting?"

"No. You here questioning us. Scott goes missing and now a man's found dead in the house he was staying at… It sounds more like we're in danger. We've only been here a couple of days. I doubt any of us even knew this guy." She looked angry, and I wondered if I was going to lose my invitation to lunch.

"You need to see it from our perspective. We have a possible crime to investigate."

"What do you mean *possible*?"

"I should have said probable. Until the coroner has done an autopsy, we won't know for sure what his cause of death was. Let's just say I feel confident that the man was killed. Do you know for a fact that no one on your production knows him?"

"Of course not. You haven't even told me his name."

"He was a cameraman and everyone here is involved in the film industry. Does it seem like a stretch to think one of your people might know him?"

Arianne didn't like it, but she took her time and thought about it.

"I see your point."

"I've got a better chance of getting to the bottom of this with your cooperation. If we can eliminate the cast and crew, no one will be happier than me. The more people we eliminate, the closer we'll be to finding the monster who killed this man and was possibly involved in Scott's disappearance."

"I... Maybe I shouldn't even suggest this, but is there a chance that... this is going to sound crazy... is there a chance that *Scott* killed this man?"

"We're not taking that off the table yet. If the foot we found belongs to Scott, then obviously the odds plummet that he had anything to do with it. A man who loses a foot isn't going to be up moving around the next day."

"And if it isn't his foot?"

I just shrugged. "If that's the case, then who knows?"

"You can talk to whoever you want, but if they want a lawyer, they can get one."

"That's how the system works. Don't tell anyone else

about the dead man yet. I want to see their reactions when I tell them."

Arianne nodded. "Let's get some lunch."

CHAPTER TEN

Lunch was catered by the taco truck which parked in downtown Calhoun. They had sent a van out with a nice variety of food, and I helped myself to a couple of tacos and a glass of tea. I watched the cast and crew as I ate and noticed that the mood seemed to be one of concern and an odd optimism. I decided that false optimism was likely a requirement for work in the movie and TV industry.

The guy who was playing Bigfoot was from Adams County and a regular in the local productions at the Grove Theatre. He'd been given a special place in the shade where he could take off his Bigfoot boots and head and soak his feet in ice water. He was tall and muscular, filling out the hairy suit as a passable sasquatch. Cody Morgan gave the man a glare and nodded to me as he took his food and went off to sit in his truck.

Eli and Jackie sat in folding chairs facing each other as they ate and spoke quietly. When I saw Jackie get up and walk over to throw her plate away, I intercepted her.

"Can I speak to you for a few minutes?" I asked, gesturing toward my car. It was parked in the shade and we'd have some privacy standing beside it.

"Of course. Have you found any sign of Scott?"

Realizing what she'd said, she stuttered, "I mean… other than the, you know… any new sign?"

"Nothing yet. There are a couple of search efforts underway. I need to ask you a few questions about Scott and the group dynamics. You've been part of the production since the beginning, right?"

Jackie nodded. "I heard a pitch for the show and thought it would be a great vehicle for me, so I signed an agreement with the creator and became a producer. I was the one who recruited Eli and Scott."

"So you knew Scott before the show?"

"I knew of his work. He'd done a short-lived reality show about haunted archaeological artifacts. The show was… not good, but I saw Scott's potential. I say the show wasn't good and that's true, but it had a small fanbase. Being a related topic, I thought we could harness Scott's fans and bring them over to the new show. I was right. They helped launch the show with better ratings than was expected."

"But you're the real star of the show?"

"I don't know about that. I get a lot of attention because I'm the woman on the show. Plenty of people swoon over Scott and his antics." She looked down at the ground. "They're going to be disappointed if we can't get Scott back."

"What do you think happened to him?"

"At first, I thought he'd just gone off with a local woman. He's quite the Lothario. When he didn't show up on location yesterday, I felt bad for Kayla. She's been wearing her heart on her sleeve for weeks."

"Did he ever make a play for you?" I asked.

"That was *not* going to happen." Jackie gave a little laugh. "I'm sure even he knew it."

"For some guys, being turned down is a challenge."

"He was… persistent for a few weeks, but that's not really his game. He's a member of the If-They-Don't-Like-Me-They-Don't-Deserve-Me Club."

"I guess that's better…" I left it open to see if she gave

an opinion.

"At least he doesn't assault women. He hooks women who are already predisposed to be a bit... obsessed with him. Which would be fine if he took it seriously. The trouble is, he doesn't take any relationship seriously. In the last couple of years, I've seen a dozen women crushed because he cut them off when he got tired of them."

"Did you ever speak to him about it?"

"Only casually. This is a business." She waved her hand around at the production. "As long as he acted professionally during business hours and the relationships were consensual, I had to consider it his business. If I didn't and we clashed over it, that kind of infighting could affect the show. Everyone here depends on the show for their livelihood."

"I guess I see your point. Still, it must have been hard to watch him hurt women and not do anything about it."

"I didn't say I didn't do anything. I needled him on the show and off."

"Yeah, I've noticed the adversarial relationship between your characters."

"I'm glad you called them our characters. With reality TV, too many people blur the line between the actors and who they play on TV."

"Don't blame the people watching. Y'all are the ones that call it reality TV," I pointed out.

Jackie grinned. "You're right. I've made the same point myself. Still, it's the beast it is. Of course, it's not just reality TV. The audience has been confusing actors' on-screen characters with the actors themselves since the first days of Hollywood. And then the actors kill themselves with drugs and alcohol when they forget who they really are."

"You seem to be well grounded. My wife loves the show, by the way."

"I'm glad. It's supposed to entertain people. That jerk 'local expert' we've got working for us on these Florida locations takes all this Bigfoot nonsense way too seriously. I think he's argued with everyone on the production."

"Including Scott?"

"Especially Scott. Do you want my opinion?" Jackie asked conspiratorially.

"Of course," I answered like we were hanging out and gossiping over the back fence.

"I think Scott was some type of idol for Cody, that he really believed. Then when Cody saw the type of person that Scott really is and that he doesn't even believe in Bigfoot, it popped the man's balloon."

"That could be a blow. It's always dangerous to meet your heroes. Do you think he was upset enough to hurt Scott?"

"I don't know. Cody Morgan is clearly a hothead. Always blowing up at someone who doesn't agree with him. If he hurt Scott, it would have been in the heat of the moment. From what I understand, Scott was walking back to his house after taking Kayla home when he disappeared. I guess there could have been a confrontation that got out of hand." Jackie shrugged.

"Scott was seeing Kayla and had made moves on you. Are there any other women in the group that he'd had a relationship with?"

"I hate to use the word 'relationship' because he doesn't do those. Fling isn't right either, because the objects of his attention often thought it was more than that. There should be a word for a one-sided relationship. I guess unrequited relationships might be the best way to describe his interactions with woman."

"So were there others?" I asked again.

Jackie avoided my eyes. She was obviously reluctant to mention other women.

"I'll find out one way or the other. If you tell me, I'll at least have your viewpoint on what was happening between Scott and the other women."

She sighed. "Guess you have a point. Arianne has been having sex with Scott off and on since the production started."

I had already heard about this from Arianne and Eli, but I was interested in another perspective on the affair. "I noticed that Arianne didn't seem overly concerned when he went missing. I understand that Kayla had to push her to call and report his absence."

"Arianne's almost as ruthless as Scott is. I don't think it was Kayla as much as it was the threat to the production that his absence posed that made her call and report him missing."

"You said that Scott only went after women who were interested in him. How does Arianne fit into that?"

"Theirs was the most balanced affair that I've seen Scott engaged in. Oddly, I think that's what caused him to be so cool about it. From what I saw, most of the encounters between the two of them were initiated by her."

"So the affair meant more to her than to him?"

"Physically, yes. I really don't know about emotionally. It was clear that he was using her to get more freedom on location than the rest of the crew received."

"Do I hear resentment in your voice?"

"Not from me. As a producer, I have a lot more leeway than anyone else. I just hated to see him get special privileges."

"What about Arianne? Was she jealous of the attention Scott was paying to Kayla?"

"I'd call it irritation. A couple of times, just lately, when she wanted Scott's attention and Kayla had his complete focus."

"Did she ever confront him about it?"

"Not that I know of. Arianne can turn her professional demeanor on and off like a light switch. It's on most of the time when she's around anyone in the production."

"Except for Scott."

"That's right."

"Can you think of anyone else that might have a grudge against Scott?"

"There have been a couple of jealous boyfriends that came close to getting into a fight with Scott. There are probably a bunch more we've never seen."

"Have you ever seen Scott take drugs?"

Jackie smiled at this change of direction.

"Is that amusing?" I asked.

"Scott's a health nut. He would get all bent out of shape if he had to take an aspirin."

"So there's no chance he might have been talked into trying something?"

"He once told me that he played on his high school football team but quit because he got hurt a couple of times and had to take anti-inflammatories and pain killers. Said he wasn't going to do anything that meant he had to take a bunch of drugs."

"Drinking?"

"Moderate. No more."

"So his only vice is women?"

"Bingo." She nodded.

"Where were you last night?" Jackie's aura of control made me want to shake her up and see if I could get more candid responses.

"When last night? We had food delivered. Arianne thought we should all stay close to home and close to each other and I agreed. After dinner, I went up to my room and answered emails and posted on my social media accounts. Later, when I was done with my bath, I reviewed the shooting schedule for today. The producers had decided that we should try and stick as close to the original schedule as possible. They've had Em working on rewrites of the script."

"Em?"

"The skinny guy over there, late thirties, with hair that's too black. He's Emerald Wolfe, the show's main writer."

"Writer? I'm still confused about the difference between a scripted show and reality TV. I didn't realize you have a writer." Obviously, I knew that reality shows weren't real, but I'd also heard that they didn't have writers.

"Maybe I should call him a plotter rather than a writer. None of the interviews we do with witnesses are scripted. Just the interactions between the hosts. So, for example, I might get a notice that Eli and I should get into an argument over some piece of equipment that he wants to use. Or Scott might be told that he should complain about the conditions at a particular location. All of these notes, if it's done right, make it look like we're having natural interactions that all mesh together to form our on-air characters and create some tension and plot points."

"So that there's a narrative between the hosts that stretches across episodes," I said, beginning to understand the nuances.

"Now you have it. Everything is designed to make our characters relatable. If people don't like the hosts, then it doesn't matter what the show's about. And that goes the other way too. If they like the hosts, the audience will watch the show no matter what it's about."

"What time did you go to bed?" I asked to get us back on track.

"Midnight, or a little after. We get to sleep in most mornings. It's rare that we have an early call time. It's one of the great things about doing a paranormal or cryptid reality show. They like night shoots and late afternoon when the sun is low in the sky. I'm a night person, so that was a consideration when I jumped on the idea for the show."

"Did you see or hear anything last night?"

"I'm a heavy sleeper. Don't tell anyone, but I snore too."

Remembering something else Arianne had mentioned, I decided to ask her about Jake Nash, the cameraman. "Was Jake jealous of Scott?"

"Jake is jealous of everyone who gets facetime on the show. He's got a serious case of actor wannabe."

"He's not very good?"

"Jake can do silly, overly dramatic bits that we'll use to drop a bit of humor into the show, but real acting? I'm afraid not. He tries too hard."

"Did he butt heads with Scott?"

"I think he sees Scott as his rival for a position on the show, but that's ridiculous. Jake's a good cameraman and that's all he's ever going to be. Looking back, it was a mistake to let him get in front of the camera in the first place. Before this season started, he tried to get a new contract that would've had him featured on every episode with equal billing. He was told no. His contract makes it clear that he's paid as an actor only when he has a part in a show, and there is no guarantee that he'll get facetime in any episode."

"How'd he take that?"

"He was pissed, but he didn't have any choice. Jake is egotistical, but not stupid. The odds of him getting a real acting job with any other show are nil."

"Any confrontations with Scott?"

"No. Since the new season started, he's been in full suck-up mode with the three of us and Em. He'll do anything to get a spot on an episode."

"A man was found dead this morning in the house where Scott was staying." I dropped the bomb to see how Jackie would react.

I was rewarded with a shocked expression, her mouth opening as though she was going to say something, but closing again before any sound came out. Finally, she gave herself a little shake and seemed to compose herself.

"Who?" she finally asked.

"A cameraman for a local TV station."

"Is this related to Scott's disappearance?"

"We don't know much at this point. We can't even be sure the man was murdered."

"That's why you were asking questions about last night." She seemed to be taking this all in. I knew she was a good actor, so how much could I go by her reactions?

"Yes. Though, as I said, we don't know what connections there are to Scott or your production company."

"Maybe it has to do with the house or its owner," she

suggested.

"I've thought of that. And another investigator has already talked to the owner about Scott, and we'll be following up on any enemies they might have. Though I'd think it would be pretty extreme to kill a man in order to financially hurt or send a message to a landlord."

"I guess so. Still, what could he have to do with us?"

"Now that I've told you why we're interested in everyone's movements last night, can you think of anyone in your production company who was acting differently, or was gone for a period of time last night?"

"No, I really can't."

I pulled up Saint Mendoza's driver's license photo on my phone and showed it to Jackie. "Have you ever seen this man before?"

"That's the man that was killed?" She shook her head. "I don't recognize him."

"Does the name Saint Mendoza sound familiar?"

"No."

I asked her not to tell the others, thanked her for answering my questions and asked her to send Jake to me. He wandered over carrying a taco and a Dixie cup of sweet tea.

"Sorry. I had to transfer some footage and just got my lunch," he said and leaned against my car.

"What's your position with the production company?" I was curious to see what he would say.

"Have you seen the show?" he asked with enthusiasm.

"A few times."

"I'm getting more parts. I kinda play the cowardly cameraman." He set his taco and drink down on the hood of my car so he could use both hands to talk about himself. "I've had some small roles in other productions. Mostly indie stuff, but my roles have been well received." He stopped talking as though he'd forgotten the question.

"But right now, you work as a cameraman and get *some* time in front of the camera?"

"Right. Good spots, though. The show gets emails and comments all the time about how I should get more airtime. Humor is the life blood of paranormal reality shows."

"What do you think about the other actors on the show?" I was particularly interested in what he would say about Scott.

"Jackie's a hardass. She's a… Wait, you won't tell her what I'm saying, right?"

"This is all confidential," I lied.

"Okay. She's the reason I didn't get made a regular on the show. See, she's a producer as well as one of the actors and she's never liked me. Honestly…" He leaned in toward me. "I don't think she likes guys."

"She seems to get along with Scott."

"Yeah, that's true, but she teases him. Not that Scott doesn't deserve that kind of treatment. He's a pu… goes after women. I told one of the producers that Scott was going to get them in trouble one day with his sexual harassment. They were real interested in what he's been up to. I know they even talked to Jackie about it. Which pissed her off. I had to deal with that for weeks." He rolled his eyes.

"If she doesn't like guys, why does she defend Scott?"

"That's easy. Scott's a big part of the show. She's not stupid enough to cut her nose off. You know what I mean?"

"Any chance that they'll move you up to fill in for Scott?"

"Funny you say that. I was talking to Em last night about letting me have a few spots to help fill in while Scott's gone."

"You told me what you think of Jackie. What about Eli?"

"Eli's okay. Minds his own business. Kind of stand-offish. But he'll go out for a beer with us, which is pretty cool of him. A lot of the above-the-line people won't socialize with the crew."

"Does he mind you being on the show?"

"No. He and I play off each other pretty good."

"And Scott?"

"Scott's another story. I heard him tell Jackie and Dante—Dante's another producer—that it's too confusing for the audience to have another pretty boy on the show. He was, like, pushing for Dani to get airtime instead of me. She does some camera work, like second unit stuff."

"That must have pissed you off."

"Yeah, it did…" He caught on to where I was leading him and narrowed his eyes at me. "Hey, don't go down that rabbit hole. I didn't do nothin' to Scott. Yeah, I might have had some… issues with him, but I'm not going to, like, *do* anything to him. Geez. That's crazy."

"I'm not pointing any fingers. Just talking to everyone," I said, trying to placate him. "Do you know a guy named Saint Mendoza?"

"Yeah, yeah, I met the guy a few nights ago. First night we were here. He was at a bar in Tallahassee. Saint is a weird first name, so even though I'd had a few beers, I remember it. The guy told me he was a cameraman too. Why?"

I tried not to look like a poker player who'd been dealt the card he needed to complete his royal flush.

"How did that come about? Were you in the bar by yourself?"

"There were four of us. Me, Dirk, Eli and Koby, our sound guy. We were maybe getting a little loud, and a waiter came over and asked us to keep it down. It was after that that Saint introduced himself. He said he heard us talking about the production and said he worked as a cameraman for a TV station."

"Were you talking about the production?" I asked and watched Jake think hard about his answer.

"Probably. How else would the guy have known we were with the show? Hey, what's up with this guy? Do you think he had something to do with Scott's disappearance? Did they ever find out if that foot… you know… belongs to Scott?"

Jake was at full throttle with the questions, which gave me the option of answering the ones I wanted to answer and ignoring the others.

"We should find out soon if the foot is Scott's. We're still looking into a number of possibilities when it comes to Scott's disappearance. What else do you remember about Saint?"

"He was kind of quiet once he joined us. Offered to buy us drinks. Let me see." He put on his thoughtful expression again. "He was Hispanic, did I mention that? Guess with a name like Saint Mendoza, that goes without saying. His English was good. I was kind of glad he didn't want to talk about cameras. A lot of cameramen, you go out and all they want to talk about is cameras. I like the art, not the mechanics. Get me?"

"How long did he hang around?"

"I guess as long as we hung out."

"Did the other guys talk to him?"

"A little. Not much. He seemed most interested in Eli. You know, said he'd seen him on the show. Though he must not watch the show much, 'cause I had to tell him who I was. He thought that was cool, a cameraman getting in front of the camera."

"Did you see him again after that?"

"I don't think so. I'm not real good with faces. Why'd you say you were so interested in this guy?"

I thought now was a good time to drop the grenade into the conversation.

"He was found dead in the house where Scott and the others were staying."

Jake's mouth opened and closed at least four times before he was able to get any words to come out. "Dead? Like dead, dead?"

"The body was discovered this morning." I didn't ask any questions because I wanted to see where he would go if given free rein.

"Oh, wow! I don't understand. How could he be dead in the house? I mean, what killed him?"

"We're still trying to figure that out. Where were you last night?"

Again, his mouth went through the fish-out-of-water routine.

"You can't possibly think I had anything to do with… with… him dying." Jake was very indignant. I wasn't sure if it was real or put on. All of his reactions were dramatic, so it was hard to judge.

"I'm not focusing on anyone right now. I do find it interesting that you all met him a few days earlier and now he's dead in a house that was rented by your production company."

His expression was one of confusion mixed with calculation. "Do you think I need to hire a lawyer?"

"How involved in Scott's disappearance and Mendoza's death are you?"

"Not at all!" He said this loudly enough that several other members of the production company looked over at us.

"Then why would you need a lawyer?" Of course, innocent people needed lawyers all the time, but it wasn't my job to tell him that.

"This has me rattled." Jake pursed his lips. "I like my job, and I want to become a member of the cast." It was clear that he was talking to himself more than me.

"What we need to do is figure out what happened to Mendoza and find Scott," I told him. "You could help me do that."

"How?"

"Be honest with me."

"Sure." He nodded.

"Where were you last night?"

I could see that Jake wanted to protest his innocence again, but he bit his first response back and answered the question.

"We just hung out at the house. Arianne thought it would be best if we didn't go anywhere. So we had dinner brought in. Good food. Chicken and macaroni and cheese, you know, down-home stuff. After that, I went on my laptop and looked over all my social media accounts before calling Em and talking about the show. I guess we did that for an hour or more."

"What did you and Em talk about?"

"Just the show. He thinks I should get more spots in the episodes, so we were kind of talking about that."

"After that, what did you do?"

"I laid in bed and played a game on my laptop. Chatted with my girlfriend in Atlanta for a while. She was in a play and got home late. After talking to her, I went to sleep."

"What time was this?"

He pulled out his phone and tapped it a couple of times before turning the screen toward me. "My last text to Bree was just before two."

I asked a few more questions, but all of his answers led back to Jake, the most important person in his own life. I warned him not to tell anyone else about Mendoza's death before I had a chance to talk to them and let him go.

CHAPTER ELEVEN

As Jake walked away, my phone buzzed.

"What's up?" I asked Mick.

"The K-9 search teams are out in the woods. I keep thinking it's a waste of time 'cause he's in the lake."

"I know, but we'd be stupid not to cover all the bases."

"Roger that. I walked through the house with the landlord, who said she didn't think anything was missing. The poor woman is in shock. All she wants to do now is sell the house. Anyway, it looks like robbery isn't a motive in Mendoza's death, though I think we knew that too."

I told him about Mendoza showing up at the bar where Eli, Jake and a couple of others were having beers.

"I don't believe in coincidences," he grumbled.

"Not in this case. My guess is that Tina learned that *The Big Search* was in town and decided to sniff around."

"Mendoza seems to be her favorite tool for sticking her nose in where it doesn't belong."

"Yep. And it got the poor guy killed. I think that just reinforces my thought that this was about him seeing one of the production company members at the house. He would have recognized them, so they had to kill him."

"If they were guilty of making Scott go missing, then

being seen snooping around the house when it's marked off as a crime scene would have been a red flag that even a dopey detective like me might have noticed," Mick said.

"Question is: Why was that person at the house?"

"They forgot something?"

"That's my guess. Or they were there to meet someone."

"Scott?"

"I doubt that, because I'm pretty sure that's his foot we have in the morgue. If that's true, I can't see him limping around on a stump."

"Does seem like a stretch," Mick agreed.

"I'm going to finish interviewing the folks out here. Let me know on the off-chance the search team actually finds anything."

I walked over to where the cast and crew were getting ready to go back to work. Emerald Wolfe was the only one not actively doing anything other than staring at his phone. I stood next to him for a full minute before he looked up at me with strangely penetrating eyes.

"You want to talk to me?" he asked in a monotone that went with his emo black hair and lanky, listless stature.

"Just need to ask a few questions."

"Fascinating being a suspect in a murder." His mouth turned up a bit on the right side.

"Are you?"

"Nice riposte!"

"You got me with that one. I have no idea what a riposte is."

"In fencing," he said, going into a stance as though he were pointing an épée at me, "it's the term for a comeback… basically."

"Nice, I'll write it down in my notebook," I said with a smile that told him I thought he was a clever boy. *Catching more flies with honey and all that jazz*, I told myself.

"What are these questions you want to ask me? Where was I when the murderer struck? Do I own a candlestick? Is my name Colonel Mustard?" He smiled crookedly as he followed me over to my car.

"That's the type of thing. Let's start with easy stuff. Do you like Scott Nicholl?"

"Present tense. So we're pretending that he's alive, are we? Or are you waiting for me to use the past tense and you can yell 'Gotcha!'"

"As far as I know, he's still alive. A severed foot does not a body make." I continued to smile. "So, thumbs up or thumbs down on Scott?"

"Thumbs down on this whole miserable experience. They pay me well for doing nothing more than telling them to add more cowbell." He waved off the peons that were so annoying to him.

"Scott?"

Em sighed and let his right hip rest against my car.

"Scott is, was, whatever, obsessed with women. Not all women, mainly the ones that were willing to fawn over him. It was a bore to watch. Sad that there are women who will let themselves be led around by the nose like that." His disdain was written all over his face.

"Does that include Arianne?"

"Certainly. One of the worst. He gave her… you know… and she let him make a mockery of the production company rules. I certainly couldn't borrow a car or show up on set when I felt like it."

"And Kayla?"

"Now that's just tragic. The girl—and when it comes to romantic relationships, that's what she is—was marked for a calamitous end when he finished with her. From what I've heard, it wouldn't be the first time he let one of his flings come down hard. I tried to talk to her, but she wouldn't listen." He brushed back his hair dramatically.

"So what about Jackie?"

He smiled and pointed his finger at me.

"Now they were a match. I tried to write more flirting into the show, but Scott hated it. Of course, that was because she was in control. He was like a moth that knew the dangers of the flame. He was attracted to the golden flickering but saw his own death in the... what... enticing glow." He was writing as he talked.

"So you thought Scott was a jerk?"

"Not so quick, Deputy Dawg. Personally, I was repelled by Scott; but professionally, I admired him. When he came on set, he had his act together and could look into the camera and... captivate. Even when he had to flirt with Jackie or perform some other bit that he didn't like, he would be the consummate professional and bring his best game. In my humble opinion, he was only held back by his own need to be loved by the fairer sex. Oh, and not just one. He needed multiple fair maidens to admire him. When he felt they were wilted, he'd cast them off like a dead rose." Em thought for a minute. "I might have gotten carried away there, but you get the point."

"Yes, I got it. When did the back-and-forth with Jackie and Scott start?"

"I'm not sure. It started before I came on to the production. I've only been with the show for the past year. An interminable year." He sighed loudly.

"What do you think happened to Scott?"

Em looked serious for the first time since we'd started talking.

"An interesting question. I listen to way too many true-crime podcasts. Unsolved mysteries and all that. If I were writing the story, Scott got drunk and went to pee in the lake where he was snatched off the bank by a monster from the Cretaceous period that dragged Scott's body down to its lair." He paused. "But I don't believe in prehistoric monsters and Scott didn't drink that much. So... maybe a scallywag shanghaied him for his crew. They certainly didn't rob him. The man never had more than a few dollars on his person, just a cheap watch, and his only jewelry was one of those wretched class rings you buy out of a brochure."

"So if you eliminate accident and robbery... then what?"

"Revenge! Maybe a jilted lover or a cuckolded husband.

But why hide the body? That's usually a sign that there is a connection between the killer and the victim. Which could fit in with the revenge motive. You might have been too quick to eliminate an accident. You found the boat on the bottom of the lake. He could have taken it out and… But no, that's not Scott. He might do that sort of thing to find a place for a liaison with a woman, but to go out on the lake by himself? No."

"Money?" I prompted.

Em snapped his fingers. "Possibly! Scott was a skinflint. Never offered to pay for a meal or a drink if he didn't have to. Didn't gamble. Seldom even took the women he was having an affair with out on the town. So he must have a tidy sum sacked away in a bank account or under the mattress at home."

"The lead investigator is following up on his financial situation."

"Scott didn't have anything to do with his family, so maybe the closest relative figured out that he could bump Scott off and walk away with the money. Only hitch in that plan is the disappearing thing. If Scott isn't found, they'll have to wait seven years to get their hands on the cash."

"Something to do with the production, then?" I suggested.

He smiled from ear to ear.

"To get him out of the way. Yes, I love it. Mostly because that would put Jake Nash square in the crosshairs." He pretended to be pointing a gun.

"You don't like Jake?"

"That ass took up an hour of my time last night trying to convince me that he should be in more episodes of the show now that Scott's gone. Ha!"

Em's eyes were alive for the first time. I recognized the look. It was the one that investigators got when they became obsessed with a single suspect.

"Do you think that Jake could get rid of Scott?" I asked.

"He's the only one of us that would stand a chance

against him in a fight. They were roughly the same size. Same huge ego too. The only problem for Jake is he doesn't have the talent to back it up."

"Have you told him that?"

"Last night and every other time he's tried to get me to write him into episodes. There have been moments in the show when his goofiness worked. He does a decent job of playing the overly dramatic coward afraid of the noises in the dark woods. But it's like a spice. The only reason it makes the show better is when it's used in moderation. Too much and you'd have the audience retching, possibly literally."

"Does Jake have the temperament to kill someone?"

"I don't know. If you're asking me if he's a psychopath, then I'd say he probably is. Certainly, he lacks empathy. If he had any, he would have noticed how bored I was last night when he was badgering me. Honestly, I don't think he has ever thought about another person in the world except for how they relate to him and his *career*." I could hear the air quotes around the last word.

"Who else benefits from Scott being gone?"

"Eli. He doesn't have the screen presence that Scott and Jackie have. With Scott gone, there's an opportunity for Eli to move to the forefront. Funny thing is, he came up and talked to me about that yesterday. A sort of *Now what?* conversation about the show. I got the feeling he'd had the same type of conversation with Jackie."

"Do you think Eli could kill?"

Em looked thoughtful. "Motive, check. Means? Eli is calculating. I don't mean that as an insult. I see him standing off watching the others. He'll read the notes I make and will suggest subtle changes that improve his part. Doesn't socialize with anyone much. Has a wife and kids, that's about all I know of his personal life. He's so closed off that it's hard for me to say who he really is."

"What about Jackie?"

"No motive there. Scott could match wits with her, but I always got the feeling she was holding back. Scott was never a threat to her career. I could see him killing *her* to advance *his* career. That would make sense. The other way around doesn't fly."

"Where were you last night?" I asked, throwing him a curve ball.

"Last night?" His eyes were wary, and for the first time he didn't look sure of himself.

"After Jake drove you crazy?"

"I spent a couple of hours writing. I always do."

"Writing what?"

"If you have to know, it's a spec script for *South Park*. I also have an urban fantasy book series that does okay. Most nights I work at that, but… with everything that's happened with Scott, I haven't been able to concentrate on the next book. And I got this reality TV show script idea for a *South Park* episode, so…" He shrugged. "It didn't turn out like I thought, kind of shit, but what are you gonna to do?"

"Would you have a problem with us looking at your laptop?"

"Do you know any producers you could share it with?" He saw my frown and added, "JK. I guess I'd let you. But why last night?"

"Do you know a man named Saint Mendoza?" I asked, ignoring him.

"No, but I love the name. I'd make him a drug kingpin or a superhero."

"You're sure you haven't heard the name?"

"I'd remember a name like that."

I pulled up Mendoza's driver's license photo on my phone.

"Do you recognize this man?"

"No… maybe… Now that you mention it, he does look a bit familiar." Em looked puzzled. "I'm good with faces, so if I saw him, it was from a distance or just a glimpse."

"Try and remember."

"No. Sorry. If that's Saint Mendoza, then the name doesn't go with the face. He's completely miscast," he assured me.

"He was found dead at the house where Nicholl and the others were staying," I said bluntly.

Em's reaction was off the scale.

"No! You. Have. Got. To be. Kidding me! Wow! How crazy is that?" He slapped the side of his head while he expressed his shock, and maybe just a little delight. All of his posturing boredom was gone. "When did this happen?"

"We found his body this morning."

"I'm right in the middle of a true murder mystery," he enthused, and I wondered if any of these people thought about anyone but themselves. "How was he killed?"

"We'll have to let the coroner decide that. Did you hear anyone leave the house last night?"

"No, but I'm a heavy sleeper." He bit his lip. "I'm being honest here. I take a little something at night to help me sleep. Writer's brain, you know. Very hard to turn off." He tapped his head and I suspected that he took a little something to wake up in the morning too.

"Can you think of a way that his death fits with Scott's disappearance and probable death?" Asking a suspect to give their version of what they think happened has been used in the past to railroad innocent people, but it can also be a good investigative tool, as long as you're taking it for what it is and not trying to turn it into a confession.

"Let me think. I always like to go straight to the crazy idea first. Scott wanted to kill this man and, in order to do so, he faked his disappearance, going so far as to amputate his own foot, and then lured his victim to the house and killed him." He saw my face and shook his head. "Yessss, that's *too* far out there. Then how about Saint was blackmailing Scott's killer and had to be silenced. That's a classic. Absolutely, I'd go with that."

We went back and forth a few more times, with Em becoming more animated with every wild theory he threw out. Finally, tired of his writer's affectations, I told him to withhold the news of Mendoza's death from the other members of the production, then sent him away.

I had four more members of the crew to talk to: Koby Cheong, the sound guy; Dirk Grey, the gopher and driver; Dani Young, a general gopher and sometime camera operator; and, finally, Gabriella Taliaferro, who did make-up, set dressing and wardrobe.

I had to wait for a scene to be finished before I could talk to Koby and Dirk, so I asked Dani to come over and answer questions. Dani was in her early twenties, slim with brown hair and sad, busy eyes.

"I don't know what I can tell you." She had her phone in her hand and was constantly fiddling with it. Every minute or so, she would turn the screen up and look at it.

"Are you expecting a call?"

"What?"

"You keep looking at your phone?"

"Sorry." She blushed and held her phone up. For a moment, I wondered what she was going to do with it, then she twisted her hand and the phone was gone. Just gone. I stared at her empty hand.

"What the hell?" I asked, amazed in spite of myself.

"Sorry again. I'm a little bit of a showoff. My dad was a magician and taught me all his tricks. I worked my way through college doing magic shows. Too bad no one is interested in magic acts anymore," she sighed.

"How well do you know Scott?"

"Not that well. I've only been working on the production for six months."

"Did you know that he wanted to give you some time in front of the camera?"

"Really?" For the first time, her eyes focused on me.

"According to another member of the crew, he talked to them about it."

"I didn't know that. I thought…" She stopped and looked down at the ground.

"If you know something, you should tell me," I urged.

"Yeah, okay, I guess." She paused for a minute. "When I

started, Scott kind of made a, you know, pass at me. I didn't know then that he did that with every woman he saw. Anyway, I told him I don't do guys. I thought he might hold it against me. I didn't want a bunch of crazy drama, and it kind of freaked me out 'cause I wanted this job. They promised me I could do second-unit camerawork and they have. So, wow, he tried to talk them into letting me do a bit in front of the camera? What would they do with Jake? I mean, they've already established him in the running storyline. I guess they'd have to sort of move him to the back. Or was he going to leave?"

I think she would have continued to talk until she collapsed from hunger or lack of sleep, whichever came first. I raised my hand to get a word in edgewise and told her that I had other questions for her.

All her answers were the same. She would tell me that she didn't know anything, then vomit up nonsensical word salad until I stopped her. She didn't know Saint Mendoza or recognize his photo. I thought about telling her that he had been found dead in the house, but decided I didn't want to see how she would react to that. If she was the murderer, then I'd let Mick do all the interviews with her.

Koby came over next. He was thirty-five, short and muscular.

"This is all crazy. I can't believe that Scott isn't back yet," he said, holding his hand out to me.

I shook it and introduced myself.

"I'll tell you anything I can," he promised.

"Tell me what you know about Scott."

"Scott is very professional on set and very unprofessional off set. I get along with him fine. He isn't like some actors who think they're better than the crew."

"Did anyone else have a problem with him?"

"Not really," he said without much conviction.

"Tell me about it," I pushed, and he gave me an embarrassed smile.

"He chased a lot of women. The big problem was that he

would chase a couple on the production at the same time. I know that if I tried a move like that, I'd end up in the emergency room." He heard himself and stopped. "Not that I know what happened to Scott."

"What about Jake?"

"Jake?"

"How'd he feel about Scott?"

"I don't want to point fingers."

"Other people have said things," I assured him.

"Well… everyone knows that Jake wants to take over Scott's part on the show, which is crazy. Scott has talent. Jake, not so much. He's a good cameraman who'd be better if he didn't think he was an actor."

"What if I told you that Scott wanted Jake replaced with Dani?"

"Wow, yeah, I can see that. Dani doesn't have the camera skills that Jake has, but I think Scott had gotten tired of Jake running up his ass and backstabbing him."

"Do you think Jake and Scott could have come to blows over it?"

"Sure. It would be like Jake to throw the first punch." Koby looked at me. "You said other people have been talking. What did they say?"

"Sorry, Koby, that's not the way the game is played. You don't get to cheat off of someone else's test. I want to know what you've seen and heard and what *you* think."

"Jake has a temper. He's good at hiding it, but a couple of times I've seen him go into a rage and throw equipment around."

"What was he mad about when he did that?"

"Most of the time it's been the type of thing that pisses all of us off. Equipment failing just when you need it. With a job like this, when they're ready to shoot, you'd better be ready too. There isn't a high tolerance for mistakes. Of course, equipment will fail just because it does. If it happens at the wrong moment, it makes me or the camera guy look bad."

"But that wasn't the only time he got mad, was it?"

"No," Koby admitted. "A couple of times, it was at Scott 'cause Scott had pushed him out of a scene. One time he found out that Scott got Arianne to cut Jake's scene after they looked at the dailies. Jake punched a hole in the wall of the hotel we were staying in that time. I was rooming with him, and he begged me not to tell Arianne what happened."

"What'd you do?"

"I'm not risking my job for anybody. I've got two kids going to private school. I told him if he went to Arianne and admitted he put the hole in the wall, then I'd back him up when he said it was an accident. I mean, in a way it was." Koby looked down.

I wasn't sure how punching a wall was an accident, but I let that slide.

"Do you know a man named Saint Mendoza?" I asked.

Koby's face lit up. "Hey, yeah, we met some guy at a bar the other night named Saint. Not sure if his last name was Mendoza, but he was Hispanic."

"Tell me about meeting him."

"Is this guy a suspect in Scott's disappearance?"

"Maybe."

"Okay, the guy came up to us… I guess we'd been talking kind of loud. I'm a cheap date. A couple of beers and everyone is my friend. Anyway, this guy Saint must have heard us talking about the production, 'cause he comes over to our table and tells us he's a cameraman and wants to buy us a drink. Only beautiful women turn down free drinks, so we shuffled chairs and made room for him to sit with us."

"What was your impression of him?"

"He wasn't lying about being a cameraman. He started out saying he'd like to move from doing local TV to a production like ours. For a few minutes we talked about the job, then moved on to sports and everything else."

"Did he ask questions about Scott or any of the other cast and crew?"

"Sure. When we were talking about the show, he asked if

working with stars was difficult. You know, are they prima donnas, that type of thing."

"Did it seem odd?"

"No, he kind of apologized to Eli and said he didn't mean him. Eli is cool. He waved it off, you know. The rest of us are used to people coming up and asking questions about the stars. You give them a few funny anecdotes and most of the time they're happy."

"Was Mendoza happy with a few anecdotes?"

"I guess. After the initial meet-and-greet stuff, he talked to Jake most of the rest of the time we were in the bar. Which made sense, them both being cameramen. I was kind of surprised he didn't focus more on Eli. That happens a lot if one of the stars goes with us to dinner or a bar. When people come over to our table, they'll ignore the crew and focus on the stars."

"Have you seen Mendoza since that night?"

"No," he said without any hesitation.

I wanted to make sure we were all on the same page, so I pulled up the picture of Mendoza and turned the phone toward Koby.

"Do you recognize this man?"

"That's the guy, Saint."

"He was found dead this morning in the house that Scott and the others were staying in."

"No way!"

I almost said, "Way," but stopped myself. Instead, I asked, "Where were you last night?"

Koby told me the same story about Arianne wanting everyone to stay together before saying he'd spent the time after dinner and before bed Zooming with his wife and kids.

I asked a few more questions, then sent Koby on his way with the same admonishments as the others.

Next, I talked with Dirk the driver. It didn't take long. Since I knew he'd been out with Eli the night Scott had disappeared, he was low on my list of suspects. I asked him about meeting Saint Mendoza in the bar, and his version of events corroborated everything that Jake and Koby had already told me.

Then I looked around for Gabriella and didn't see her, so I asked Arianne where she was.

"She's staying with Kayla, who's not taking Scott's disappearance well."

"I'd like to see both of them. And I'd like to walk through both houses while I'm over there, if you don't mind."

"At this point, the only thing that matters is everyone's safety. I can give you my key. Just give it to Gabby or Kayla when you're done." Arianne sounded like she was trying to harden herself for further bad news.

"We'll have a deputy at both houses tonight," I assured her. *Better deputies than Greer*, I told myself.

CHAPTER TWELVE

I took the house key and went back to my car, starting the engine to let the air conditioning run while I looked through my messages. I answered several texts before I returned a call from Dr. Darzi.

"Not every law enforcement officer has my private phone number," he told me. "But you are such a good customer."

"Gee, thanks," I said with an appropriate amount of snark.

"I have finished the autopsy on the foot. All jokes aside, this is a boating accident. The damage done to the bone and tissue is consistent with something like a boat prop. There are a few other things that could cause similar damage, but since it was found in the water then Occam's razor would tell us it was most likely caused by a boat."

"Not a chainsaw?"

"Definitely not."

"I guess that's good. Any ETA on the results of the DNA tests?"

"I did confirm that the lab now has what it needs. I will call them shortly. If not this afternoon, then tomorrow morning."

Next, I called Major Parks and brought him up to date on the two cases. He wasn't very happy but agreed that we needed to post deputies at all three houses tonight. We couldn't afford to let anyone else disappear or get murdered around *The Big Search* production.

I headed toward the lake, watching as dark clouds rolled in from the Gulf. It had been a couple of days since we'd had a real Florida thunderboomer, and it wouldn't break my heart to get a little relief from the heat.

A few knocks on the front door of the house where most of the crew was staying brought a bright-eyed woman in her late forties with a surprisingly attractive shade of fake blonde hair.

"Gabriella, I'm Sergeant Macklin."

"Call me Gabby. Everyone does. I remember you were talking to Arianne yesterday. You're searching for Scott." Her accent was a little exotic, something with an island flavor.

"That's right. I would like to ask you some questions."

"Of course. What's happening over at the other house? I noticed lots of cars around it this morning. Did they find poor Scott?"

"May I come in?"

"Yes, yes." She backed away from the door and escorted me into the living room.

"How are they managing without their make-up artist?" I asked with a smile to put her at ease.

"Jackie and Arianne are able to do a little, you know, for the closeups. The real work is with that monster costume. The first one we had was awful. This one is a bit better. I still have to do much work around the eyes and mouth. With this humidity, I told them no medium shots. All long shots."

"How long have you been with the production company?"

"Since we started. Jackie said to me, 'Gabby, we couldn't have a show without you.' She is a very nice lady. Such tragedy in her life. Still, she smiles."

"What sort of tragedy?"

"Lost her daughter, got a divorce soon after. This was several years ago, before the show. Still, she is strong."

"What happened to her daughter?"

"Some sort of accident. She doesn't talk about it. It almost broke her, but no." Gabriella looked up at me as though she suddenly remembered why I was there. "Mr. Scott, have they found him? Please tell me that's not what those cars are doing at the house. I saw them and got such a chill."

"We still don't know what happened to Scott. Can you tell me what it was like working with him?"

"He was very nice to me. Always bringing me snacks or flowers. I'm not embarrassed to say I work extra hard to make him look good."

"How did he get along with the other people in the production company?"

She blushed and looked down at her perfectly manicured nails.

"He likes the ladies too much. I tell him he's going to end up in trouble with some husband or another woman. I wish now I hadn't said those things." She fingered a silver cross she wore around her neck.

"How's Kayla doing?"

Gabriella frowned. "I think she takes it too hard. Everyone tells her that Scott is a… playboy. Don't take it seriously. I told her that many times and still she would whisper how they would get married. 'Wait and see,' she told me. I told her no. If he wanted to get married, he'd had many other women who were… well, I didn't tell her this, but women who were more… you know." She stuck her chin up and her chest out.

"Do you think Kayla might be violent if Scott broke her heart?"

"I've asked myself that same question. When I was little, there was a girl in my village, a silly little girl. When this girl was sixteen, her mother got tired of her disobedience and boy-crazy behavior, so she punished her by locking her in her room and telling everyone that she was going to spend the last three months of school… Um, what do you call it? Ah yes, grounded. No more boyfriends and no more drinking in cars. That silly little girl killed her mother with a shovel. It was awful. The silly ones can be dangerous." She wagged her finger at me in warning.

"You think Kayla could be like that girl?"

"With the silly, emotional ones, you can't know." She raised her eyebrows. It was clear that Gabby didn't like Kayla.

"Were you with Kayla last night?"

"No. She took a sedative that the doctor, one from the computer, so I'm not sure it even counts, prescribed for her."

"May I talk to her?"

"Please."

I followed Gabby up the stairs, studying the layout of the house. The stairs and floors were all carpeted, which would make it easy for someone to sneak out of the house without being heard.

Gabby knocked firmly on the door to the right at the top of the stairs. Without waiting for an answer, she opened the door and looked in.

"Wait," she told me and slipped inside the room. A few minutes later, she opened the door for me. "She's awake."

Kayla was lying in the middle of the bed with a laptop on one side of her and her phone on the other. She was propped up on a couple of pillows and looked like she'd just been wakened from a deep, perhaps narcoticized sleep.

"Have you found him?" Kayla asked in a breathless voice.

"Now, I told you they hadn't," Gabby admonished her.

"I thought maybe you were just trying to spare my feelings," Kayla said sullenly.

Gabby turned to me and rolled her eyes.

"I'll let you two talk," she said and slipped quietly out of the room.

"Mind if I sit?" I reached for a chair and pulled it over to the bed.

"I don't know what I can tell you. I… I can't even think, I'm freaking out so much about Scott. My mother wants me to come back to New York. I told her I don't want to go without Scott. She doesn't believe that we're in love. Mom always treats me like a baby. She didn't want me to take this job. Said a girl traveling around the country with a bunch of actors would end up in trouble. I guess she'll say, 'I told you so.' I told her that Scott could come back and this might just be a mistake." Kayla stopped abruptly and stared at me as though she expected me to assure her that everything would be all right.

"I think you should prepare yourself for bad news," I told her instead.

"I know about the… what Eli and you found. We don't know that's his." There was a whiny tone to her voice, like a spoiled child hoping that her birthday party wouldn't be rained out.

"That's true," I said, wishing that the results of the DNA comparison would come in soon so that I could give her a solid answer. "You told me about the night Scott went missing. Have you remembered anything new?" I asked her.

"No. It was a perfect night. I guess that's a blessing, as my gramma would say. Our last night together was one I can always look back on."

"Does the name Saint Mendoza mean anything to you?"

"Who?"

I repeated the name, and she shook her head.

"Are you sure that Scott never mentioned him to you?"

"Is he a criminal? Was he in the area?"

I took that as a no. Once again, I took out my phone and brought up the picture of Mendoza.

"Have you ever seen this man?"

"No. He looks dangerous."

I looked at the photo again, but I couldn't see Mendoza

as dangerous. He had the same deer-in-the-headlights look that eighty percent of people had in their driver's license photos. Other than that, he just looked like a normal guy. I put my phone back in my pocket, wondering what this woman was trying to do. Was she just providing a masterclass in playing the victim or was she trying to misdirect the investigation.

"Where were you last night?" I asked.

"Here in bed. I took a sedative and slept all night. I haven't been able to eat much, so with my empty stomach I think the sedative is affecting me more than it would otherwise."

She's even a victim of the sedative, I thought, which made me think that her whole relationship with Scott might have been aimed at making her a victim. Maybe Kayla wasn't as naïve as she let everyone believe. Maybe she'd known that Scott would eventually dump her and had been prepared all along to play the victim.

I looked at her staring up at me with puppy dog eyes. Could she have killed Scott? It wasn't impossible. Kayla was slightly built and would have had to take him by surprise. But that wouldn't have been hard, as I doubted that he would have been suspicious of her. If she had come up behind him and knocked him over the head, could she have also dragged him to the boat? Probably only if she could have convinced him to walk to the boathouse with her.

"Why are you looking at me like that?" she asked.

"I'm just worried about you," I lied. "I'll leave you alone now."

"Please find Scott," Kayla said pitifully.

I assured her that we were doing everything we could.

Why doesn't she want to be out helping with the search? Wouldn't that be a more natural reaction? Does she know he's dead? These questions swirled around in my mind while I checked out the rest of the upstairs. The door to each bedroom opened and closed almost noiselessly. Anyone could have crept out during the night without disturbing the people in the house.

I was surprised to see Dani when I got downstairs.

"Where's Gabriella?" I asked.

"She had to go out and do some shopping. If you ask me, she's just tired of babysitting Kayla. Can't blame her."

"How do you think Kayla is doing?" I asked.

She rolled her eyes. "My dad would say she was milking a cow that's run away."

"Meaning?"

"You know she's pretending that she and Scott had this big romance. Now she's all weepy and dramatic. Geez, you should read her posts on social media. Over the top, seriously."

As I was leaving, I noticed that the hinges on the front door had been recently oiled. I checked the back door and found the same thing. There were fresh drops of oil down the edge of the door and spots on the ground underneath the hinges. Had someone wanted to make completely sure that they could open and close the doors without being heard?

I walked to the other house. It was only about five minutes away, midway between the house where the crew was staying and the one where Mendoza's murder had taken place.

As soon as I arrived, I checked the doors and found that they had also been recently oiled.

What did that mean? I knew that both houses were owned by the same person and used solely as rental properties. Was this just evidence of regularly scheduled maintenance? If not, and one of the production company had done it, could there be any reason other than to sneak out of the house with nefarious intent? I doubted it. And if the murderer had done it, oiling the hinges at both houses looked like a calculated move to keep us guessing. *Or,* I thought, *they didn't know for sure which house they would be in when they needed to sneak out.*

Inside, the layout of the second house was almost

identical to the first. All the interior doors were quiet, and the carpeting would make getting around without disturbing others easy.

I called Mick.

"You've talked to the owner of the house where Mendoza was killed, right?" I asked after he'd given me a report on the futile land search.

"Yeah, I told you she's not happy with the dead body in her house. She called me back about an hour ago and I was getting a definite sue-the-county vibe."

"As soon as we fire Greer, I'll call her up and give her his phone number and address. She can sue him into poverty. Is she the owner of the other two houses?"

"No. That's a man named Harper. I don't remember his first name. I can text you the information. I didn't see any reason to contact him yet."

I filled him in on the oiled hinges.

"That looks like a breadcrumb to me. I figured this for an inside job. With Nicholl missing and the murder, there are two connections: the production company and the house."

"Did you ask the owner if she has any enemies? Maybe it's not the production company and someone is focused on that house in particular."

"I thought about that. The owner, Mrs. Robin, didn't like me suggesting that it might be an enemy of hers. She lives in Calhoun, so you'd think that someone who was after her would target where she lives, not her rental property."

"Have there been any disputes over the property lines, building permits, noise complaints, that sort of thing?"

"She says no, and we haven't had any calls for service at the house except for once last year when she needed our help removing a renter who'd stayed past the dates of their contract."

"Send me the info on the owner of the other two houses."

Seconds after I disconnected, Mick sent me the contact information.

Adam Harper answered on the second ring with a gruff, "What?"

After I introduced myself, he was more civil.

"I've got twenty-five rental properties. I thought it would be a good way to retire. Now I work sixty hours a week. It's crazy, but I guess it's better than sitting around the house listening to my wife tell me what I've done wrong over the last twenty years."

I explained why I was calling.

"If I'd known they were actors and such, I never would have rented the place to them. Figures there'd be trouble."

"Have you oiled the hinges on the exterior doors lately?"

"I've got two apartments that were flooded last month. I don't have time to oil hinges. I've got a man that helps me with the maintenance, but I haven't sent him over there since one of the docks had to have some boards replaced this winter. And I can promise you that the maid service I use for the rentals wouldn't do something like that. I can hardly get them to change the sheets."

I asked him to send me copies of the lease agreements with the production company, and any correspondence he'd had with them before renting the properties.

After I hung up, I looked at my watch and saw that it was just after four, which meant I stood a chance of making it home before seven o'clock that night. Not that I wouldn't have reports to read and reports to write, but at least I'd be at home with Cara while I was doing it.

I called Pete next.

"Everything's running smoother than when you're here," he said, and I could see the smile on his face in my mind.

"Thanks, pal. Phil and Julio will be back on Friday so you can go back to malingering at home."

"Don't worry about me. I rearranged your furniture so I can keep my foot propped up. I solved a string of auto burglaries without leaving the comfort of your office chair."

"You're my hero."

"Aw, shucks," Pete said, and then his tone turned

serious. "How are things going with the mess at the lake?"

I filled him in on the investigation.

"It's one of the women he's been fooling around with," he declared.

"Getting conformation that Scott is dead would move the investigation along. Once it's officially a murder investigation, then search warrants will follow. Right now, we're still trying to get the judge to sign off on one for Scott's phone data."

"Darzi will come through for you."

"If he doesn't, we'll have to wait until the body surfaces."

"Odds are good it's in the lake. You just hope a gator hasn't stuffed it in a hole."

"We may have to let a few more days go by. Eventually the body will degas, and we can bring cadaver dogs out on the lake. I'd enjoy an investigation on the lake a bit more if the temperature wasn't hovering just south of one hundred."

"It's not breaking my heart that my recovery is taking place in the air conditioning," Pete said.

"Lucky you," I said and hung up.

I was driving back out to the shooting location to ask a few more questions when my phone rang.

"We've got Scott's body and it's not pretty," Mick told me. "A teenage kid found it floating under his family's dock."

With mixed feelings, I headed back to the lake. I wouldn't be home before midnight, but at least Scott Nicholl wasn't missing anymore.

CHAPTER THIRTEEN

The road around the lake was clogged with news vans and gawkers. I called and told the watch commander that we needed more deputies to help with traffic control and to cordon off the crime scene. He grumbled and said he'd have to call in some from off-duty, but in the meantime he'd ask the Florida Highway Patrol to send anyone they had available to help.

I kept an eye out for Tina Knightly, who I expected to jump out and ambush me as soon as I left my car. There was no Tina, but plenty of other reporters shouted questions at me. I called Major Parks, who said he was on his way to give a short statement to the press.

"Get me some solid facts to lead with," he ordered.

"I'll give you an update as soon as I talk to Mick."

I heard awful screams coming from inside a two-story lakefront home, a huge Spanish-modern mix-up that didn't really work, in my opinion. The screams were so loud and uncontrolled that I couldn't tell if they were coming from a male or female, and they were incredibly distracting as I walked down toward the substantial dock that extended fifty feet out onto the lake. There were two boat lifts, one of them holding a classic 1968 cabin cruiser. I didn't have to be an investigator to know that these folks had real money.

Mick was standing on the dock with two paramedics. I recognized one of them as Alejandro "Hondo" Valdez, a wonderful guy and a great EMT. The three of them were casting uneasy looks under the dock.

"He's caught on the dock's pilings," Mick told me as I walked up.

I greeted Hondo and his assistant, a medium-built young woman with short hair who introduced herself as Angie.

"Who's screaming in the house?" I asked, amazed that whoever they were hadn't already run out of breath.

"That would be Bray Carr, sixteen. He found the body about an hour ago," Mick said.

"Is he all right?"

"I'd say he's tipping the hysterical scale at a solid ten."

"I checked him out," Hondo told me. "His parents didn't want me to give him anything. They've called their family doctor."

"They have a doctor that makes house calls?" I asked.

"A personal friend," Hondo said.

"In my day, kids *wanted* to find dead bodies." Mick shrugged.

"Were you able to get anything out of him?" I got down on my knees and tried to see the body that bobbed a foot below the surface.

"Simple story. He came home from school at three-thirty. By the way, he drives a new Mustang. Anyway, he came down here to sit on the dock and make videos to post on social media. He heard a noise and thought it was an alligator or a fish. When he looked under the dock, he saw the body and dropped his phone into the drink. I'm not a hundred percent sure that most of that screaming isn't about his phone. Bray made a point of telling me the phone was less than a month old."

"How long did it take them to call us?"

"His parents said it took a while to calm him down

enough so they could understand what he saw. Then they came down and took a look before calling 911," Mick said.

"How did all the media get here so fast?"

"The little snot called a local station and asked if they would pay him for his story."

"While he was screaming hysterically?" I asked with my eyebrows raised.

"I'll give you my opinion," Hondo said. "That boy is faking much of his hysterics. He probably thinks there's a trip to the islands or a new jet ski from Mommy and Daddy in this."

"Great." I thought about Kayla. "I've got a girlfriend for him."

The glare from the late afternoon sun made it difficult to see the body. There was no doubt what it was, but I couldn't make out many details.

"The body is missing its right foot," Mick said. "Which I'm sure will match up with the foot we have. We hung Angie over the side to get a closer look."

"The body has on a pair of jeans and a polo shirt," Angie said, sounding proud of her work.

"That matches what Scott was wearing when he went missing. Shoes?" I asked.

"No, but there's only one foot and the body has been underwater and picked at. I guess by turtles and stuff." Angie didn't sound the least bit bothered by the gruesome find.

"Linda is on her way. She said it's her pickup since she got the foot. She told me it will give her a sense of completion." Mick shook his head.

"I hate retrieving bodies from the water," I sighed, thinking about the effort it was going to take to get the body to shore and into a body bag without losing valuable evidence.

"The media is going crazy up there." Mick was looking up at the house, where I could see reporters trying to creep around through the trees on either side. Meanwhile, a few of our deputies were trying to herd them back to the road.

I pulled out my phone and called Parks. He told me he was pulling onto the road now and could see the news vans.

"We don't have enough yet for a positive ID. But you can tell them that we're calling off the land and air searches for Scott Nicholl and let them come to their own conclusions."

Parks vented for a minute without ever using a single curse word. I was impressed. Finally, he said, "I'll try and get them to move most of the vans to the sheriff's office and get out of this neighborhood. They'll be mobbing us until we can tell them who the body is and, if it's Nicholl, what he died of." Parks sighed. "Last thing we needed."

My phone continued to vibrate after I put it up, but I ignored it. I'd flipped it to sleep mode, which only allowed calls from Cara, dispatch and Dad to get through. All of our investigators knew that if they needed me in the middle of the night, they should ask dispatch to call me.

I looked up to see Shantel coming down the bank with her camera bag while Clark Macon, one of our civilian crime scene techs, walked behind her with a duffle bag full of equipment.

"I assume you just want us to document the scene," Shantel asked, looking at the dock. "I could have brought my fishing pole. Except I don't think I want to eat any fish that have been chewing on your corpse."

"It ain't pretty," I told her.

"Yours never are."

"Stop calling it my corpse. I gave this one to Mick. All I'm doing is running interference for him."

"He means he's stirring the pot," Mick joked. "And I can't tell you how much I appreciate you making this my first murder case in a decade."

I helped Shantel and Clark get started, then Mick and I went up to the house to interview the witness, who had finally stopped screaming.

Bray's parents let us in and hit us with a barrage of questions before we could get a word in.

"How could this have happened? Is our son in danger?" his mother asked.

"I demand to have police protection for my family. Can't you get those reporters out from in front of our house? They're blocking our driveway. I want a meeting with the sheriff to discuss all this mess. Who authorized a TV production company leasing houses in our neighborhood?" The father was talking over his wife.

Fredrick Carr—he made it a point to tell us he didn't want to be called Fred—was dressed in fashionably casual clothes that included a silk button-down shirt, silk slacks and a pair of shoes that would have cost a month's salary for me. All of this was topped off by hair that was cut and styled to look like he'd just gotten out of bed and an ear pierced with a two-carat diamond.

"I don't think your son is in any danger. However, we're here to talk with him and make sure that he doesn't know anything that might put him in the crosshairs of a bad actor." I thought the "bad actor" bit was particularly relevant.

"Yes, well, we may need to get our lawyer to sit in on any questioning," Fredrick said, and I knew what was coming next. "David Thorne is our neighbor and friend."

I smiled and cursed under my breath.

"Of course, Bray can have a lawyer present, but I don't think it's necessary since he is only a witness." I tried to sound as nonthreatening as possible.

"The sooner we can speak with him, the sooner we can take care of those other matters you'd like us to deal with," Mick said in a subservient tone that I'd never heard him use. I looked over at him to make sure it was the same Mick who was always ready with a smart comeback. He was looking like butter wouldn't melt in his mouth.

"I guess it won't hurt to let you talk to him, as long as we can both be there to stop it if things get out of hand," Fredrick said in a passive aggressive manner. He looked over at his wife, who seemed at a loss whether to attack us or thank us.

"If we're there," she agreed.

"Before we talk to him, I'd like to get some background information," I said, being careful not to disturb the delicate agreement we'd reached. "You're Fredrick Carr and…" I looked at his wife.

"Philippa. I'm the CFO for Capital Online Mortgage Broker." She spewed it out as though her job title was part of her name. She stood an inch above her husband and didn't look like she paid nearly as much attention to dress and coiffure as he did.

I wondered what he did for a living but decided to find out later. From the looks on their faces, I figured it would be best to skip straight to talking with Bray.

"Where would be a good place to talk to your son?" I asked.

"We'd better go upstairs. He's settled down, and we don't want to get him worked up again," Philipa said, sounding like she was talking about a rabid chihuahua.

We followed the parents upstairs to a door covered with images of anime characters. Philippa knocked twice before opening the door as cautiously as a bomb disposal squad. The way they were acting, I expected to find a sasquatch-sized monster behind the door. Instead, lying across the king bed was a young man who looked like he still had a few years before he would be shaving regularly.

The room was almost half the size of my entire house and was filled with every electronic gizmo I'd ever seen advertised over the last ten years. On the bed were a tablet, a laptop and a game controller for the sixty-five-inch TV mounted on the wall across the room.

"What?" Bray snapped.

"We wanted to make sure you're all right, and these men need to ask you a few questions." Philippa's tone with him was the opposite it had been with us, more like a cowed chamber maid for Elizabeth Báthory.

"I don't know if I can talk to them. I'm too, arrgghhhh!" He pounded the bed with his fists. "Too upset!" His voice was rising like he might start screaming again.

Mick stepped past me and said, "We have our crime scene team down on the dock, and I wanted to make sure they knew where to find your phone."

The boy's eyes lit up like he was looking at presents around the Christmas tree.

"I can show them exactly where it went into the water," he said, starting to clamber out of the bed.

"I don't think you should go outside right now," his mother told him, and Bray glared at her.

"If I don't show them the right spot, they might not be able to find it." His tone spoke volumes about the household hierarchy.

"Maybe," she said, making it clear that he'd won the argument.

"We'll only be a minute and we can talk as we walk out to the dock." Mick sounded like there wasn't anything he wanted to do more than walk down to the lake with Bray. Of course, the truth was he'd have liked nothing more than to chuck the brat into the lake.

Wearing sweats emblazoned with characters from a video game I'd never heard of and slippers that looked like mutant fish, Bray headed for the door. His father hadn't said a word since we'd entered the room.

"When did you get home?" Mick asked Bray as we followed him down the hall.

"Three-thirty. I'm in a split enrollment with the community college, so I get out at noon."

"What did you do between getting out of school and arriving home?"

"I went to Cosmic Cat in Tallahassee to pick up my comic order," he said as though that were the most natural thing in the world to do.

"Tell me what you did when you got home," Mick asked with an interested smile on his face.

"You know, came in, grabbed a sandwich and checked my YouTube Channel for views and subscribers. I have ten thousand subscribers. That's when I thought I'd go out on the dock and film some shorts. That's the thing right now."

"So you got your phone and headed down to the dock?" Mick prompted him.

"I filmed my feet walking down the path. There's another trend, filming your feet. Maybe because of pervs, but views are views. I'm monetized, so who cares."

"Okay, you filmed your feet," Mick said, making encouraging motions with his hands. It was obvious that he was having a hard time sounding like he thought Bray's life was fascinating.

"Everything was, like, totally normal. Hot and miserable, you know, 'cause it's summer in Florida. I'm moving to Chicago or New York as soon as I can." The way he spat this out made it clear that it was meant as a rebuke of his abusive parents and the rotten decisions they had made. "I thought I'd do a monologue about the shithole I live in while I filmed the lake. At first, I couldn't decide if me standing or sitting would be best. While I was trying to decide, some ass in a ski boat went by and their wake hit the dock. That's when I heard a thumping sound. Kind of felt it too. I guess it was the gross body."

We were halfway to the dock now and could see Shantel and Clark finishing up their work, while Linda and Avery stood waiting their turn.

Bray started to hurry toward the dock.

"Wait. We have to let them give us the okay," Mick told him, then added, "You know, if you put your phone in a bag with uncooked rice, it will dry it out. You might be able to salvage it."

"You think?" Bray asked as he watched the techs work. "Is the dead guy really Scott Nicholl from *The Big Search*?"

"Kind of hard to tell," Mick said.

"He was messed up," Bray agreed.

"Have you seen anything odd on the lake in the last couple of days?"

"I don't come out here very often. Between school and

the video game I'm working on."

"What's your dad do for a living?"

"Him? He tries to sell his lame internet ideas." There was scorn in Bray's voice.

"You all live well. He must make good money."

"He had a website, like a zillion years ago, that you could use to do real estate searches or some crap. I guess it was lit for the time. A mega company paid him millions of dollars for it. Bam, that's it. He hasn't done anything since. Lays around the house drinking half the time."

"Where was he today?"

"Went to Tallahassee for a 'entrepreneur' meeting with a bunch of other freaks." He pronounced *entrepreneur* like it was a dirty word.

"And your mom?"

"She was at work. I blasted her after I saw the body."

"Blasted?"

"Blew up her phone. She works on the south side of Tallahassee. Took her forever to get here while I was freaking out. I took, like, three hot showers. Gross! Still, it sucks I didn't get a good video of his body floating under our dock. That would have given me a hundred million views. Instead, I dropped my phone. I did get some video of you all down here trying to fish him out of the water."

"When?" I asked, alarmed.

"Just now. With my camera from my bedroom." He spoke over his shoulder to me like I was a peasant.

"You don't want to post that footage," I said.

"I was live-streaming it," he said, and I felt a headache coming on.

I tried to figure out what he could have seen from his bedroom window, but it wasn't much. Just Shantel and Clark photographing and videotaping the area. Linda hadn't even begun to try and bring the body out from under the dock and get it into a body bag.

"The woman in the fishing waders looks weird," the little rat sneered, looking at Linda. "Pervs might like that."

I was impressed with Mick's ability to pretend that the kid wasn't a pimple on the butt of humanity. *Mick must be a master poker player*, I thought. I knew he must have wanted to slap the kid upside the back of the head. I knew I did.

"Did you see anything else worthy of filming while you were down here?" Mick asked.

"Like what?"

"Something floating in the water, some weirdo watching you, anything."

"Nothing like that," he said.

We let him explain to Linda and Shantel where his phone went into the water, and they came up with a plan to retrieve it while they worked at getting the body out from under the dock.

We walked Bray back to the house, then told him and his parents that we would find a criminal charge to pin on all three of them if Bray filmed the retrieval of the body from the lake.

"Doesn't he have the right to film…" Philippa started to say until Mick stepped an inch into her comfort zone.

"I don't care if the Supreme Court says he can do it. It would be the moral equivalent of kicking old ladies and I'd find some way to see that karma paid you a visit."

"Hey, that's a threat," Fredrick said.

Mick turned to him. "Would you like to debate the moral acceptability of filming a dead body and posting it on the internet? You want to go in front of the world and tell people you want to let your son do that?"

Fredrick turned a light shade of red, but kept his mouth closed.

When we were outside again, Mick shook himself like a Labrador getting out of a pond.

"That kid makes me want to scream. Every day we see young people who grew up rough. Some of them turn out bad, but most turn out good. Here's this brat with more toys and opportunities than ninety-nine-point-nine-nine-nine-nine percent of the world and he appreciates nothing."

"He might grow out of it," I said, not believing my own words.

Mick looked at me and I shrugged.

"Could be worse. You could have to live with him," I said.

"I couldn't imagine. I hope he tries the rice trick for his phone someday. It doesn't really work, you know?" he said with a mischievous wink.

We spent an hour watching Linda, Shantel and their help recover the body of Scott Nicholl while documenting the entire disturbing event. Every few minutes, I'd look back at the house to make sure our friend wasn't trying to get an extra million views on social media at the expense of Nicholl and his family.

Once the body was ashore, it was clear that it was Scott Nicholl. As bloated and partially eaten as the body was, the clothes, facial features and body structure matched those of the TV star.

"I did talk with his mother yesterday," Mick said. "The falling out they had was almost twenty years ago. When Nicholl went off to college, he never looked back. From what I gathered, he and his stepfather never got on and it just got worse the older Nicholl got."

"Must be odd to have a son you don't have any contact with."

"I could hear the pain in her voice. It sounded like he blamed her for siding with his stepfather, and she couldn't forgive him for his anger toward his stepfather. The son was as stubborn as the mother, or vice versa." Mick pulled out his phone. "No sense waiting. I don't want her to hear it from the news."

"Probably too late." I pointed across the lake to where I could see a couple of reporters and cameramen down by the water. They were either trespassing or had paid some homeowner to let them into their backyard. Even though they were two football fields away, I knew their cameras would be able to get usable footage from there. We could only hope they had some professional integrity.

Mick stepped away and made the call to Scott Nicholl's mother. He couldn't tell her that we knew beyond a doubt that it was her son, but he could tell her that the odds were heavily weighted in that direction.

"Even though they haven't been together for twenty years, his mother is crying for him tonight," Mick said when he got off the phone, and I could hear the hitch in his voice as he turned his head away and wiped at his eyes. It was never easy to deliver the news of the death of a family member.

With the body bagged and Bray's phone recovered, we left the Carr residence. Bray almost had a fit when we told him that we would need to take his phone. Mick got him calmed down by assuring him that Lionel West, our forensic IT guy, would do his best to recover all of Bray's data. Of course, we didn't tell him that we would look at everything on his phone to make sure there was no connection to the death of Scott Nicholl.

Dr. Darzi called and told me that he was going to perform the autopsy as soon as the body arrived at the morgue.

"Really?" Not only would that be the quickest turnaround I'd ever had from Darzi, but it would also mean that he would be working late into the night.

"My voicemail is full, and the reporters have gotten ahold of my home phone and my wife's phone. I am willing to do anything to get rid of them." His usual easygoing demeanor was being tested to the limit. "I won't have any conclusions, but I'll at least be able to give them bullet points and send them off to harass the toxicology lab."

"Mick will be there." A part of me wanted to attend too, but this wasn't my case, and it wouldn't be fair to crowd Mick. Besides, I had days of work to catch up on. Even though Pete was able to cover a lot of it for me, he couldn't make all the decisions involving the day-to-day management of CID.

"I'll call you as soon as the autopsy is over and let you know what he finds," Mick promised.

CHAPTER FOURTEEN

I called Cara and told her I'd be heading to the office for a couple of hours before coming home.

"Have you had anything to eat?"

"I had a late lunch with the production company. I'll grab a burger or something."

"I've got a better idea. Dad sent a ham. I'll make some sandwiches and meet you at the station."

"One of their honey smoked hams?"

"Yep."

"Make it two sandwiches and you have a deal," I told her.

Her parents, who were old-school hippies, lived in a co-op near Gainesville that was just a few steps up from a commune. Anna grew and collected herbs and, um, *other* botanicals while Henry occasionally indulged his Viking heritage by hunting and curing his own meat. They used honey from the community's bee hives and cured the ham with wood they cut themselves.

Cara pulled into the parking lot right after I got out of my car, so I helped her carry our dinner inside. The office was eerily quiet and strangely lit at night. While the building was always open, the majority of the workforce was on a normal eight-to-five schedule, and our dispatch was located across the street in the jail complex. Only the patrol deputies' break room saw much traffic at night.

I turned on some lights and opened my office.

"I'll even sit with you in front of my desk," I said, giving her a kiss as I pulled the two guest chairs in my office up to the front of my desk and moved papers so we could lay out the food.

The sandwiches were exactly what I needed. I ate the first one without saying a word as I savored the flavor. With my hunger temporarily sated, I leaned back with a cup of iced tea and relaxed for the first time that day.

"Bless you." I rubbed her knee with mine.

"I know this is a crazy time. I can't believe that Scott Nicholl is dead." She caught herself. "Sorry, I didn't mean to bring it up."

"Like I can think of anything else anyway."

Taking this as permission, Cara asked, "Was he murdered?"

I tapped my phone which I'd placed on the desk so I could see the caller ID when it vibrated.

"Hopefully, Dr. Darzi will be able to give Mick an answer. We won't know all the details yet, and Darzi won't write up a final report until the toxicology results come back."

"Do you have any suspects?"

"At this point, it could be almost any of the cast and crew. The problem is, no one has a great motive. We're still trying to get enough of his records to see if anyone had a monetary motive. Several people could benefit from him being gone from the show. The problem with that theory is that, just like a rising tide lifts all boats, a receding tide lowers all the boats."

"I get that. The show isn't going to be the same without Scott."

"It might not even survive."

"Maybe more people will tune in because of the murder?" Cara suggested.

"I originally thought there was a chance the disappearance was staged for ratings. I'm not sure about a murder, though."

"Maybe Scott and someone else planned to stage his disappearance, but it went sideways." Cara always had unique ways of looking at cases.

"If Darzi comes back and says he thinks it was accidental, I could see that. But there's another wrinkle," and I proceeded to tell her about Saint Mendoza's death.

"Has Darzi done an autopsy on Mendoza?"

"He said tomorrow at noon. He may charge the county extra for all the work we're sending him," I joked.

"How's your dad handling all this?" Cara knew that Dad had been having a harder time dealing with the stress of being sheriff since the previous winter when he'd been the subject of a near-fatal knife attack that had caused him to suffer a traumatic brain injury.

"I think he's taking it in stride. The media drives him crazy, but Parks is great with the reporters and takes on most of the burden of communicating with them."

"Maybe Mendoza found out about the faked disappearance and he was killed to cover it up?"

"That seems extreme for an elaborate prank. Albeit a prank with some legal consequences. This ham is great, by the way." I paused and squinted suspiciously at Cara. "This gift from your parents wasn't a precursor to them coming up here next week for the Fourth of July, was it?"

"Relax. They're having a big Fourth of July picnic at the co-op."

"You know I love your folks, but I've got enough on my plate right now."

I finished the second sandwich and my potato salad as I told Cara about my experiences with Kayla and Bray.

"Young people are turning into monsters these days," I said, only partly kidding.

"You're just good at finding the ones who are spoiled rotten. What about Jessie?"

Jessie Gilmore was a young woman I'd run into on a case and had helped to get into the public safety academy.

"True. She's doing great at the academy, as I knew she would. That's one." I held up a finger.

"Jade and Taylor who work part-time at the vet are terrific. Hardworking and super polite."

"You're right. Maybe it's living on the lake that does it to them." I thought of David Thorne's son, who had ridiculed Phil Eccles and me when we'd shown up at his house mostly naked following a low-speed canoe chase and gun battle that had ended with an impromptu swim in the lake.

"I think some parents just focus too much attention on providing their kids with material wealth, and not enough on their spiritual wealth. And I'm not talking about religion. Parents don't have, or don't make, the time to be with their kids. And some of them don't want to spend the time *training* their children. We see it with animals at the clinic all the time. The owners think they're loving the pet by letting it do whatever it wants, when what they're really doing is stressing the poor animal out because it doesn't know what it should or shouldn't do, and it can't understand when the owner gets mad. I think kids are the same way."

"Ha! I guess we talk big for not having kids. People like Pete and Sarah are walking the walk."

"Their girls are two more examples of good kids," Cara reminded me.

"No argument there."

Cara kept me company for another couple of hours while I worked on reports and other paperwork. By the time I was ready to leave, it was after eleven. We spent a few minutes cleaning up, then I saw my phone start lighting up with calls and messages, one after the other. Curious, I reached out for the phone to check all the caller IDs and saw a text from Pete that read simply: *911 call me.*

"What's going on?" I asked when he answered.

"You must have really pissed off Tina. She just aired a hit piece on you, your dad, the sheriff's office and almost everyone you've ever known. That's only a slight exaggeration. You can watch it on WTHA's webpage."

I barely thanked him for the heads-up before I hung up and opened my laptop. I found the webpage and Cara and I sat back to watch.

Tina was sitting in front of the official WTHA backdrop, looking groomed and professional as she stared at the camera.

"Tonight, I have information that I want to share with you. Normally, I finish a story before presenting it to the viewers. In this case, I feel the consequences of the facts I've learned are too dire to wait until I have all the loose ends of my news story neatly tied up. As we've seen in big corruption cases, it's not always possible to follow every lead to the end. I'm going to give you a number of facts tonight and I'm sure that you, the viewer, are intelligent and will be able to come to your own conclusions.

"The story involves a local law enforcement agency and the widespread nepotism and possible mismanagement of that organization. The Adams County Sheriff's Office has received little scrutiny in the past, even as the sheriff promoted his own son to a position where the son's connection to drug addicts and other criminals could be problematic.

"If you want proof of Larry Macklin's connections to drugs, you need look no further than the long friendship he has maintained with a man whose family was deeply involved in the drug trade. He paid this man as a confidential informant, even though he knew that the man's father was a drug dealer and a murderer. Eddie Thompson even avoided imprisonment when he turned on his family's extensive crime organization. Eddie only did this once the secrets couldn't be hidden any longer.

"In addition, Macklin's wife works as a distributor of veterinary medications and her parents both have convictions for drug offenses.

"Many of you have probably noticed that Sheriff Ted

Macklin is often accompanied by a large-breed dog. The animal weighs close to two hundred pounds and has injured more than one person. Still, the sheriff has taken this animal into churches and hospitals. Why does he need the added protection of this gargantuan guard dog?

"Just recently, a friend of Larry Macklin's was promoted to sergeant and is being paid as a frontline supervisor, even though he is unable to fulfill his duties due to his own reckless behavior. Pete Henley purposefully rammed into a vehicle driven by a young woman. At the time of the incident, she had not been charged with any crime, though later it was revealed that she was a suspect in a murder investigation.

"Who is the sheriff's henchman when it comes to protecting the rash and dangerous officers in the department? That would be Major Samuel Parks, a long-time crony of the sheriff. Though he is well past retirement age, the sheriff keeps Parks in place to run interference with the media. Major Parks also presides over internal affairs investigations. When you look at these so-called investigations, it's surprising how many result in the exoneration of the officers involved.

"I'm sure many of you have heard that I lost a dear friend and colleague, Saint Mendoza, today. He was cruelly cut down in Adams County and now the discovery of his murderer rests in the hands of Larry Macklin. Can we expect justice from the Macklin clan and their cronies?

"Questions need to be asked and public officials need to be held accountable for what looks like a sheriff's office that has lost its moral compass."

Unable to stomach anymore, I clicked off the video and stared at the screen. Cara put her hand on my arm and rubbed it.

"At least my parents won't mind. Now they won't have to worry about bringing up their possession charges in conversation anymore." Cara laid her head on my arm.

"This is bad." I stated the obvious in a low, tired voice. I couldn't believe that Tina had the gall to fling out her web of innuendos in order to damage not just me, but Dad and the entire sheriff's office.

I picked up my phone, which had continued to vibrate the entire time we'd been watching the video. I was going to call Dad and see what he wanted me to do, but when I opened my messages, I saw that I'd already received one from him. It read: *Don't call now. I'm taking a bottle out to the back porch. Meet me at my house at seven in the morning.*

I looked at my watch.

"Of course he's upset. Y'all can come up with a gameplan in the morning." Cara was making an effort to be upbeat, but I could hear the concern in her voice.

I saw a message from Eddie that just read: *Sucks.* Eddie had risked his life to help bring down his family's backwoods drug empire and had accomplished a lot over the last couple of years to become a sober, productive member of the community.

Sorry, I texted back.

Yeah.

"Mauser's the only one who came out of this with their reputation enhanced," I grumbled.

"Everyone in town already knew about Eddie's family, and anyone that matters knows what he risked to help you and law enforcement put his family behind bars," Cara reminded me. She stood up and rubbed my shoulders. "Come on, you need to get some sleep so you can meet your dad in the morning."

"How am I supposed to sleep after this bullshit!" I groused but got up.

"At least you can rest your feet if not your mind." Cara gathered up the trash and took a second to straighten the office.

Since we'd come in separate cars, I was able to stew on the way home without having to pretend this wasn't eating me up inside. Dad had warned me not to bear-bait Tina. Why hadn't I listened to him? Now I was going to have to spend time I didn't have trying to clean up this mess. And how was I supposed to do that? Get Tina to retract her allegations? There wasn't a snowball's chance in hell of that happening.

When we got home, I tried to push some of my anger and fear to the back of my mind, but it didn't work. I took a twenty-minute, steaming hot shower before crawling between the sheets to spend the next five hours staring into the darkness. It took an effort of will not to restlessly toss and turn and disturb what sleep Cara was able to get.

She'd told me not to worry about the insinuations that Tina had made against her and the fledgling vet supply business she ran in addition to managing Dr. Barnhill's office. But people weren't always reasonable. I would hate it if my stupid antics hurt Cara.

CHAPTER FIFTEEN

I rolled out of bed at six, already imagining the conversation I was going to have with Dad. Every permutation ended with me looking like an idiot, so I resolved to take my knocks and not try to engineer a soft landing for myself.

The first thing I noticed when I pulled into his driveway was that Dad's SUV was gone. Before I had time to wonder why, the front door opened and Genie came down the steps toward me.

"What's going on?" I didn't like this at all.

"Sam Parks is in the hospital. They think it might be a heart attack. Your dad left about half an hour ago."

I started to get into my car, but Genie put her hand on mine. "Your dad is pretty upset. You might not want to go right now."

"I have to," I told her, and she gave me a quick hug.

I don't remember much of the drive to the hospital. I kept thinking about the fact that Dad hadn't called or texted to tell me about Parks and what that might mean.

I had to flash my badge before reception would tell me where to find Major Parks's room. The good news was that he wasn't in the intensive care unit. I hurried past the nurses' station and found Dad and Lilly Parks face to face in the hallway.

I stopped just within listening distance. Lilly's eyes were narrow and angry as she faced Dad. For his part, Dad looked like a sailor on the bow of a ship facing into a nor'easter.

"You are not going to see him. Not today and, if I have my way, not ever. You've used him every chance you got. He should have retired years ago, but every time he told you he was going to go home and enjoy the years he had left, you begged and manipulated him into just another year, just one more year. No more! Do you hear me? God has granted him a reprieve and we're taking it. He will *not* come back to that blood-sucking office. I'll send someone to get his things."

By this point, there were several nurses and orderlies pretending to be busy within sight of the one-sided argument.

Lilly pulled her husband's department-issued phone out of her pocket and shook it in Dad's face. Then she slammed the phone to the floor and stomped on it. Everyone on the floor jumped at the sound as it smashed to pieces. Dad's face was bright red, and he couldn't have looked more shocked if she'd slapped him.

"You can lose his number. By the time he gets out of the hospital, he'll have a new one and you'll get it over my dead body." With that, she turned to the nearest nurse and said in a loud, clear voice, "This man does not have permission to see my husband. I have his power of attorney and forbid it."

She turned back to Dad. "If you try to get into his room, I'll have security haul you out of the hospital." She spun around without another word and entered her husband's hospital room, leaving Dad staring at the door as she slammed it in his face.

I was frozen in place, embarrassed for Dad, worried about Major Parks and terrified of what was coming next.

Dad slowly began to move. He looked at the hospital employees, many of whom knew him, and then his eyes met mine. I could see a maelstrom of anger and pain in their green depths. His quickly looked away from me to a point on the floor in front of him. He started walking, picking up speed with every step. By the time he reached me, he was moving at a brisk pace and never looked at me.

"Dad…"

"I can't talk to you." His voice was full of controlled fury.

I watched him go down the hall and waited long enough to give him time to enter the elevator and get out of the building without us having any awkward encounters. Then, with as much dignity as I could muster, I walked over to the nurses' station and showed the woman on duty my star.

"Will Major Parks be okay?"

The nurse looked around as though hoping to be rescued from this awkward situation.

"I… We can't give out…" She leaned in and, with a quick glance right and left to make sure no one saw her, said, "He should be fine."

It was clear that this was all the information I was going to get out of her.

As I drove back to Adams County, I called Pete.

"How's Major Parks?" he asked right away.

"Apparently, he'll be okay. I didn't get much information. I'll fill you in later. How'd you hear about it already?"

"Marti was on the night shift and called me after the 911 call came in."

"I think it's safe to say Major Parks won't be coming back to work," I said.

"I thought you said he's going to be okay."

I gave Pete a quick recounting of what I'd witnessed between Dad and Lilly Parks. I was still shocked by what I'd witnessed. Lilly had always struck me as a friendly, gregarious type and I'd never sensed any sort of resentment toward Dad or the department. I knew that much of her reaction had been based on fear, but I wondered how much of it she'd really meant.

"You are in so much trouble." Pete whistled.

"Thanks for the news flash. I'm surprised *you* aren't mad at me."

"Tina was really reaching with me. I got a bunch of positive social media cred when I saved all those school kids from that crazy… woman. Most people still remember *why* I ran her off the road. Besides, I should be certified fit for duty in a couple more months. Sorry, you'll have to look elsewhere if you want someone to kick you while you're down."

"Shouldn't some of Mrs. Parks's anger be aimed at Tina Knightly?" I complained.

"She's the scorpion in this story. It's her nature to be a venomous insect. You're the one everybody expected better of," Pete explained.

"Are you coming into work today?" I asked.

"I'm going to leave the house in a few minutes. Where are you going to ground?"

"I can't hide. I still need to talk with Mick and see how the autopsy went."

"Didn't he get up with you last night?"

"There was a text from him. I think he heard about the Tina hit piece. All it said was that we'd talk in the morning."

I pulled into the sheriff's office parking lot.

"Who do you think will take Parks's place as the department spokesperson?" Pete asked.

"And our financial guru. I don't know. Most of the work is going to fall back on Dad and that's not good." I felt the weight of the trouble I had caused and almost didn't park the car. *You can't hide,* I told myself and pulled into my usual spot. "I'm at the office. We'll talk later."

"Good luck," Pete said with a sincerity that gave my spirits a gentle boost.

It was eight-thirty by the time I got out of my car. Other deputies in the parking lot avoided eye contact with me. Dill Kirby, our semi-retired desk sergeant, shook his head and said, "Never tangle with the press. Especially when they come in a blonde-headed, toxic little package."

I started to respond and he just put his hand up.

Most of the desks in CID were still empty, so I went

straight to my office and briefly thought about closing the door. But I decided it would be cowardly to hide out in my office, so I left the door wide open.

I hadn't even had a chance to start scrolling through my emails when Mick called. My phone was still on silent since the rate of calls and texts was running about two a minute, but I saw Mick's name and answered.

"Where do you want to meet?" he asked like we were two crooks doing a money hand-off.

"I'm in my office."

"Is that safe?" He didn't sound like he was joking.

"I'm not hiding."

"Good luck with that. I'll be there in five."

When he walked in, he pulled the door closed.

"Less chance of someone throwing a grenade in here."

"It hasn't been that bad."

"Most of the deputies know what a rat Tina is, but still…"

"You were the one spitting onion at her," I reminded him.

"A minor point. How's Major Parks?"

I gave him the few facts I had.

"And you *still* came into the office." He shook his head.

"What did Darzi find?" I wanted to move the conversation on to the work at hand.

Mick opened his notebook.

"The back of Nicholl's skull was crushed. Darzi created a 3D image of the damage and said he'd try to determine what had caused it. What he feels comfortable saying is that Nicholl didn't just fall down and hit his head. The damage was too severe for that. To do that kind of damage, he would've needed to fall twenty feet or more and the injuries would have looked different."

"So we're looking at murder."

Mick nodded. "Of course, Darzi's still hedging his bets and won't give an official cause of death until he's finished his investigation. As part of that, he wants any photos we have of the boat and anything we believe might have been on board that could have caused the damage to Nicholl's head."

"What about the foot?"

"He's sticking with his theory that the foot was severed by a prop, or something very similar to a boat's prop. The possible time of death is very wide, but it covers the time that he disappeared. The body was in bad shape due to animal predation and the time it spent submerged in water." Mick shrugged. "Oh, yeah, and the DNA results on the foot came in about the time I showed up at the morgue."

"Glad they rushed it," I said with a dose of sarcasm.

"Still doesn't hurt having conclusive evidence that the foot fits our Cinderella."

"True. At least we can be definitive." I had a moment when I thought we should tell Parks so that he could relay it to the media. It was going to be a long while before I got used to the new reality. "You might want to let Dad know so he can put out a press release."

"You don't want to…? No, I guess not. Sure, I'll do it."

"Any luck with security cameras around the lake?"

"No. The houses are too far apart and set too far back to do us much good. I have a few dark and blurry images that might be boats on the lake the night Nicholl was murdered. They come from security cameras mounted on the back of one house, and a couple come from houseboats. They won't do us any good, though, not even if we have a suspect."

"I'll ask Shantel to send Darzi the photos of the boat and the evidence we collected."

We talked about my interviews with the cast and crew of *The Big Search.*

"Dr. Darzi doesn't think Nicholl's murder would have produced a large amount of blood. Chances are his scalp only received minor abrasions from whatever impacted his head. But the timeline is important. Whoever killed Nicholl took time to put his body on the boat and take it out onto the lake to dump it."

"And had to swim out of the lake," I pointed out.

"When they killed Mendoza, they likely got some blood on themselves and possibly bleach."

"Mendoza's murder was a spur-of-the-moment killing," I said, thinking out loud.

"I agree. The murderer didn't expect to confront Mendoza. That's probably why they threw bleach on him. If he had grabbed them or come into close contact, they might have been afraid that their DNA would be on his body."

"We need to come up with a plan for moving forward. I—" Before I could finish, there was a knock on my door. It was Captain Roy Grant, which instantly gave me a sinking feeling. Grant was the patrol division commander.

"I want to see you in my office," he told me after a nod to Mick.

"I hope this doesn't mean you need to order more uniforms," Mick said once Grant had closed the door.

"Make some notes while I go find out if I'm still in CID." I stood up and felt a little lightheaded. Over the last few days, I'd had less than ten hours' sleep.

Grant's door was open and he was sitting at his desk, wolfing down one of the latest confections made by Beth Miller, the head of our records department. Grant was an effusive mountain of a man who usually set anyone in his presence immediately at ease. But today my knees were almost shaking.

"Would you like some?" he asked, indicating another slice of pastry on a plate in front of him. I shook my head and he pointed to the chair in front of his desk. "Close the door and sit down."

"You wanted to see me?" I knew I sounded like a twelve-year-old, but my heart was in my throat. Would Dad really let me find out I was being transferred like this?

"How soon can you change into your patrol uniform?" Grant asked me, but after a second his mahogany face blossomed into a smile. "Sorry, bad joke. My wife tells me I'm not half as funny as I think I am. Don't worry, you aren't being transferred… yet."

"Okay," I said, feeling only a little relief.

"The sheriff has moved me to Major Parks's position, including heading up internal affairs investigations. So I'm informing you that we are opening up an investigation into you and your known associates." He sighed. "Off the record, we all know that everything Tina Knightly alleged in her report last night was bullpucky. On the record, we're going to do a thorough investigation of your background, including the decisions that led to your transfer into CID, your promotion to sergeant, etcetera. The sheriff has no choice but to do this. If things get any stickier, we'll ask FDLE to do the investigation. We discussed it and think it won't come to that."

"I understand completely." And I did.

"What we *aren't* going to do is suspend you. We decided that a show of confidence in your work is warranted and will help offset any repercussions from attorneys who represent any offenders that you or anyone you supervise arrested in the past."

I understood this too. Whenever an investigator or crime scene lab came under scrutiny for misconduct, attorneys rushed to file appeals based on that fact. They hoped that the arrests and the evidence could be brought into question.

"Will you be taking over as spokesperson for the sheriff's office?"

"Yes, but not immediately. The sheriff thinks he needs to be front and center for the time being. You and Mick will report your findings directly to the sheriff. Now go forth and solve crimes." He waved his hand toward the door.

I felt stunned as I walked back to my office. Dad's strength never failed to amaze me. I knew how shocked and hurt he'd been this morning after the confrontation with Lilly Parks, yet he'd already managed to fill Parks's position and come up with a plan for dealing with the PR issues stemming from Tina's on-air tantrum.

Mick was still in my office going through his notebook

when I got back.

"Sorry to report, but I'm still your supervisor." I tried to make it sound lighthearted but failed. Then I told him what I'd learned from Captain Grant.

"Sounds like you might land on your feet after all. I'm glad I don't have to break in a new boss," Mick said.

"The bad news is, we still have to solve these murders." I settled back in my chair and pulled out my own notes as I tried to push away all my personal concerns and concentrate on the investigations.

"There were half a dozen houses around the lake where I missed talking with the occupants. I can try and run them down today," Mick said.

"I need to follow up on Cody Morgan." I pulled out my phone and texted Darlene Marks. *Free for lunch?*

Figured your dad would have you chained up in the basement.

I'm free if you are.

Not sure it's safe to be seen with you. Tina the Terrible might come after me.

The taco stand and I'll pay.

Around noon. I'll text you when I'm on my way.

I put the phone down and turned back to my notes.

"One killer or two?" I asked.

"Without evidence to point to two, I say we assume there's just one," Mick said.

"Agreed. The primary target was Nicholl."

"Yes."

"Mendoza was killed because he was in the wrong place at the wrong time."

"Or he knew something, and it was a prearranged meeting."

"We need to interview Tina Knightly," I said, feeling my blood pressure go up at the very thought.

"I should probably do that." Mick smiled. "We don't want any bloodshed or new breaking news reports from the intrepid reporter."

"Agreed. We didn't find a camera at the scene of

Mendoza's murder. Did he have a camera with him?"

"I didn't find one. I searched the apartment he shared. He lived like a monk. Three sets of clothes. Two pairs of shoes. His bed was just a metal frame with a mattress on it. Two pillows and a sheet on the bed. A lamp on a wooden box beside the bed. The only thing that stood out were a couple dozen photos of his family. There was also a binder with financial records. From what I could see, the majority of his earnings went back to his family. The beater car he drove wasn't worth the insurance he paid for it."

"And his car was found at his apartment complex," I mused. "How did he get to the lake?"

"I think his car had been moved by someone else. When I talked to his roommates, they said he always backed into his parking space, and it was parked head in."

"I have a thought."

Mick raised his hand. "I've already gone there. He drove over to the TV station where he met Tina, who drove him out to the lake."

"If that's the case, then she's in this up to her eyeballs." I couldn't help but let myself smile, just a little bit.

"I've asked the apartment complex to provide me with their surveillance footage. I already sent Lionel a text to follow up with them. Now that we've got confirmation of Nicholl's death, I've submitted new affidavits for search warrants for his phone, laptop and other belongings."

I looked at my watch. I'd been in the office for an hour and a half. I figured that was enough time to prove to everyone I wasn't running scared.

"Let's go to the rental house and collect Nicholl's stuff," I said. "*After* you get up with Dad and let him know what the autopsy showed and update him on the other aspects of the case."

"Dr. Darzi's going to be doing Mendoza's autopsy at three this afternoon."

"We'll toss a coin to see who goes to that. You go talk to Dad and I'll go see who's available from crime scene to meet us out there."

Pete was sitting at a desk outside my office.

"Can I have my desk now?" he asked.

"It's still not your office, but, yes, you can use it," I told him.

"At the rate you're going, it's just a matter of time before it's mine." He stood up on his crutches.

"Need help?" I offered.

"I'm getting better every day," he said, shaking his head. "I badgered the doctor long enough that he told me I don't have to use the wheelchair anymore."

"Don't screw it up," I admonished.

"Yes, dear," he shot back.

I held the door for him and helped move some chairs around so he could prop up his leg. With him situated and looking way too comfortable behind my desk, I left and headed down to Shantel's lair.

CHAPTER SIXTEEN

"I ought to spank you," Shantel said, wagging her finger at me when I walked into her office. "Getting that crazy woman to air our dirty laundry on the news."

"That laundry wasn't really dirty," I reminded her.

"I know that and you know that, but does the guy on the street know that?"

"I admit it. I screwed up and shouldn't have poked the news viper."

"What did I tell you when you were just a snotnosed rookie?"

"Never talk to the press."

I could remember her saying that when I was at my first crime scene as the responding deputy. There'd been a motorcycle accident and a news van just happened to be passing by. Shantel had grabbed my sleeve as I headed toward the van.

"Just treat them like they're anyone else who pulled up to an accident and, whatever you do, don't give them any information. Always play dumb with the press," she'd advised me.

"I guess I didn't listen very well," I told her now. "We need someone to come out to the house Nicholl was staying in. We've got a warrant to search his possessions and collect his electronic devices for Lionel to go through."

"It won't be me. I'm collecting the photos that Dr. Darzi wanted. Lots of photos of parts of the boat with a ruler next to them. Marcus can go. He's putting together a packet for one of the county prosecutors, but it doesn't have to be done today."

Marcus looked content in his office and frowned at me when I delivered the directive from Shantel.

"You know how hot they're saying it's going to be today?" he asked. "I had my whole day planned out and it involved me sitting in the air conditioning in front of my computer." He stood up with a shake of his head. "I figured you'd be fired by now. Guess that's what nepotism will do for you." Marcus gave me a wide grin and took the light punch in the arm I gave him with grace.

When I got out of my car at the lake, I took another look at the house now that the news vans were gone and the street was pretty much back to normal. *What happened here?* I thought.

Marcus and Mick arrived a few minutes later. After we donned protective clothing, Mick used the key he'd gotten from the landlord to let us inside.

"I shouldn't have put my gloves on before unlocking the door," Mick said, fumbling with the lock.

"Why was the killer here the night Mendoza was killed?" I asked as we walked into the house.

"If we're going to play twenty questions, here's one. Did Nicholl ever make it back to the house the night he was killed?" Mick asked.

"I've thought about that one too. Maybe we'll find an answer to that on his laptop," I said as we reached the stairs.

"Let's hope he doesn't have an unbreakable passcode on it."

"Lionel has some new tools for breaking passcodes,"

Marcus said as we entered Nicholl's room. Everything looked the way it had yesterday when we'd discovered Mendoza's body.

"I wish we'd taken an inventory of everything in the room before Mendoza was killed," I said.

"You think that's what the killer was doing here that night?" Mick asked.

"Somebody killed Nicholl for… some reason or something. Maybe when they didn't get it from Nicholl then they came back the next night and got caught by Mendoza."

"No one was here the night Nicholl disappeared. Not until the others got back from Tallahassee. So the killer probably had a couple of hours to search for anything they wanted," Mick pointed out.

"Did they *know* they had that much time? They would have had to know that the others were at a bar in Tallahassee. We need to ask for everyone's phones. There might be a text message or phone call that clues us in."

"Cell tower ping data could eliminate Eli, Dirk and Koby, though they alibi each other anyway, so that's not new information," Mick said.

"If they were in it together, one of them could have taken the phones to Tallahassee while the other one or two killed Nicholl. They all alibied each other, eliminating themselves as suspects. It would be a nice play."

"Agatha Christie and Alfred Hitchcock, all rolled into one. The trouble with multiple killers is that their agendas seldom overlap that neatly. Each one needs to have a motive for wanting the man dead. On top of that, they have to be able to trust each other," Mick said.

"I agree that's a tall order."

We let Marcus dust and photograph each item before we bagged and tagged it. We didn't find anything of interest.

"We need to collect the sheets too," Mick said. "Biological material could show evidence that another person or persons were in the victim's room. The way this guy courted women, who knows what we might find on the sheets."

"That's a revolting thought," I said, grimacing.

Marcus gave us bags to collect the sheets and pillowcases.

After we'd gone through Nicholl's suitcase and the few clothes and personal items he'd put out in the bathroom, I stepped back and thought about the man. Scott Nicholl had spent a good portion of his life on location living out of suitcases. He hadn't set out any pictures of family or loved ones. I wondered what we would find on his phone if we ever found it. Did he have a picture of his estranged mother? His stepbrothers? Was there any woman that he really loved?

"It wasn't much of a life," Mick said, echoing my thoughts. "Our victimology for Nicholl doesn't have much joy in it."

"Being a hound dog isn't going to bring much joy," Marcus said as we helped him carry the evidence down the stairs. "Not everyone can find the one woman for them, but to be constantly chasing every woman who gives you a second look would make for a crazy life."

"I want to go back in and look around the house. The killer came back for some reason. Marcus, I know you processed most of the house last time, but let's all go through it one more time and see if there's anything we've missed."

"Let's walk around the outside first," Mick suggested. "It's a shame they don't have a ring camera or some other security cameras on the house."

"None of the three rentals do. These days that's getting to be less common."

"I wouldn't have a rental without security cameras," Marcus said.

"Tina needs to be more forthcoming. We need to know what Mendoza's plan was. Was he going to wait around outside or did he intend on entering the house?" Mick asked.

"As bad as Tina is, I can't imagine that she would encourage him to break into a crime scene," I said, wondering if I was giving her too much credit.

"I agree. It's one thing to send a guy over here to watch the house in case something interesting happens, and a whole 'nother thing to be a part of a break-in at a crime scene."

"Was it a coincidence that Mendoza ran into the crew at the bar?" I asked.

"No way. Tina heard that there was a big-time TV production crew in town and got some insider information so she could arrange for Mendoza to cozy up to them and fish for gossip," Mick replied, stating my case for me.

"Agreed. Unfortunately, we might have lost the ability to grill Tina over all this. Unless…"

"Unless we can catch her on video surveillance driving around with Mendoza on the night he was killed."

"I have all my toes and fingers crossed," I admitted.

"I can't believe she even went after Mauser," Marcus said.

"That was low. I might have deserved it, but poor Mauser never did anything to the woman."

"She hit Eddie Thompson pretty hard too," Mick reminded me.

"I need to run by and talk to him. He's managed to remake himself into a respectable citizen. I'd hate for this to damage his rehab."

"I looked around the backyard. Anywhere I thought would be a good vantage point." Mick put us back on track. "Trouble is, the armadillos, squirrels and every other type of animal have mucked up the ground to the point where it's impossible to find tracks or a disturbance where someone might have kneeled down to wait."

"Not like the old days where the guy smoked half a dozen cigarettes while he was waiting, so there was a nice pile of butts to mark the spot," I said wistfully, dreaming of all that DNA evidence we didn't have.

"What about the killer? Do you think they had the place staked out?" Marcus asked.

"No. I think if they had, they wouldn't have run into

Mendoza and he'd still be alive."

"Or the killer had a meeting set up with Mendoza," Mick suggested.

I thought about that. "Let's look at it logically. If Nicholl's killer came here to kill Mendoza, it would have been a prearranged meeting, or he followed Mendoza. If it was prearranged, then the killer planned it out. Under those circumstances, why kill Mendoza in the utility room?"

"We haven't mapped out how the killing took place." Mick pointed to the back door into the utility room.

"Let's go take a look."

"I've got the crime scene photos on my camera." Marcus held up the camera he had around his neck.

The utility room still smelled of bleach, so we left the door open to let in fresh air.

"Is this a reasonable place to plan on killing someone?" I asked as we stood in the narrow space in front of the washer and dryer.

"I don't feel like I have room to maneuver." Mick swung his arms around.

"The body was here lying on its side," Marcus said, pointing as he looked at the screen on his camera. "The bleach smeared and messed up the blood evidence on the floor, but there was some blood spray on the wall there." He pointed to the wall away from the washer and dryer. The spots were still visible.

"The killer hit Mendoza with the murder weapon, and when the killer swung the weapon back for the second blow, blood was flung against the wall," Mick said.

"The attack was to the front left side of Mendoza's head," Marcus said, looking at another photo.

"We'll know more about the wounds after the autopsy, but that looks correct from the pictures," I said.

"Which means that the killer was inside the utility room and was surprised by Mendoza coming in. The killer used the murder weapon without hesitation," Mick said. "Otherwise, Mendoza would have tried to block the attack with his arm."

"Unless he had a camera in his arm," I said.

"Evidence marker seventeen and eighteen," Marcus said, and showed us a picture where two small pieces of plastic were labeled with evidence markers. "They are black plastic, broken off of something."

"He tried to block the blow with the camera, and the murder weapon either bounced off or knocked the camera out of his hands," Mick said.

"Where is the camera?" Marcus asked, and we all looked out the utility room door toward the lake.

"Which is probably where the murder weapon is," I said.

"I'll see if your dad can get the dive team back out here to look. We can get a drag magnet too, and go out in the boat to fish around for anything that might have gotten tossed in there," Mick said.

"We need to look at the pictures you took the day Nicholl disappeared and see if there are any differences between those and the pictures you took the day Mendoza was found dead. Maybe we'll find something is missing or moved that might give us a clue as to what the killer was looking for, or what he or she used to kill Mendoza," I said.

"I downloaded all those photos," Marcus said.

"I think using a big screen to do side-by-side comparisons will be the best way anyway," I told him.

"In this day and age, there's probably software that can compare photos and note differences," Marcus suggested.

"I think our eyeballs will work. Besides, we might notice other things that could be important."

"I can take a look at them," Mick offered.

"Let's both do it. What one misses, the other might catch."

We spent another half hour walking through the house before admitting we were just killing time.

"I've got to check on that CCTV footage from Mendoza's apartment complex before the autopsy," Mick said as we headed back to our cars.

We all went our separate ways. I looked at my watch and decided I had time to run by the library and talk to Eddie before I met Darlene for lunch.

Eddie was at the front desk, checking books out for a kid who looked like he was stocking up for the rest of the summer. Eddie looked up and quickly averted his eyes when he saw me.

"That's quite a load of books you've got," I told the young man, who looked like he'd just hit his teens. He proceeded to tell me about the books he'd checked out and gave me a rough rundown of the reasons he'd chosen each of them.

"He's quite the reader,'" I said to Eddie after the boy had left.

"Are you looking for any book in particular?" Eddie asked as though he'd never seen me before. "I can point out where you can find it if you tell me what you're looking for."

"Eddie, I'm sorry about Knightly's report. I didn't know she was going to do that."

"Books on Bendict Arnold would be in history or biography."

I sighed. "Look, I'm not minimizing what happened, but you *did* testify at your father's and grandfather's trials. Everyone knows who your family is."

Eddie leaned across the counter and looked me in the eyes. I was surprised at the amount of anger I saw in his.

"That's not the point. Besides, a lot of people I work with and who come in here don't know I took drugs or realize just how close I was to... all that mess with my family."

"You were the hero in that story," I reminded him.

Eddie seemed to think this over. I got out of the way as an elderly woman came up to the counter carrying several *The Cat Who...* books. Eddie and the woman made small talk as he checked the books out for her.

"See, no one cares."

"I *was* the hero, wasn't I?" Eddie asked.

"You were," said a voice from behind me.

Startled, I turned to see Albert Griffin, the county's unofficial historian and Eddie's landlord.

"I tried to tell him last night that it wasn't a big deal. Worse for you, I imagine?" he said gently.

"Dad's not real happy," I confirmed.

"Tina Knightly is a nightmare to deal with. I could have told you to beware of antagonizing her."

"Plenty of people did, including Dad. That's why he's particularly furious with me."

"I can't believe she went after Mauser," Eddie said. "That made me angrier than what she said about me. Your dad brought him into the library a couple of weeks ago and the kids are still talking about Mauser the Mountain. That's what one of the kids from public housing called him. The boy's mother told me he wants to come to the library now just in the hopes of seeing Mauser."

My phone buzzed with a text from Darlene. *Done in 15 then headed that way.*

"I've got to go meet Chief Marks for lunch. I just wanted you to know I didn't mean for your name to be smeared across the airwaves."

"If anyone is to blame, it's my father and grandfather," Eddie grumbled.

"I'll walk out with you," Mr. Griffin said.

"I feel bad about dragging Eddie into all this mess when he's come so far with his sobriety," I confessed to him when we were outside.

"He was upset last night when he first saw it, but I told him the same thing you did. A heroic story always involves overcoming personal flaws. Everyone who knows Eddie is proud of what he's accomplished."

"I hope it doesn't cause a rift between him and Jessie."

"Not that woman. She called up this morning after she'd seen it and told him that there are bad journalists just like there are bad actors in every profession."

"She's a keeper. I hope we can hire her on when she

finishes at the academy. Maybe I should say I hope she *wants* to come work for us when she gets done with her certification."

"I think that's her goal. How's Jackie holding up? I wanted to see her while she's in town."

"You know Jackie King?" I asked, surprised.

"Yes. I'd gone back to teaching for a few years and she was in my class. Very smart young lady."

"I didn't know she'd lived here." This was all news to me.

"For just two or three years. Her father worked for the forestry service, or maybe it was the state agricultural service. Anyway, they moved around the state a lot. She was around fourteen when she was in my history class."

I wondered why Jackie hadn't mentioned it, but then again, what did her living in the county twenty-five years earlier have to do with anything happening today?

"I'd ask you what she was like, but I don't see how it can be relevant."

"Like I said, smart and determined. I know Cody Morgan too."

"How do you know him?" I was used to Mr. Griffin knowing everyone in the county and their history going back a hundred years, but I was always surprised when his knowledge extended past the boundaries of the county.

"He came up and gave a talk to the historical society about ten years ago. The presentation was on North Florida weirdness. UFOs, Bigfoot, ghosts, that sort of thing. He was a little stiff, but very knowledgeable. It was one of our most well-attended talks. When I saw him the other day, I told him we'd pay his gas if he'd come back and give another talk."

"When did you see him?"

"Friday. He came into town to have lunch with Chief Marks."

"He said he knew Darlene. I feel like I'm the only person in the county who doesn't know him." I frowned.

"Nice guy. A bit socially awkward, and smarter than he

acts sometimes."

I got some more local gossip out of him, then left to meet Darlene.

She was sitting in her fancy chief's SUV, talking on the radio to one of her cops.

"There are days I wonder who would hold their hands if I wasn't around." She shook her head and smiled. "Reminds me of when we were partners and I had to do everything but wipe your nose."

I gave her a discreet one-finger salute.

"See, and that's the attitude that has you in Dutch with the local news witch." Darlene smiled. "Why the hell were you even talking to her? We have some good reporters around here. Go to them if you need to share information with the public."

"Tina has put herself in the middle of a murder investigation and I got carried away," I admitted.

"That can't turn out well." She pushed me toward the taco truck. "I don't have all day and I'm hungry as a hippo on a treadmill."

Darlene ordered two pork barbecue tacos and deep-fried garlic potato wedges. I got a hamburger taco and my own bag of wedges.

"Tell me what you know about Cody Morgan," I said after Darlene had finished her first taco.

"He's good friends with Kay Lamberton and her brother. I know he worked for them at least part-time back in the 1980s. Even helped out with a couple of murders they got involved in through their funeral home."

"That sounds a little dodgy," I said and got the look from Darlene.

"Don't be throwing dirt at Kay." Darlene would go to the mat for a friend, which was part of what made her a great cop.

"She seemed like a very nice person when I met her," I said innocently.

Darlene gave me a hard look before she decided I hadn't meant to disparage Kay.

"Cody showed up one time when I was visiting Kay, and we got to talking about the woods. Cody has spent more time in the wilderness than anyone I know. Anyhow, he took me out and showed me some things I didn't know about the wilds of Florida. Stoic backwoodsman kind of guy. I got the feeling his early years were rough, and it doesn't help that he's obsessed with Bigfoot, skunk ape, whatever you want to call it. He told me he saw one when he was a kid. The image never left him. He's been tracking the creature ever since."

"Talking about Bigfoot all the time is going to bring some ridicule down on your head." I nodded.

"If you understand how well he knows the backwoods, it's a lot harder to dismiss his stories about Bigfoot," Darlene said with a sincerity that caused me to look at her. She didn't meet my eyes. I thought about asking if *she* believed in Bigfoot but decided to leave that on the table for now.

"You would vouch for him?"

"Never say never, but if he did hurt someone then there would have to be a reason, deep and personal," she assured me.

"So how would you deal with Tina Knightly?" I figured I'd gotten as much out of her about Cody Morgan as I could.

"You've grabbed a tiger by the tail and now you're asking me what you should do?" She shook her head. "I thought I taught you better."

"Apparently, you and Shantel didn't beat it into my head well enough."

"How's your dad taking the bad publicity?"

"Not well." I went on to tell her about Major Parks.

"I know your dad leaned on Parks."

"He's already given over most of Parks's responsibilities to Captain Grant."

"That's smart. Grant's a great logistician. That's what made him perfect for running the patrol division. Of course, now your dad has to find someone to take over patrol,"

Darlene said.

"I thought about that. Both lieutenants in patrol are good, but I'm not sure either one is ready for more responsibility," I said.

"Says the boy who's just proved *he* wasn't ready for more responsibility." She gave me a lopsided grin.

"That cut to the bone. You aren't wrong, and Dad's mistake promoting me might make him think twice before doing the same thing again."

"He didn't make a mistake," Darlene said with more certainty than I felt was warranted.

We packed up our trash and tossed it into the can on the way back to our cars.

Mick called as I was pulling away from the taco stand.

"I've got some security footage that looks promising," he told me. "I tried to get the footage from the TV station's parking lot, but they told me to pound sand if I didn't have a warrant. The convenience store a block away was more accommodating after I got a friend of mine with the Leon County Sheriff's Office to talk to them." He paused expectantly.

"What'd you find?" I asked, taking the bait.

"Tina driving by the convenience store toward the TV station about twenty minutes after Mendoza did the same, and then Tina driving away again. Unfortunately, the footage is too grainy to make a positive ID on Mendoza, who's in the seat away from the camera."

"But Mendoza's car wasn't found in the TV station's lot," I pointed out.

"I couldn't find her in the footage driving away in his car later, but she could have gone east instead of south and not passed that camera. The footage at his apartment complex is going to be crucial."

"Fingers crossed. I could use some leverage over her. I know she's involved in Mendoza's death. I don't mean directly. I don't think she *intended* him to get hurt. Still, she threw him into harm's way."

"Careful. You played with fire and got burned once," Mick reminded me.

CHAPTER SEVENTEEN

At the risk of running into Dad, I went back to the office. I knew sooner or later I was going to have to face him. I just wasn't sure how much time I should give him to cool off, or how it would go when he did.

I got Marcus to place copies of all the photos of the house where Mendoza had been killed in a shared folder so I could obsess over them in my office after I kicked Pete out of it. I sorted the two sets of photos into ones that had been taken after Nicholl disappeared and ones that had been taken after Mendoza was found dead, so that I could look at each original photo beside the corresponding one from the later date. Not all photos of the same room had been taken from the same angle. Any photo that didn't have a close mate went into a miscellaneous folder.

I went back and forth, trying to find differences between the photos. If the killer had come back for something, I was hoping I'd notice it.

After an hour, my eyes were getting sore and I was about to give up when there was a knock at the door. I could see through the vertical window in the door that it was Pete. He was making a stupid face in the glass. With a roll of my eyes, I waved him in.

"You've been locked in here for a while." He hobbled on his crutches over to a chair and sat down. "Sorry, I didn't get the door."

"That's okay. Unless you're going to tell me all your deep, dark secrets," I joked.

"So you can let Tina spread them all over the internet? No, thank you."

"That was low."

"So what are you doing in here? I know you aren't reading CID reports, because I'm doing that and all of your other work."

"I'm going over the crime scene photos. I feel like we'd be making progress if I could just figure out why the killer was at the house the night Mendoza was killed."

"You think you can find something missing?"

"I could just be looking in the wrong direction. Still, if the killer went back to the house, then there had to be a reason."

"Turn your laptop around so I can get a look."

I spun it around and moved it toward Pete before getting up and coming around the desk to sit next to him so we could look at the pictures together.

"I didn't know the utility room was so narrow. That's an odd place for a planned confrontation," Pete observed.

"When you're there, it feels claustrophobic. I'd never attack someone in such a confined space unless I didn't have a choice."

"Definitely not enough room to maneuver."

"That's my point. I think the killer came to the house looking for something. Mendoza had been watching the house at Tina's bidding. At least I'm eighty percent sure at this point that Tina was directing his actions."

"So he's watching the house, sees the killer enter and decides to… what?" Pete asked.

"Get in their face with the camera. Videotape them. I don't know. But as Mendoza entered the utility room, the killer attacked him."

"With what?"

"I was hoping I'd see an object missing between the first set of photos and the second."

We spent another half hour comparing the photos when Pete pointed at a pair of pictures showing a wall of the garage.

"There." Pete indicated a spot against the garage wall. There was a workbench, and a couple of nails had been hammered into the side of the bench. You could see this clearly in the more detailed photos after the murder.

"What?" I asked, not sure what he was seeing. He was pointing back and forth between the post-murder picture and a picture taken when we'd first gone through the house after Nicholls disappeared. In that set of pictures, there was a photo of the bench, but it was from head-on and didn't show the side with the nails.

"There, see, hanging down? You can see the dark line against the bench." Pete was pointing at the head-on shot of the bench, and there was a clear black line extending down the side. Something had been hung on the nail.

"What is it?"

"I can only see about six inches and that isn't too clear. Could be anything. Large screwdriver, pipe, maybe a crowbar," Pete suggested.

"The murder weapon?" I nodded.

"The two rooms in a house with the most murder weapons are the kitchen and the garage." Pete smiled.

"Maybe the owner of the home would know what that was." I peered at the picture, trying to get more information than the image had to offer. "I'll check. Whatever it is, the killer could have tossed it into the lake from any point on the shore. I would bet money the murder weapon is somewhere at the bottom of the lake."

"Good luck finding it."

"We're going to use divers and at least one drag magnet," I said.

My phone rang with a call from Mick. I answered, but

before I had a chance to ask how the autopsy had gone, a bull came charging into my office. Mauser had heard my voice from the hallway and came storming through CID and into my office, thumping everything in sight with his near-lethal tail. I told Mick I'd call him back and hung up to deal with the invasion.

"Watch it!" Pete said, trying to protect his leg and face at the same time. Mauser tried to lick both of us to death before attempting to climb into my lap.

"What are you doing, you big monster?" I tried to push him back off of me, but it was a challenge.

"I'll go now," I heard Pete say as he struggled to safely get up in the presence of the goliath. It was at that point that I saw Dad in the doorway and understood why Pete was in a hurry to escape. Dad stepped back to let Pete hobble out of the room, then came inside.

"I guess he heard your voice. Come on, let's go." The command was for Mauser, who pretended not to hear it.

"Dad, we're going to have talk this out," I said, and immediately regretted it when I saw his face turn a menacing shade of red.

"Not now." His words were clipped. He looked at Mauser and frowned. "Fine, stay with him."

"I've got work to do," I said, but Dad had already turned on his heel and walked out, leaving me to babysit my four-legged brother.

"I don't think you made him happy. Now we're both in the doghouse." I got an enthusiastic headbutt from the Dane. "Now what am I going to do with you?"

I struggled up and kept him off of me long enough to get to the door.

"Good news and bad news," I told Pete. "The good news is that I'm going to let you use my office."

Pete looked at Mauser. "I can see this one coming. What do you think your reporter girlfriend would say if she found out that deputies were being forced to babysit your father's dangerous beast of a dog?"

"That's why I'm asking you to volunteer," I said, grimacing while Mauser drooled on my shoes.

"I guess if I can't go running around the county questioning people, I should take care of the monster so you can." Pete looked at Mauser and made googly eyes at him. "Come to Uncle Petey."

Mauser bounded over, tail wagging, and I had a moment when I saw us taking Pete to the emergency room to have his leg once again pieced back together. But, to the giant lunkhead's credit, he stopped just short of crashing into Pete and laid his head against his chest.

"You'll need to help me get settled and maybe take him for a walk before you leave," Pete told me.

I found a leash in my desk. *Why do I have a leash in my desk?* I asked myself. *Because Dad is always dropping his black-and-white elephant off with me.*

I was heading for the back door with Mauser in tow when I decided to sidetrack to Lionel's office and see where we were with Nicholl's laptop and phone data. Lionel was a charter member of the Mauser fan club, so I had to wait through five minutes of greetings and ear-scratches.

"You know Mauser doesn't have a say in who gets a raise and who doesn't," I joked with Lionel.

"That's not what Tina Knightly says," he answered with an evil grin.

"*Et tu, Brute?*" I grumbled. "Enough with the ear-rubs. Have you gotten Nicholl's phone data?"

"I was just putting the report together." Reluctantly, Lionel swiveled his chair away from Mauser to face one of the half dozen monitors in his office.

"His last answered call was at nine-thirty on Sunday. There's the number." He pointed to a number on the monitor. "Don't worry, I'll send all of this to you. His last sent text was to Dirk, just before eleven-thirty: *How long will you all be?* The response was: *Around one. Do you need to go somewhere?* Nicholls responded: *no get soaked but be safe.*"

"His last text wasn't to Kayla?" This was news to me.

"No. That one was sent fifteen minutes earlier." He pointed to the screen, and I read the text over his shoulder.

"Can you find the phone?"

"I can tell you where it was located before the battery and SIM card were pulled out of it, or maybe the phone was destroyed. Either way, it has quit sending information."

"How do you know the battery didn't just run down?"

"I was able to pull some information from one of his exercise apps, which uploads a ton of information, including how much power the phone has left. When it quit sending info, the phone still had sixty-two percent battery life."

"Where is it?"

Lionel shifted over to another monitor and pulled up Google maps. On the satellite overlay, a pin was stuck in the middle of the lake. From what I could tell, it was a hundred feet or so from where the boat had been found.

"I don't think you have to be a genius to figure the phone is at the bottom of the lake," Lionel said.

I tried to calculate the odds of finding the phone. Ten thousand to one? A hundred thousand to one? A million to one? The bottom line was that we could drag a magnet across the bottom of that lake for a long time before we ever came up with Nicholl's phone.

"Whoever killed Nicholl and dumped his body wanted to know when the others were coming home," I said.

"Stands to reason. Also, they probably hoped to delay anyone looking for him."

"Standard Criminal Behavior 101. Use the victim's cell phone and text people. Can't blame the people getting the messages. Who thinks that the text they receive might not be from the person they think it is?"

"If anyone should, it's the two of us after working all of these cases. Still, if I get a text, I assume it's from the person my phone tells me it's from," Lionel admitted.

"What else can you tell from the data?"

"I can tell you exactly when he was killed."

"What?"

"He was wearing a FitNow band, and it sent data to the app on his phone. At eleven-ten, his heart rate soared for about thirty seconds and then zeroed out. That was five minutes before the text to Kayla."

"So we know for sure that the texts came from his killer. I wish our suspects were somewhere other than in their rooms alone."

"You can eliminate the three who were at the bar."

"True." I would have to think about this new information. Did it do me any good? Only time would tell. "I want any other information you can give me about the texts he sent and received. Particularly during his last week."

Lionel gave me a thumbs-up.

"What about Mendoza?" I asked.

"I'm still working to get his phone data. I think he used a pay-as-you-go phone. The data you get from them isn't nearly as good as from major carriers with name-brand phones."

"Looks like our killer took it too, which means it's swimming with the fishes along with Nicholl's phone."

I thanked Lionel and left to take Mauser for his constitutional outside, which wasn't that easy. As soon as I opened the door and the summer heat hit us, Mauser tried to back away.

"Come on! We're all Floridians here and, unfortunately for you, you can't use the indoor facilities," I told him, and finally succeeded in getting him outside after a lot of pushing and shoving.

I called Mick while Mauser sniffed around some live oak trees.

"What did you learn from Mendoza's autopsy?" I asked.

"The murder weapon was about an inch and a bit wide, and came down three times with some force on his skull. The first blow was lighter and a glancing blow. Now this is me talking, not Dr. Darzi, but I'd say that Mendoza partially blocked the first strike with his camera, but took enough of a hit that it gave the killer the opportunity to come in with the second and third blows."

"Makes sense. There were pry marks on the door. Whatever the killer used to pry the door open could have been what he used to kill Mendoza."

"A crowbar is the prying device of choice. I can testify to that after ten years investigating burglaries."

I got a funny feeling thinking about a crowbar.

"Text me the number for the owner of the house," I asked him, and went on to fill him in on what Pete pointed out in the pictures of the house before and after Mendoza had been killed.

"I think I see where you're going with that, and it would be an interesting development."

"Not too surprising, though."

As soon as I hung up, I cleaned up after Mauser and headed back to turn him over to Pete.

An hour later, I was meeting with the woman who owned the house.

"My niece talked me into renting the house out through that Airbnb website. Now I'm sorry I did it," Chelsea Robin told me. She was thin, with brown hair heavily mixed with grey. I guessed that she was in her late fifties.

"How long have you been renting it out?"

"Two years. My husband left me for a thirty-year-old podcaster, like that's a career. The woman talks about fantasy books she's read. I listened to one and thought I was going to throw up. Six months ago, he called me up and asked if I wanted to get together and talk. Can you believe his nerve? Anyway, when he walked away, I got myself a good lawyer and ended up with this house. I wanted to be closer to my job in Tallahassee, so I got an apartment and have been renting this house out through the website. Now I don't know what I'll do."

"There are more houses than we'd like to admit where terrible things have happened. Life goes on. I don't think you have to tell your renters that someone was murdered here. Especially since I don't think the murder had as much to do with the house as it did with the people staying here."

"The funny thing is, I was kind of excited when I found out that it was a TV production company that wanted to rent the house."

"I can get you the name of a couple of outfits that will clean up the utility room for you," I offered.

"I don't have to go in there today, do I?"

"No. I just want you to come into the garage and tell me if there's anything missing," I said. "We can go through the house and avoid the utility area."

"Most of the stuff in the garage was my husband's. He wanted to come back and get some of it. Like that was going to happen. Walk out on me and then think you can come back and get whatever you want. Not likely." It was clear she was still mad. If it had been her husband lying dead in the utility room, I'd have had a prime suspect.

I saw her shudder as we entered the house.

"Who exactly contacted you to rent the house?" I asked, not sure how the online rental system worked.

"I got a notification, and it was from a production company. I didn't know it was *The Big Search*. I've got a son who watches the show. He's in school up in Tennessee. I don't like all that weird stuff. Bigfoot, UFOs, ghosts. But I do like that actor, Eli. I saw him in that documentary about the ocean. He was great and looked good in a dive suit."

We reached the door to the garage and she put her hand out, but paused before opening it. Her hand returned to her side, and she shifted from foot to foot.

"I know it's silly, but I'd feel better if you opened the door and went in first."

"No problem." I stepped past her and went into the garage. I flipped on the light switch and walked to the middle of the garage. "It's fine. No one is here."

"What about the utility room?" she asked, pointing to the door.

I walked over and opened the door. "All clear," I said, then closed the door.

Once it was shut again, she took a couple of tentative steps into the garage.

"If you think there's anything missing, let me know." I stood back and gave her room.

Chelsea walked around looking at the walls and cabinets. After a few minutes, she shook her head.

"Gives me the creeps to be in here," she said. "I can't tell if anything is missing. I did look around the other day with that other detective."

"I want you to look over here." I pointed to the table where Pete had spotted the missing tool.

Chelsea looked where I was pointing, then walked over and felt the pair of nails that extended out from the side of the workbench.

"Looks like there was something hanging here. As you can see, my husband hung tools all around the garage." She waved her hands at the wall.

"Could we call your husband?"

She looked at me like I'd suggested she hold a cobra.

"I… No. I don't even have his number."

"Is there anyone else who might know what was hanging there?"

"My son might. He worked on projects with my husband."

"Could we talk to him?"

She called him and didn't seem to be able to make him understand which spot she was talking about. Finally, he talked her into taking a picture of the area and texting it to him.

"A crowbar," I heard her son say after he saw the photo.

"Is he sure?" I asked.

Chelsea held the phone out to me, and I took it.

"This is Sergeant Macklin. Can you describe the crowbar?"

"It's a crowbar. You know, black, I guess, about two feet

long, maybe a little longer."

"When was the last time you saw it there?"

There was a long pause.

"I guess maybe two years ago." He didn't sound very certain.

I thanked him and handed the phone back to Chelsea.

Why would someone who'd broken into the house, presumably with a large screwdriver or crowbar, need to grab another crowbar from inside the house in order to kill someone? The answer was pretty obvious to me. They hadn't actually pried the door open to get in. They had unlocked the door with a key, and then used the crowbar to pry the exterior door open so that an investigator would think the killer didn't have a key. Staging a crime scene was all too common and seldom worked.

"I'd like to take another look in the utility room," I told Chelsea.

"Fine. I'll wait outside." She started to walk away, then stopped and turned back to me. "Would you like to buy the place? I'll make you great a deal."

"Not today." I gave her a kind smile and watched her turn and go.

In the utility room, I again tried to recreate the scene in my head. I was standing at the dryer and turned toward the door into the garage when I saw the killer coming toward me and involuntarily jumped.

"Ass!" I said, my heart pounding as I scowled at Mick, who had poked his head into the utility room from the outside.

"I decided to swing by on my way back from the autopsy. You almost pissed your pants." He grinned.

"I'll get you back someday," I promised. "I think on the night of the murder, the foot was on the other shoe." I told him what I learned about the crowbar. "A possible scenario is that the killer came here, unlocked the back door, went inside and then saw or heard Mendoza approaching. The killer went into the garage, but decided that they needed to confront Mendoza, so they picked up the crowbar and, as Mendoza was entering the utility room, the killer attacked him."

"Mendoza attempted to defend himself with his camera, which explains the pieces of plastic Marcus found."

"Right, but the crowbar slid past the camera and hit Mendoza's head. He either fell to his knees or all the way down on the floor."

"At which point the killer finished him off with a couple of sharp blows with the crowbar."

"Then, satisfied that Mendoza was dead, the killer went outside, closed the utility room door and then pried it open to make it appear like a break-in," I said.

"The fake break-in is a classic," Mick admitted.

"I just wish we knew why the killer was here."

"I got the footage from Mendoza's apartment complex while I was in Tallahassee." He held up his hand. "Don't get excited. The video is underwhelming in its quality. Why they even bother to have the cameras when they're that bad, I don't know. It's an ancient system where the cameras take one image every three seconds, and the resolution is pathetic. All you can see is that a person, probably a woman, drove the car back to the apartment complex and left it there."

"But you can tell it's not Mendoza?"

"Too late to be Mendoza. It's at three-forty-five. He was most likely dead by then."

"You say it's a woman. Clothes?"

"The image is black and white, so all you can tell is that her pants are dark, maybe jeans, and her shirt is lighter."

"Maybe we can use it anyway."

"How?"

"Bluff. We pretend we know it's Tina. Show her the best still image of the bunch and see if she crumbles," I said.

"With anyone else, I'd say go for it. But first of all, I don't think your dad is going to let you play tough with Tina. You've been bitten once. Second, I would bet she doesn't bluff easily."

"You're right," I said, discouraged that we didn't have what we needed to charge Tina, and irritated that she had created a situation where we weren't going to be able to bluff our way to a confession.

"And this is a sidetrack anyway. You and I both know she dropped Mendoza off here at the house, but she didn't have anything else to do with the murder."

I nodded. "I know. Let's let Mrs. Robin go."

We walked back through the house and found her standing by her car.

"Who else would have a key to the house?" I asked.

"I have five keys that I use when I rent the place. One is mine. The other four are for the guests. Most of the time, they just want two. Oh yeah, the maintenance man has a key."

"When was the last time you changed the locks?" Mick asked.

"About a year ago. I had a renter that we had to get you all to kick out; I told you about that," she said, looking at Mick. "I changed the lock after that."

"So anyone who has rented the house since then could have made a copy of the key?" I frowned.

"I suppose." She looked thoughtful.

"When you rented the house, who did you give the keys to?"

"They said to just leave them in the lockbox."

"Lockbox?"

"It's like the ones that the realtors use. A friend gave it to me. I put one key inside and gave them the code to open the box. The other three keys, I left on the hall table."

"So they had four sets of keys to the house?"

She nodded and I just shook my head. Anyone could have a set of keys to the house at that rate. I didn't know why I was obsessing on the keys. Whoever had killed Nicholl could have taken the set he had with him. They hadn't been found in his pockets or anywhere else.

"I'm not kidding about selling the house," Chelsea told

us as I handed her a couple of cards for crime scene cleaners.

"You'll need to wait until we give you the all-clear to call the cleaners. After that, you're free to sell the house if you want to," I told her.

We watched her drive away as we listened to the grumble of summer thunderstorms moving in from the coast. The breeze had picked up, giving us a little relief from the heat.

"What now?" Mick asked.

"You're the lead investigator," I reminded him.

"I've got the boat and divers scheduled for tomorrow. Maybe we'll get lucky and find the murder weapon or the phones."

"I'm not sure how much any of that would help. Maybe they could get DNA off of them, though our killer has been pretty savvy."

"Submerged in water for days will make it difficult. And if we're talking about the people in Nicholl's inner circle, their DNA could be expected to be found on his phone."

"Not the crowbar," I pointed out.

"True. I guess we go fishing tomorrow."

"Let's go on a fishing expedition now. I want to ride over and talk to the group. I'm particularly interested in who rented these houses. What are the odds that none of the three would have security cameras of any sort?"

"Yeah, not even ring cameras. Okay, I'm game."

CHAPTER EIGHTEEN

I called Arianne and found out that they had finished shooting for the day and were getting pizza delivered to the houses.

"Let's hit the below-the-line folks first," I said to Mick.

"I see how comfortable you're getting with the lingo. You'll be working in LA before you know it."

"I'd rather be staked out on an anthill," I assured him.

Mick followed me over to the house where Kayla, Jake, Dirk, Dani, Koby and Gabriella were staying. When I knocked on the door, I was surprised by how quickly it was answered until I figured out they'd been hoping I was the pizza guy.

"Sorry. No pizza," I told Koby, who was standing at the door looking at me expectantly. He backed up and held the door open for Mick and me. "We just wanted to ask a few more questions."

"Why not?" Koby said, sounding tired and depressed.

All the other members of the crew were in the living room except for Kayla, who I assumed was still languishing dramatically upstairs. They were all sitting with their phones in hand as if waiting for a plane to take them far away from here.

"Do you all know who made the original reservations for the three rentals?" I asked.

"I did." Dirk half raised his hand.

"Hey, can I move over to the murder house? At least I could have my own room," Jake asked and received glares from everyone else.

"That's disgusting. How could you stay there?" Koby asked.

"Could I talk to you alone?" I asked Dirk, who frowned and got up off the couch like a teenager told to take out the trash.

"I'd like to see Kayla," Mick said to the others. All of them rolled their eyes in unison.

"Talk to her, kick her ass, throw her out the window," Koby told him.

"I'll take you upstairs." Gabby got up and Mick followed her to the stairs.

"Let's go in the kitchen," I told Dirk, and once again received the spoiled teenager look. I expected him to stomp his feet as I followed him to the kitchen.

"Sorry, man. I'm just sick and tired of this." He waved his hand around. "Traveling with the crew is stressful enough, but with all the drama and being crammed in together… it ain't fun."

He was still holding his phone and glancing at it from time to time. I had found myself more often than not having to ask people under forty to put their phones up when I was interviewing them. He must have seen me looking at his phone, because he slipped it into a pocket of his jeans and gave me his full attention.

"Are we going to be able to go home next week for the Fourth of July?" he asked.

"Regardless of what you've seen on TV, we can't tell people not to leave town. It will be up to the production company."

"Sorry, I don't mean to be callous or anything. We've just been on the road for weeks."

"Do you always make the reservations?"

"I have for about a year. I like it. I can get a few perks, like being in the house with the above-the-line people. I also know where we're going and find out a little about the place before we get there. I like that."

"How does it work? Do you just go online and pick the places?"

"I don't have that much freedom." He smiled. "Jackie gives me the places she's picked out and then I make the reservations and deal with all the transportation and other details."

"Jackie always picks the rentals?"

"Sometimes we stay in hotels. It all depends on where we're going and where our budget is at any point. But, yeah, she always tells me where I should make the reservations."

"Is there ever a problem when you go to make them?"

"Sure, sometimes they don't have the houses or rooms for the dates we want, then I have to go back to Jackie."

I knew that Jackie was a producer as well as a star of the show. Still, I was surprised that it wasn't Arianne who took care of the details.

"Why doesn't Arianne arrange for the accommodations?"

"She did until Jackie got mad at her 'cause her room sucked."

"When was this?"

"Not long before I started making the reservations. Prior to that, Arianne did all of it."

"Was there any problem making the reservations this time?"

"No."

"And you communicated with the landlords?"

"All I did was email them and tell them when we'd be coming in and what we expected. They told me where the keys would be. Actually, the landlord for this house and the other one met us here and let us in."

"Who all had keys to the house where you and Scott Nicholl were staying?"

"Me, Scott, Eli and Jackie."

"I thought Jackie was staying at the other house?"

"She held on to the extra key for any of the other producers who might come down. We always have an extra room set aside."

"And Jackie always keeps the extra keys?"

"Yes."

"Eli told me about y'all taking the jon boat out for a spin. When was this?"

"Saturday."

"Who came over to the house?"

"Everyone. We ate dinner there. I think Scott ordered food for everyone. If it wasn't Scott, then it could have been Arianne or Jackie."

"Was that unusual?"

"No. We often have a get-together at a new location. We have lunch or dinner and sit around and discuss what the next couple of days shooting are going to cover. You know, and we go over any script notes."

"So everyone was in the house?"

"Sure, in and out. Most of us went out on the lake and hung around after we ate and talked about the show."

That was wonderful news. DNA evidence would be pretty much useless in this situation. The only way it would be of any value would be if the killer had been injured and left some of their blood behind. Blood evidence would be harder to explain.

"Did anyone get hurt that night?"

"No."

"Did anyone *not* go for a ride in the boat?"

"Gabby. She said she was nervous in a small boat. Some folks teased her a little. No big deal. It was all in fun."

I had one more question I wanted to throw at Dirk.

"Why didn't you tell me that you were the last one to get a text from Scott?" I used my best neutral-cop voice.

His brow furrowed as he thought about this information. "I didn't *know* I got his last text."

"May I see the exchange between you and Scott on your phone?" I held out my hand.

Robotically, Dirk reached into his pocket, pulled up the text message and handed me the phone.

The text was there exactly as Lionel had found it on Nicholl's phone records. It would have been telling if Dirk had deleted the text.

"I feel sick now thinking I was the last person to text Scott," he said. I didn't tell him that he had in all probability communicated with the murderer instead.

I asked a few more questions that didn't yield anything useful, then we went back into the living room. Mick hadn't come back downstairs yet, so I asked Koby to come into the kitchen with me.

"We heard about what that reporter did to you," Koby started. "You know she came out to the location today?"

I'm sure I made an ugly face because it got a little smile from Koby.

"I know. She's a snake. Tried to get me to say that you were harassing us."

I felt my blood pressure rising. "Did she talk about her cameraman?"

"Jake asked her what he was doing at the house that got him killed."

This made me smile. "What did she say?"

"She pretended the question didn't bother her. Still, you could see how mad it made her. All she said was that he must have been looking for a story. After that, she kind of went after Jake. Asked him why he wasn't a regular on the show, and when he made excuses, she started asking questions about comments that had been made about his appearances on the show. She read out some nasty ones that people had left online."

"That couldn't have made Jake very happy."

"He got red in the face and walked away."

"Did she talk to everyone?"

"Everyone that would talk to her, which wasn't many of

us. We all know better than to talk to reporters. If you say something that the producers or stars don't like, you can get your ass kicked off the show."

I asked a dozen questions, but Koby didn't have anything to add to what he'd already told me.

When I took him back to the living room, I noticed that Dani was gone. I assumed that Mick had come back and was now talking with her.

"Jake, would you follow me?" I asked.

He looked at me as though considering his answer. After a minute, he stood up and put his phone in his pocket. I went back to the kitchen with him reluctantly tagging along.

"I don't know what I can tell you." His eyes challenged mine. I didn't like his attitude and decided to see what would happen if I nudged him a little.

"You know you have one of the strongest motives for killing Scott."

His jaw clenched and his eyes narrowed.

"You can't accuse me of murder. I haven't done anything." The words sounded rehearsed.

"Have you talked to Arianne about replacing Scott on the show?" This was a shot in the dark. From the look on his face, it was clear I'd hit the mark.

"So what?" he asked, flipping into defensive mode. His voice was high with a touch of fear.

"So, a man has been murdered and before he's even buried, you're fighting over his job."

"You're crazy if you think I'd kill someone for a job." He was very indignant.

"A starring role in a show," I pointed out.

"No." Jake shook his head vigorously.

"Where were you the night that Scott disappeared?"

"I was in my room. I'm sorry I didn't arrange for an alibi."

"You went to the bar the first night. The night you met and talked with Mendoza. Why didn't you go to the bar the night that Scott was murdered?"

"I didn't want to. This is summer in a college town. The night scene isn't worth the effort. I wanted a drink the first night and I didn't want one the night that Scott… disappeared."

"And you were also hanging out in your room the night Mendoza was killed." I made it a skeptical statement instead of a question.

"Yes!"

"Why did you go back to the house the night that Mendoza was killed?"

"I didn't go back to the house!"

"Someone killed Scott and Mendoza. Someone with a motive." Now I was trying to see who he would throw under the bus.

"It was Kayla!" he said without lowering his voice. Then he apparently decided that he shouldn't let everyone know he was pointing the finger at others, so he half whispered, "She's crazy with all of that fake grieving. And why was she pretending to be so distraught before we even knew he was dead?"

It was a question I'd asked myself.

"Do you think she could have snuck out and not been seen?"

"Easy! No one was checking under her tongue to make sure she swallowed those sedatives. She was a gymnast in school. She's agile enough to get down the oak tree that's right outside her window!"

I was getting the feeling that not only did Jake think it might be her, but he also actually *wanted* Kayla to be the murderer.

"Could she run the boat?"

This question caused him to pause for a moment before his eyes lit up.

"Yes! When I was standing near her and Scott, she told him that her father used to take her fishing on a lake back home all the time!" He was literally bouncing up and down like a gameshow contestant who's gotten the right answer.

"What's her motive?"

"Scott wasn't going to marry her. Hell, he wasn't even serious about her. No way, not at all. He probably told her that night and her psycho switch flipped on." Jake was loving this idea.

"Do you have any evidence?" I asked.

"You mean besides the way she's been acting?"

"Like real evidence. Did anyone see her coming and going from the house? Did you see dirt on her clothes, or were they ripped from climbing down the oak tree? Did you see any bruises on her? You know, evidence."

"I guess not." Jake paused, and I let the silence grow to see what he would say to fill it. Finally, "There's no evidence against me either."

"Are you going to get the job?"

I could see that the switch back to this topic made him uncomfortable.

"No. They're going to pause production of the show. When I talked to Jackie, she said she's not even sure she can continue to support it."

"How many more shows did you have left in the upcoming season?"

"Two more. We would have finished up before the end of August. Now they think they have enough unaired footage to piece together two more shows."

"That's a blow."

"Jackie said the producers have agreed to pay us for the two shows we won't film. I'm still bummed. Now I have to start fighting for a job on another show. You don't know how competitive this business is. I've already reached out to friends in the business, but right now everyone is having a tough time keeping themselves employed. Too many amateurs putting out content. On top of that, all the high-tech stuff allows the big producers to put out more content. Us guys in the middle don't have a lot of options."

Jake looked down at the floor of the kitchen, and for a minute I thought he was going to cry. *Is this how someone who has killed for a job might feel if the job fell through? Maybe,* I thought.

I spent a few more minutes with Jake, including getting him to show me his texts and phone calls for the last couple of days. I was looking for any numbers or texts that could have belonged to Mendoza, but I didn't find any. Just lots and lots of show business contacts.

When I got back to the living room, Mick was done with Dani. He'd talked to Gabby when they were upstairs, so there was nothing left for us to do when I asked for one more thing.

"We want to walk through the house again."

Everyone shrugged.

"I'll walk with you," Jake said, which surprised me, but I didn't argue. The more time I spent with a suspect, the better chance I had of seeing them slip up.

When we got to the top of the stairs, Jake pointed to Kayla's room.

"I'm telling you, check out the oak tree."

He knocked on the door and received a pathetic response from Kayla.

"Sorry to bother you again. I'd just wanted to look around your room, if you don't mind," I apologized.

"Anything that can help find the monster that killed Scott," Kayla said with a heavy sigh before falling back against the pillows. I looked at her half-opened eyes. If she'd been pocketing her sedatives at some point, it was clear that she was taking them now. Her eyes were lifeless and dilated.

Jake was right about the tree. Anyone with moderate athletic ability could manage to clamber down the sprawling oak outside her window. There was a branch as big around as a person three feet below and two feet away from the window. It would be tricky, but not impossible. I wouldn't want to be wearing shoes when I tried it, but I was sure I could do it.

I went back to the bed as Mick walked around the room looking at the few personal items that Kayla had set out.

"May I look at your feet?" I asked, feeling like a pervert.

Kayla looked at me through her drug haze and gave me a strange little smile.

"Yeah, sure." She wrestled with the sheets for a moment before pulling her bare feet out of the covers.

Her feet were clean and unmarred, though well-calloused like a child that likes to go barefoot.

"Thank you," I said and helped her get the covers back in place, which seemed to take a huge effort on her part.

We looked around the rest of the rooms and noticed nothing out of place. I wasn't even sure what I was looking for.

"We're leaving tomorrow," Jake told us as Mick and I finished looking around upstairs. Mick and I looked at each other.

"And you're just telling us now?" I asked.

"Apparently, they just decided. I would have thought they might have talked to you first," he said, and it was a reasonable assumption on his part.

"I would have too," Mick mumbled under his breath.

Like I'd told Dirk, we didn't have any way of holding them in town. Still, it would have been nice to get a heads-up.

"When are you leaving?"

"Right after we're done shooting tomorrow. Arianne just sent out a text telling us to pack up in the morning so we don't have to come back to the rooms when we get done."

Mick and I nodded and headed down the stairs.

CHAPTER NINETEEN

The rain had passed just west of us, leaving the night air cooler.

"It's after six. Do you want to go over and talk with Arianne?" I thought I would give Mick a choice. He'd been working as many hours as me over the last week.

"You bet, now that we know they're hightailing it out of town tomorrow."

We stopped at the cars and compared notes from our separate interviews.

"I can't eliminate Kayla from my list of suspects," Mick said. "Her behavior and drugged state could represent a reaction to having killed her lover and Mendoza."

"Why Mendoza?"

"She went over to the house for something. As lovesick as she acts, maybe it wasn't even for some piece of evidence. It could have been for a memento from Scott's possessions. Seeing Mendoza caused her to go into fight-or-flight mode, and when he was blocking the doorway out of the utility room, she attacked him."

"It's not impossible," I agreed. "From everything we know about her, she had a tenuous grasp of reality before Scott was killed. Murdering him would not have made her any more mentally balanced."

"And taking drugs wouldn't help either."

"She stays on the list. Close to the top." I nodded. "What about Jake?"

"Not off the list. His deflection is suggestive of someone with something to hide."

"Guilty of what? That's the question. Guilty of being a schemer who moved in as soon as Scott's body turned up? We *know* he's guilty of that."

"Ambition could drive a person to commit murder."

"What's his financial situation look like?" I asked.

"He's been delinquent on bills in the past. Mostly before he joined the show. Credit rating in the low six hundreds. Doesn't own a home or have a big bank account. Looks like he carries about three thousand dollars in credit card debit. His biggest red flag is a car payment that's close to a thousand dollars a month. I checked and he owns, or I should say the *bank* owns, a Porsche Panamera."

"I'm not surprised. A guy with his ego needs a flashy car. It would also be a symbol of his ambition."

"Exactly."

"He has the means and opportunity. He stays on the list," I said.

"We need ways of eliminating suspects."

"Unfortunately, we're dealing with a lucky or smart killer. Either way, they haven't left us much solid evidence."

We got in our cars and drove down the street to the other house. As soon as I got out of my car, I froze. A high-pitched voice bombarded me from behind. I turned to see Tina and the cameraman from the onion incident coming out of an unmarked van parked across the street.

"Macklin, have you been suspended by the sheriff's office?" was the first question she shot at me. The next one was, "Are you involved in the drug trade in Adams County?"

I had managed to turn back toward the house and was making my feet move toward the front door while my teeth ground against each other in an effort not to answer any of her ludicrous accusations.

I heard Mick tell her to back off when she shot out her next question. "How much money does your wife make distributing drugs?"

The question was outrageous, but my reptile brain told me that she needed to be confronted there and then. I turned and managed to get within ten feet of her before Mick hit me like a freight train. The impact pushed me five feet back, while his bear grip kept me from breaking free.

"Not now!" he growled into my ear. "She wants this. Don't fall for it."

What he was saying wasn't getting past my anger. Mick realized this and took his head and banged it into mine. The hit rattled my teeth while bringing me to my senses. I forced my muscles to relax.

Mick wasn't taking any chances. He maintained the bear hug while pushing me toward the front door.

Everyone inside had heard the ruckus and Eli opened the front door for us.

"She's been stalking us all day," he said.

Arianne was in the foyer and watched us come barreling into the house.

"Knightly is a hellcat." Arianne shook her head. "She's tried to get me to spill dirt on you *and* the production."

I stopped and took a couple of deep breaths to compose myself. I gave Mick a quick nod of thanks, then turned to Arianne.

"We heard y'all are leaving tomorrow," I said, not wanting to discuss Tina Knightly.

"Yes, after we get done shooting. Is that a problem?"

"It's a problem for us. Not that we can stop you."

"We can't afford to stay here indefinitely while you conduct your investigation," Arianne said flatly.

"I understand. Just don't expect me to be happy about it. We'd like to talk to each of you again before you leave."

If I'd known they were leaving, I'd have brought them all in for formal interviews where we could have gotten signed statements about their whereabouts at the time of the murders and any interactions they'd had with Mendoza.

"Of course. I don't think anyone will object to answering your questions," Arianne told us. "We're all upset about Scott's murder and want to see the person who did it arrested."

"There's also the murder of Saint Mendoza," Mick reminded her.

"I know. I didn't mean to… make less of his death. I just never met the man. It's like reading about a murder in the paper. The death of a friend hits differently."

"Is there a place we could talk in private?" I asked her.

"The living room. Everyone else is upstairs."

"While they're talking, why don't we step out back where I can ask you a few questions?" Mick said to Eli, who nodded solemnly and led him through the house to the back door.

There were a couple of chairs and a couch in the living room. I took a chair across from Arianne.

"Who chose the houses and made the reservations?" Crosschecking answers was always a good way to find out who was hiding something.

She gave all the same answers as Dirk.

"Did Jake talk to you about replacing Scott on the show?"

"I couldn't believe him. Jake has always been pushy about getting airtime. Still, to go after Scott's role so soon after… I thought I was going to be sick. I'm used to people in the business being cutthroat, but not like that." Her face reflected the repulsion she'd felt.

"Do you think he might have had a hand in what happened to Scott?"

"You mean kill him?" Arianne paused and thought about her answer. "Until he came to me asking for Scott's job, I wouldn't have thought that he could be that vicious. Now…"

"I understand that the show is going to be put on hold."

"Jackie told us this afternoon. I… It's a blow to all of us. Whoever killed Scott not only ended his life but made all of ours harder. I hope that doesn't sound too selfish."

"Everyone has a right to see a tragic event from their own position. The only time you're on shaky ground is when you swoop in like a vulture."

"Like Jake."

"Do you think this was foreseeable? Would Jake have expected the show to move him into Scott's role and move on?"

"I'd say most shows that are as successful as *The Big Search* would have tried to put the train back on the tracks. Before today, I would have placed the odds at seventy to thirty that the show would continue."

"Why do you think they decided to shut down?"

"You'd have to ask Jackie. As a producer, she was involved in the decision."

"What's your guess?"

Arianne looked thoughtful for a few moments before answering. "The show's been on for three years now, which is a good run. They might have figured that they were coming to the end of the life of the show, so why fight this? Take the money and run." She shrugged.

I went over some of the same questions I'd asked her before. Her answers hadn't changed, so I asked if I could go up and talk to Jackie.

"Sure, knock on her door. It's the first door at the top of the stairs."

Jackie answered at the first knock. "Is everything all right?"

"Fine, I just want to ask you a few more questions."

"I saw that woman badgering you." Jackie nodded toward her window, which faced out toward the street.

"Tina has it in for me."

"I've had my own run-ins with journalists," she said with some fire in her eyes.

"I understand that the production is shutting down

tomorrow?"

"Tomorrow's filming will wrap up the tenth episode of the season. We have two more and are just going to use some footage and interviews that we have in the archive to do those."

"My wife will be disappointed that the show is ending."

"We've had a good run. The other producers agreed that we would be better off to dedicate this season to Scott and call it quits rather than try to milk a couple more seasons out of it."

"Did you ever consider replacing Scott?"

From Jackie's expression, I could tell she knew who I was referring to.

"Jake? Don't make me laugh. His acting is minor league. He's a good cameraman who should stick to his skill set and be happy he got a little bit of airtime."

"Do you think he really believed, that with Scott out of the way, there was a chance you'd let him be the replacement?"

"If so, he's a bigger fool than I thought he was."

"What's going to happen to Kayla?" I asked.

Jackie didn't react the way the others had. Instead, there was a sadness in her eyes.

"I'll see that she gets some help. I've talked to her parents, so they understand what's happened to her."

"The other members of the cast and crew aren't as sympathetic as you are."

"Empathy is in short supply these days. What some of them can't comprehend is that while there was never a chance that Scott was going to take the relationship with Kayla seriously, she didn't know that. To her, it feels like she lost a loved one. They need to learn what that kind of pain is like." Jackie spoke with conviction.

I could see that there was some real personal pain behind her feelings. Of course, she was right. If Kayla really was the naïve woman she presented herself to be, then she would be feeling real pain now. I wished I could feel more sympathy for her. *It would help if Kayla wasn't so annoying in her grief,* I thought.

"Kayla is lucky that you're looking after her," I said.

"It's the least I can do. In a way, I got everyone into this mess when I picked up the show." She sighed.

"I'll need a list of any of Scott's romantic partners and anyone who was hurt by his actions. That includes any relationships he caused to break up due to his actions."

I saw an odd hesitation in Jackie's reaction. She seemed to freeze for a moment before giving me another sad smile.

"I'll do my best, but there were so many of them. I'll go back over what I know with some of the crew who've been with the show the longest and send you a list. I also have some emails that were sent to the company from people who were angry with him."

"Did the show ever investigate any of the claims?"

"No one ever claimed he forced himself on them. Most of the emails were from men who were angry that Scott had had affairs with their wives or girlfriends. One that I remember was from a parent. There were even a couple from women who wanted us to make him see them again. I responded to each of them and explained to them that they had no legal recourse."

"Still, I would think that there was a moral obligation on the show's part…"

"Scott had a contract that was very specific. He had to actually break the law in order to be terminated. We had the right to take him off the show for any reason, but if we did that, he was entitled to full compensation under his contract. I should have argued for him to be removed from the show and paid off, but I don't think the executive producers would have been very keen on the idea. Scott was popular and, after the second year, his agent had negotiated a nice salary."

"It's always money."

"In the real world, that's often what it comes down to."

"Are those your parents?" I had been casually looking

around the room and noticed a few pictures on the nightstand. I pointed toward the center one, where an older couple were holding hands in front of a sign for a national forest.

"Yep. Dad always wanted to work in one of the national forests."

"Who's this?" I pointed to a younger man in a flannel shirt and jeans, standing beside a pickup truck.

"Royce. My ex-husband."

"Not many women carry around a picture of their ex-husbands." I smiled.

"He's a nice guy. We hit a few road bumps. Sadly, we were both too inwardly focused to keep the marriage alive. I still see him a couple of times a year."

"Is King his name?"

"No, it's my maiden name," Jackie said.

The other pictures were of Jackie on the set of various productions with friends.

"It's nice that you carry a piece of home with you," I said.

"I found out long ago that if you're going to spend a portion of your life travelling, you should take a few photos to remind you of what's important."

"Has Cody Morgan gone home?"

I saw her tense up.

"He's required to be on set tomorrow, and I won't be sorry to see the back of him."

"Cody seems like a nice enough guy."

"Like Kayla, he doesn't seem to have a good grasp of reality. At least Kayla is pining after a man, not a monster." She sounded more irritated than I would have thought.

"I can see that he gets under your skin."

She took a couple of deep breaths.

"I take my job on this show seriously, and he's made it much harder to do my job."

"As actor or producer?"

There was another slight hesitation.

"Both. His insistence that we're lying to the public..."

She threw up her hands. "I didn't know there were people in the world who still think reality TV is real. I had to explain to him a dozen times that the show is entertainment. He also has a nasty habit of lurking around where he shouldn't."

"Cody is a true believer. I gather he's spent a lot of his time sitting in the woods waiting to catch a glimpse of Bigfoot."

"I get it. I do. Doesn't make it easier to deal with. One thing I won't miss about the show are the crazy people. I've had to humor people who are, frankly, looney."

"Text me where you'll be filming tomorrow. Mick or I might want to come by. I would like to talk to Cody one more time."

I asked a few more questions, then thanked her and left her putting her suitcase up on the bed and getting ready to pack.

Downstairs, Mick had finished questioning Eli and Emerald Wolfe, who had come down for a cup of coffee while I was talking to Jackie. Before we left, we double-checked everyone's home address and phone numbers.

On the way to the front door, I took a minute to look out the window to make sure that Tina wasn't lurking outside to ambush us. I'd had about enough of her.

"I don't like watching our suspects fly away," Mick said as we walked out to the car.

"Nothing we can do to stop them. We'll ask them to write up statements and send them to us. At least that way we'll have statements to compare with any future interviews or testimony they might make later." I was telling Mick things he already knew, but I was just running it over in my own head, trying to see the best path forward.

"I've done background on all of them. Nothing jumps out at me. A few minor criminal offences. Em, the writer, has a possession charge that he pleaded down to a misdemeanor. Gabby got in a very public fight with her husband, now ex-husband, and they both got charged for public drunkenness and disturbing the peace. Dani's finances are a shambles. They've all had the usual mix of ups and downs. Guess this is going to be a down time now that they've lost their jobs."

"Put all the background information in our shared folder. I'll read through it tonight and see if I can come up with anything."

CHAPTER TWENTY

The sun was below the horizon by the time I got home. Cara met me at the door and gave me a bigger than usual hug as Alvin squeezed by and trotted down the steps to do his business.

"It rained here." I was looking at the wet deck and water still dripping off the roof.

"Helped cool the house." Cara was leaning in and holding my hand as we watched Alvin finish and come trotting back up the stairs. Being a Pug, he didn't like being out in the Florida humidity any longer than necessary.

"You seem very affectionate tonight."

"I'm always affectionate," she said, holding on to my arm as we went inside.

"Is everything all right?"

She sighed. "I'm worried about you."

"Me?" I was surprised.

"All this craziness with Tina Knightly." The way Cara said it made me think there was more to her concern than she was letting on.

"What happened?" I asked.

"Nothing... really."

"Talk to me. What?"

"She came to the clinic this morning."

"Tina Knightly came to the clinic? Why?"

"She was trying to ask me questions. There was a cameraman too."

I remembered the question Tina had shouted out to me about Cara. "Why didn't you tell me earlier?"

"Because your face is bright red now, and you're growling." She placed her hand on my chest.

I took a couple of deep breaths to calm down.

"I admit the woman is getting under my skin. But she had no right to come harass you at work."

"Dr. Barnhill came out from the examining rooms and told her to get her ass out of his clinic before he turned a rabid dog loose on her."

"He didn't?" I smiled at the thought of Dr. Barnhill, who was close to retirement age, threatening Tina with rabid dogs he didn't have.

"I think it was the look on his face that convinced her to leave. I've never seen him so angry."

"He's got a soft spot for you," I told her.

Cara smiled and stepped back. "I'm sorry. You must be starving."

"Now that you mention it."

I ate half of a baked chicken that Cara had brought home, along with a couple of biscuits and the macaroni and cheese she'd cooked. Actually, I didn't get to eat all of the chicken, as Ghost and Ivy came and begged their fair share.

I spent an hour with Cara watching TV. I tried to take my mind off of the case and Tina Knightly, but I don't even remember what we watched.

"You want to work." Cara gave my hand a squeeze.

"I don't *want* to. I just can't keep my mind from going back to the two murders. Mick was going to share some files. If I put in a couple of hours looking over then, I might be able to get some sleep."

"When are you going to talk to your dad?"

"You have that backward. I would have talked to him

today, but he wasn't having it."

"Is he that angry?"

"Look at it from his viewpoint. He tells me not to stir up the Tina Knightly hornet's nest, but the first chance I get, I give it a good kick. Knightly goes on a predictable rampage, and Dad loses one of his biggest assets and best friends at the office."

"I see your point."

"I half expected to be suspended. I think the only reason he didn't was because it would have looked like Tina won. And as mad as he is at me, I can only imagine how furious he is at her."

Cara got up and gave me a kiss.

"Study your files. I'm going to see if I can set up a drug deal." She grinned.

"We would be living higher on the hog if you were pulling down drug-dealer money." I gave her the best smile I could muster.

I went to the kitchen table and opened my laptop. Mick was true to his word, and there were a couple dozen new files in our shared folder. I was surprised at how much work Mick had accomplished. I had always thought of him as a good burglary investigator who liked his little niche in the office. It wasn't until I'd taken over CID that I'd learned just how much he hated the routine burglary investigations he'd been stuck with for years. Now, given a complex murder investigation, he was putting in the type of hours I'd expect from an ambitious young investigator.

As I looked at the files, my first instinct was to concentrate on the suspects that I thought had the strongest motives. I decided to go against that impulse and go through each person's background without regard to whether I thought they were a viable suspect or not. The only ones I put on the backburner were the three men who had been at the bar the night Scott Nicholl disappeared. They couldn't have killed Scott unless our assumptions were completely off-base.

The younger members of the crew had the smallest files, which was what I would have expected. Fewer ex-wives and husbands, less time to go bankrupt or commit petty crimes.

I wasn't even sure what I was looking for. I found Arianne's background interesting. She'd been in the Army for six years. Got into Ranger school but didn't make it through the program. Still, anyone who could get to Ranger school wasn't a person you could take for granted. She clearly would have the means to take out Nicholl and Mendoza. Motive was the problem with Arianne. Maybe she'd taken her affair with Nicholl more seriously than she was saying. Could she have been so angry over the attention he was paying to Kayla that it had set her off?

Emerald Wolfe, whose real name was Conner Duncan, had grown up in a very religious family. His father was a preacher with a sizable congregation in Huntsville, Alabama. Em had gone to New York University on a tennis scholarship. Again, someone who had the means. But what about a motive? Would there have been something in his religious upbringing? Was he repulsed by Nicholl's womanizing?

Jackie had gone to USC and studied film. Her dad was a forester, and her mother was a stay-at-home mom who had encouraged Jackie to try out for plays and musicals at school. She'd met her husband in film school, and they'd married right after graduation. After their daughter, Sylvia, was born, the family moved to Atlanta where her husband worked for a recording studio. When Sylvia was ten years old, Jackie went back to work at the same studio as her husband. She worked as a liaison and producer, creating partnerships between the recording studio and several film studios that were doing business in Georgia.

Everything seemed to be going well for them. Their daughter even followed in her parents' footsteps. After Sylva graduated from high school, she went to work for a studio in California, but then things went horribly wrong. She died of a drug overdose which the coroner had ruled as accidental.

Their marriage broke up and, three years later, Jackie became the star and producer of *The Big Search*. She was in good physical shape and was probably capable of the murders. I knew she had the opportunity, but what would be her motive?

Jake was a rich kid from a rich family until his dad's company went bankrupt. After that, the family imploded and Jake went to live with his mother in Miami. He got into trouble several times as a kid. Since he was a juvenile, the file had been sealed, but Mick had made contact with a family member who told him that it had involved stealing. Nothing big, just habitual. Seems Jake didn't like going without. For a year, he went to live with his dad, but came back to live with his mom until he graduated from high school. He was in the drama club in high school and college.

His degree was in film from the University of Central Florida in Orlando, and he'd worked at different studios in Florida while auditioning for numerous acting roles. He'd appeared in a lot of experimental and student films, but nothing that ever got on the big or little screen. When *The Big Search* was looking for a cameraman, he'd applied and gotten the job.

Did his envy and ambition rise to the level of murder? He had the means, a motive and the opportunity. He had to stay near the top of the list of possible suspects.

Ivy came and walked over the laptop, giving my eyes a break as I convinced her to settle down in the chair next to me.

Cody Morgan's file was noteworthy. He'd been more than tangentially involved in a couple of murder investigations while he was working for Kay Lamberton. His Bigfoot passion was the overarching theme of his life. He had an extensive website and his credentials as a Bigfoot researcher were as impressive as anyone's could be, considering. Physically, even at his age, I was sure he could have carried out the murders.

Mick had checked with the Roads Best motel where

Cody was staying, but their CCTV coverage was spotty at best. He could have slipped out without being noticed anytime he wanted. Motive? He hated the production. But did he hate it enough to kill the star? Scott's death appeared to have killed the show too. I admitted to myself that I would have been more focused on Cody as a suspect if he hadn't had people I respected vouching for him.

And where was he now? Mick and I had tried to call him, but he'd ignored our phone calls. Maybe he had committed the murders and skipped town. Of course, Tina could have gotten to him, and he might have been hiding from her and the other reporters.

My phone buzzed and I looked at the number. It was a reporter from WTHA, but not Tina. I almost didn't answer, but Buck Garrett had always been a standup guy and did his best to present the news honestly.

"I wanted to give you a tip," Buck said after we exchanged greetings.

"That's a switch. You're usually looking for a tip from me."

"I'm feeling sorry for you. You've been given the full Tina treatment. Look, I saw her talking to Deputy Greer. I know he's been suspended, and my guess is he's the one feeding her information about you and your father."

I should have known that Greer and Tina would find each other.

"I appreciate the intel."

"Appreciate it enough to tip me off when you find out who killed Nicholl and Mendoza. Mendoza was a nice guy. I tried to warn him about doing extracurricular work for Tina. He just kept insisting that his family needed the money."

"Will you be a witness that Tina was paying Mendoza for work that was off the books?"

"I'll consider it. She has a lot of power with the station's owners. They think she could go national."

"That's all the world needs right now."

When I went back to the files, I kept feeling like I'd read

something that should have been a red flag.

"You need to rest." Cara came up behind me and hugged me.

"I don't have the strength to argue."

As I stood up, my phone buzzed again. It was Pete. I gave Cara a *What can I do?* look and she rolled her eyes, smiling like an indulgent parent.

"What's up?" I asked Pete.

"I just put a couple of pictures in a file. Check them out."

I sat back down and pulled up the folder we used to share files. Cara sat down in the chair that Ivy had just left.

There were two new photos. From their names, I knew they were pictures from our crime scene unit. When I opened them, they both showed the utility room where Mendoza had been killed. One was taken before the murder, and the other after it.

"I've got them side by side. What am I looking for?" I asked Pete.

"Zoom in on the dryer in both pictures," he told me.

I looked at the pre-Mendoza picture first. When I zoomed in, I could see a white blur in the upper right-hand corner of the dryer. The angle in the second, post-Mendoza picture was much better, but I couldn't see anything in the dryer.

"What is that?" I asked Pete.

"I can't see it well enough to tell. I've tried a couple of different enhancement techniques, but the glass door of the dryer obscures it. All I know is that there was something in the dryer the morning after Nicholl went missing that wasn't there the day Mendoza's body was found."

Cara could overhear our conversation and moved the laptop so she could see the images.

"It's easy to leave a pair of underwear or a sock in the dryer," she said, peering at the image.

"That's my guess," Pete said.

"The killer swam back to shore from where the boat went down and needed to dry their clothes," I suggested.

"Didn't you say that someone got a text wanting to know when they were coming back to the house?" Pete asked.

"Whoever sent that text wanted to make sure that they had enough time to dry their clothes," I said.

"And they left something behind," Cara added.

"Which is why they came back to the house," Pete said, finishing the thought we'd all had.

"That's one mystery solved."

I thanked Pete. Then, after assuring Cara that it would be my last call, I rang Mick to tell him what Pete had found.

When I hung up, Cara took my hand and pulled me from the table. I closed the laptop and followed her to the bedroom, where I stripped down and headed for the bathroom to take a long, hot shower.

Cara waited to turn off the light until I'd crawled into bed.

When I turned to her and gave her a light kiss, I told her, "Sorry, that's all I have the energy for."

"I know," she said softly and gently stroked my face.

"I'm not sure if the exhaustion is more physical or mental."

"Would you get mad if I did a Pollyanna and told you everything is going to be fine?"

"Say it three times and make it so." I laid my head on the pillow and watched her smile as she told me three times that everything would be fine.

"Now go to sleep." She gave me one last kiss before turning out the light.

I would have been surprised by how fast I fell asleep if I hadn't been asleep. What didn't surprise me was when I woke up at four o'clock and my mind began to churn over all the details we'd gathered about the murders and the people involved in them.

I struggled not to toss and turn. I tried to go back to sleep, but my brain wasn't having any of it. Jake, Kayla, Dani, Gabby, Em, Arianne and Jackie. Dirk, Koby and Eli were at the bar on the night Scott had been killed, so I felt comfortable that they could be set aside as murder suspects.

With my eyes closed, I went over my last walkthrough of each house. I was convinced I'd seen a clue going through their rooms that hadn't registered with me at the time.

I thought of all the rooms I'd seen. Em's room had been messy like a teenager's. In Kayla's room, she'd been the center of attention, with pills on the nightstand and a phone and tablet on the bed. The room that Jake and Koby shared showed evidence of both their interests. Jake's side had smelled of grooming products, underscoring the fact that the man was centered on himself, while Koby's side was full of sound equipment and his high-end laptop and headphones. In Jackie's room, her laptop had been set up on one side of the room, and those framed pictures had been set on the bedside table, almost quaint in this day when everyone carried every photo they'd ever taken around on their phones. Jackie's pictures were sentimental. Even the one of her ex-husband. What was it about that tableau that rang false?

My eyes flew open, and my heartbeat scaled up to a fast-paced thumping. I looked at my watch and saw that it was almost five.

I had to think this through. What evidence did I have? None, but I felt the pieces of the puzzle fitting together neatly in my mind. For the next hour, I tried to see all the angles and come up with a plan for the next day.

Daylight was barely coming through the bedroom window when I finally got up from the bed.

"I know you've been awake for hours," Cara mumbled from her side of the bed. From the foot of the bed, I heard a couple of snuffles before Alvin resumed snoring.

"Sorry," I whispered.

"Love you," she said and rolled back over.

I shaved and showered before dressing quickly and going into the kitchen where the two cats were looking at me with sleepy eyes. Sleepy or not, they still wanted their breakfast, so I fed them and ate a quick bowl of cereal before heading to the office.

On the way, I stopped by the Roads Best motel by the interstate where Cody was staying. His truck wasn't in the parking lot, so I stopped in and talked to the yawning clerk sitting on a sofa in the office. The young man was one of the dozen family members who helped run the hotel. No more than twenty-five, he looked up from his phone when I entered the office.

"I'm looking for Cody Morgan," I said. My star was hooked on my belt, which caused the clerk to look more alert. I assured him that Cody wasn't wanted for anything. "He's been helping us out with an investigation and I haven't been able to get ahold of him," I explained.

"The murder of Scott Nicholl?" he asked, giving me his full attention now that it was something he was interested in.

"I don't see his truck outside."

"He's the old guy with the sasquatch on his hat. I tried to talk to him about the show. He's not a very talkative guy."

"No, he's not. Has he checked out?"

"Not since I've been here." He got up and went to the monitor behind the desk. "No. He's supposed to check out today. Which is fine 'cause we're already getting traffic for the Fourth of July."

"When was the last time you saw him?"

"Yesterday morning when I was getting off. I saw him standing by his truck."

"Can you call his room?"

He picked up the phone and dialed.

"He isn't answering."

As I pulled out of the parking lot, I added Cody to my list of concerns. No one was at the office when I arrived, so I did my best to work on other business until Mick came in. At seven, I texted him and asked him to come straight to my office when he got to work.

"What's up?" Mick asked, sticking his head into my office at seven-thirty.

"I want you to play devil's advocate. I put two and two

together last night and I'm not sure it adds up to four. I'll lay it out and you try to convince me I'm wrong."

An hour later, Mick was nodding his head.

"We need to get our hands on a piece of direct evidence." He frowned. "And right now, I'm not sure where that's going to come from."

"She's smart, but she doesn't know how much we know or don't know."

"There's always the classic lie-to-the-suspect approach. We can tell her we have camera footage that shows… whatever we want. Her creeping through the woods or driving the boat."

"I'm willing to include that as part of our interview tactics; though, like I said, she's smart."

We spent the next two hours like mice and men, laying plans.

"I think we're as ready as we're going to be," I said, then texted Arianne to confirm the location where they were filming. Within a couple of minutes, I got a text back with an address on the far side of the county and we headed out to my car.

CHAPTER TWENTY-ONE

They were shooting by an old barn a quarter mile past a small farmhouse. A narrow driveway ran through a field to the barn. Calling the structure a barn was being generous. Half of the roof had fallen in, but even I could see how this would make a dramatic backdrop for a Bigfoot story.

My blood pressure soared when I saw the WTHA van parked by the production company's vehicles.

"I'm not in the mood to deal with Tina Knightly this morning," I growled.

"Don't do anything you'll regret," Mick warned me.

"Like spitting onion at her?"

"Touché," he said and frowned.

I blame the next fifteen minutes' worth of missteps and my lack of situational awareness on my mind being focused on the WTHA van and a possible confrontation with Tina. The last thing I wanted was for her to get wind of who our suspect was.

We parked away from the news van and got out of the car. The whole time, I expected Tina to come charging across the field at us. Two hundred feet away, we could see members of the production company standing around the entrance to the barn. If I'd been paying close attention to them, I might have thought that the way they were just standing there and not looking at us was a bit odd. As it was, Mick and I walked toward the barn paying more attention to the cars and the news van than to the people.

We were twenty-five yards away when Jackie stepped out of the barn. I froze and my hand automatically reached for my hip. She was holding a semi-automatic shotgun at waist level.

"Don't!" she yelled. The gun in her hands wasn't pointing at us. The end of the barrel was aimed at Arianne's stomach, which was less than three feet away. I had no idea what type of shot the gun was loaded with, but it didn't matter. If she pulled the trigger, Arianne would be dead before she hit the ground.

I looked over at Mick, who was in an identical stance to mine, with his hand six inches from his Glock nestled in its holster.

"We're going to all move very slowly," Jackie yelled at us, her voice loud and firm. "Start taking off your pants."

Mick and I glanced at each other.

"Now! Down to your underwear. I don't want to find out ten minutes from now that you had a hideaway." Nothing about her words or actions suggested uncertainty. "Start by unfastening your belt and let your pants fall to the ground, then step out and away from them."

With zero options available to us, we both complied. My pants dropped to the ground, along with my phone and primary gun. Mick lost both his primary and the smaller single-stack Glock 43 he kept in the small of his back as a backup gun.

As I stepped out of my pants, I knew that my backup gun was clearly visible strapped to my ankle.

"You…" Jackie nodded at Dani. "Bring me their guns and phones."

"But the one on his ankle…" Obviously terrified, Dani looked younger than she was. She could have been a frightened teenager.

"Take it off. Don't act stupid," Jackie ordered her.

Timidly, Dani shuffled her way over to us. That's when I noticed that all of the cast and crew had their legs hobbled with shoelaces or other pieces of rope and string. Reluctantly, Dani did as Jackie had ordered her.

"Turn out all of their pockets," Jackie instructed Dani. To us, she said, "Raise your arms high above your heads and slowly turn around."

With the sun to our backs, she could see through our shirts, proving to her that we didn't have any other tools hidden away.

"Be careful. Those guns are loaded and have a round in the chamber," I told Dani. This had the effect of making her even more nervous and awkward with the guns. "Just make sure they stay in their holsters."

"Put your pants back on," Jackie told us before she turned to Dani and told her, "Drop the guns and phones in the hole."

We watched Dani go over to a twelve-inch metal pipe sticking about a foot out of the ground and drop everything into it. I could hear the guns and phones banging and rattling down the pipe for at least six seconds.

"What's this all about?" I asked, taking notice of the people I didn't see—Tina Knightly, Cody Morgan and Kayla Alvarado.

"You're a smart guy. What do you think?" Jackie answered.

"I think you killed Scott Nicholl and Saint Mendoza."

Jackie turned to Koby. "Take some of that old hay string and tie their feet together. Leave it long enough that they can move, but not too long." She turned back to us. "I didn't mean to kill Mendoza."

"I'm sure that will make his family feel better," Mick said while he watched Koby tie his feet together.

Jackie's face turned red. "I'm not that sorry about Mendoza. He was working for that reporter."

"Where is she?" I asked.

"Over in her van." A wicked smile spread across Jackie's face and, for the first time, I realized what a great actress she was. All this time, she'd come across as a kind and reasonable person. Now she'd let her mask fall and her face reflected a rage teetering on insanity.

When I looked at the van, the first thing I noticed was that the windows were rolled up and it was parked in the wide-open pasture with the rest of the cars. The outside temperature was already above eighty-five and climbing higher.

"Is she alive?" I asked.

"Probably." Jackie shrugged.

"She'll bake in there," Mick said.

"I have an app on my phone linked to a thermometer I put in the van. I checked it just before you showed up and it was a little over a hundred in the van already. What happens to her now depends on you."

"Where's her cameraman?"

"I told her to come here without him. She was so hungry for some red meat on you and the murders that she didn't even hesitate. I don't understand why you would even care about her."

I didn't think it would be a good idea to tell Jackie that it was because I wasn't a psychopath like her.

"I know that Scott had something to do with your daughter's death," I said and saw her face twitch at the mention of her daughter.

"See, I knew you were a bright boy. I had a feeling the gig was up when I had to take care of that meddling Bigfoot hunter."

"You killed Cody?"

"Not yet. But I had to knock him over the head and tie him up or he would have gone running to you," she said and saw the look of concern on my face. "He's over there."

Lying on its side against the barn was what I'd assumed to be the Bigfoot costume, but now I realized that Cody Morgan was inside the costume. He was within the shade of the barn, and I couldn't see any movement.

"You put him in the Bigfoot outfit?" I asked. I didn't know why this seemed particularly odd to me at the moment, considering everything else that was going on.

"It seemed appropriately ironic," Jackie said with a bitter smile.

"Why this big production?" Mick sounded more irritated than worried.

"Production is the right word. We're going to make a movie," Jackie told him.

"We need to get Tina out of the van," I told her. "What has she done to you?"

"You are a softy," Jackie sneered. "After she dragged you and your dad and all your friends through the mud, you're still concerned for her safety." She squared up and gave me a look that would have done Medusa proud. "She's a reporter. That's enough for me. When my daughter died, I tried to get the cops, the prosecutor, lawyers, anyone to listen to me and make Scott pay for what he did. Everyone told me that he hadn't broken any laws. So I went to the TV stations and newspapers and begged them to do a story about Sylvia. After pushing and coercing, I finally talked two different journalists into doing a story. But you know what they did? They smeared her reputation and made her out to be a drug addict and a suicide. They wouldn't even mention Scott by name. All they said was that Sylvia had a crush on some man. Some man. It was Scott Nicholl, and it wasn't just a crush. He promised her that he loved her."

Unfortunately, I couldn't argue that Tina was one of the good journalists and would never treat a victim with such casual indifference. The best I could come up with was: "Murder is murder. And while Tina may be a cretin, she's still a human being and hasn't directly harmed you."

Jackie pursed her lips and stared at me with angry eyes.

"Fine. You like her so much, you can go over there and get her out of the van. Drag her over here. She can have a starring role in my film."

Before she could change her mind, I started awkwardly toward the news van, hoping I'd find Tina alive. Koby had tied my legs too close together for me to take more than half a step at a time. The amount of time it took me to cover the couple hundred feet to the van was frustrating, not to mention painful as the string cut into my ankles.

I half wondered if I was going to get to the van only to find the door locked as part of some sick joke on Jackie's part. I was relieved when it opened, and I saw a sweat-soaked Tina lying across the seat. Above the tape across her mouth, I saw her eyes move weakly toward me. At that moment, there was no anger in her eyes, just fear and confusion.

I did my best to get her out of the car, but it was difficult with her feet and hands tied. When I went to remove the gag, I heard Jackie yell over to me.

"Leave her tied up."

"I can't get her over there without untying her feet!" I yelled back in frustration.

"Drag her!" Jackie responded.

I put the back of my hand to Tina's forehead. She was pale and her skin was wet and clammy. I checked her pulse and found it weak and rapid.

"Drag her!" Jackie ordered again. "Or someone's going to be hurt real bad."

"I'm sorry," I told Tina and meant it. As much crap as she had thrown in my direction, she still didn't deserve this.

I got behind her and tried to put my hands under her arms to drag her in a way that would cause her the least pain. It didn't work. Every time I tried to hold her up and walk backward, I would stumble over my hobbled feet. We went down twice.

"Drag her, damn you!" Jackie shouted a second time before I heard a blast from her shotgun. I turned, shaken and praying that she hadn't killed anyone. She was now pointing the shotgun at Mick, but everyone looked okay. "The next shot won't be in the ground. Now drag her ass over here and make it fast."

"Sorry," I whispered to Tina.

My only real option was to grab her feet and do as Jackie had said. I told myself that the sooner I could get her into the shade, the better. A few abrasions would be a small price for her to pay if I could save her from heat stroke and Mick from being shot.

Tina grunted and moaned as I dragged her toward the barn. It was lucky for all of us that there weren't any rocks. Even stumbling over my hobbles, I managed to get her to the barn in a couple of minutes.

"Drop her over there." Jackie pointed next to Cody in the Bigfoot suit. He still hadn't moved.

"She needs some water," I told Jackie.

"For Pete's sake! There's a cooler in the barn." She pointed with the shotgun and backed away so I wouldn't come close to her as I went to the cooler.

"Why are you doing this to us? We never did anything to you or your daughter," Dani begged.

"Don't act innocent. I heard you whine about helping Kayla. I saw you roll your eyes when I asked you all to watch her so she wouldn't hurt herself. Everyone here would have been happy if Kayla had killed herself, as long as you all could make this stupid show and stare at your phones while posting whatever inane ideas popped into your heads. It was lack of compassion like yours that allowed my precious daughter to… to slip away." There was a hitch in her voice as she spoke. Years of pain had festered into an intense hatred for anyone she could blame for her daughter's death.

"What did you forget in the dryer?" Mick asked her.

"So you're not as dumb as you look." Jackie frowned. "A sock."

"I don't understand," Koby said and received a glare from Jackie.

"Your buddy here killed Mendoza for a sock," Mick said.

Now the entire cast and crew were looking at her.

I grabbed two bottles of water and managed to stuff

them into my pockets. Next, I scooped up ice from the chest in both hands and shuffled back to Tina, who appeared only marginally better. I put the ice on her wrists and neck, trying to get her body temperature down.

"After Jackie killed Scott, she put him in the boat and went out on the lake to get rid of the body, at least temporarily," Mick said. "Next, she texted Dirk to see when the group at the bar would be coming home. When she knew she had enough time, she sank the boat, swam back to the house and stripped down so she could dry her clothes in the dryer. She'd stashed some extra clothes at the house the first day in case she couldn't finish drying her wet clothes. She changed into the new clothes, ready to race out if Eli and Dirk came home early. When her clothes were dry, she bundled them up and went back to her house. It was only later that she noticed she'd lost a… You said it was a sock?"

"If you stashed a second set of clothes, why did you bother drying your wet clothes?" Jake asked.

"That's enough talking," Jackie growled.

"I'll tell you why." Mick was trying to keep her attention focused on him. "She was going to commit the perfect murder. She couldn't take the wet clothes back to her house where someone might ask questions about them. The plan was to kill Scott and leave nothing of hers behind. If she'd thrown the clothes in the water, put them in the trash or buried them, there was a chance that they would be found and traced back to her. Drying them and taking them back to her room was part of her master plan of revenge."

"You talk too much." Jackie sounded furious now. "It's time for us to start our little production. Have you finished with the script?" she yelled over to Em, who was holding a yellow legal pad and looking frantic.

"How can I write under this kind of pressure? I never write with a pen and paper." His voice was high and frantic.

"Come on, come on. I gave you those notes."

"Her perfect murder turned into a farce when she went back for the sock and ran into Mendoza," Mick pointed out.

I pulled the tape on Tina's mouth aside as best I could so she could drink some of the water.

"You bastard!" Jackie spat. Mick had managed to ruffle her feathers. "Mendoza was spying on the house. He snuck in and surprised me. I didn't have a choice."

Tina's color was better, and she seemed more focused.

"'I didn't have a choice' is the mantra of killers everywhere." Mick was doing a good job of keeping Jackie's attention. I just hoped he wouldn't taunt her into killing him or someone else.

With Tina looking better, I moved over to Cody. When I was next to him, I could see his chest moving up and down under the heavy suit. He was alive, at least. I pulled the head of the costume off of him. He was covered in sweat and barely conscious. Blood caked his head. I still had one of the bottles of water and poured some on his face, which caused his eyes to flicker open. He opened his mouth, and I tilted the water bottle up for him to drink.

"Hey! Florence Nightengale, leave him alone and come back here," Jackie yelled to me. "I'm about sick of your sidekick and his big mouth."

"Jackie, how did you get like this?" Eli had been standing in the background, studying what was going on around him.

"Eli, I've been like this ever since Sylvia died." Jackie sounded exasperated.

"Not when we started," Eli argued.

"Why do you think I produced this show? All of this was about Scott. I've been planning this for years. Giving Scott what he deserved. Everything was planned out. I know this area of Florida and spent time here. I came down here six months ago and scouted out the houses, looking for the perfect setting. I made one mistake. A sock left in a dryer. That's all it took to unravel everything. I still might have salvaged my little project if it hadn't been for a bunch of jerks. You two." She swung the shotgun toward Mick and then me. "And the one in the Bigfoot suit."

"What did Cody do?" I asked. I knew the longer we

dragged this out, the better our chances were that the cavalry would show up. My car had a department GPS locator, so dispatch could find it, and my phone had an app they could use. The only question was how long it would be before someone became worried enough about Mick and me that they came looking for us.

"Followed her." Cody had recovered enough to talk and was sitting up. "She kept going out in the woods. I wondered why and followed her."

"What were you trying to get rid of?" I asked her.

"Her clothes. Not the ones from the first night. The ones from the night she killed Mendoza. They had bleach marks on them. Didn't they?" Cody said.

"I should have killed him." She was looking at Cody malevolently. I watched the gun barrel move in his direction and wondered at what point I'd have to make a move, even if it was doomed to fail. Could I let her shoot one of the other people without at least trying to stop her? Mick and I were both twenty feet away from her with our feet hobbled. We'd never be able to rush her without falling down or getting shot.

"You really screwed this up from the beginning," Mick told her. "See, what you failed to plan for was the unexpected."

This got the gun pointed at Mick again.

"Smart boy. Enough of this! Em, is the script done?"

"No!"

"It's good enough!" Jackie barked. "We'll adlib anything you didn't include. Bring it over here."

"This is crazy," I told her. "What are you going to gain by putting people through this farce?"

"I want to show them what Scott did to my daughter. We're going to act it out." She grabbed the yellow legal pad out of Em's hands. Now she was holding the shotgun in one hand instead of two, which improved our odds of getting to her before she could react.

I looked around at the others. Would any of them help?

Dani was the closest to her. She looked up and made eye contact with me. She was ten feet behind Jackie, who was reading the script. Dani looked down at her own hand and opened it just slightly. My heart jumped. In her palm was my four-inch-long pocketknife.

Dani must have gotten the knife when she was emptying our pockets and collecting our guns and phones. I remembered Dani's sleight of hand when she'd made her phone disappear in front of my eyes. That same dexterity had enabled her to pocket the knife without Jackie seeing her do it.

Now the question was: How could I get it and what could I do with it?

"Cody doesn't look so good. I'm going to check on him," I said. Beside Cody, I would be in a position where Dani could toss me the knife without Jackie seeing, if Jackie didn't move. It was a big "if."

"He's fine," Jackie said without looking up from the script.

Cody took the cue and dropped over from his sitting position and began breathing heavily.

"I don't think he is," I said anxiously.

Jackie looked over at him.

"Check him. Give him water, but that's it," she said and watched me as I moved toward him. Once it was clear I wasn't getting closer to her, she went back to the script.

When I was next to Cody, there was a clear path for Dani to toss me the knife without Jackie seeing her do it. What I didn't know was how well Dani could throw, or how the others would react when they saw her do it.

I caught Dani's eye and made subtle throwing motions. She looked unsure. On a straight path, the knife would pass within two feet of Jackie's back. Dani shook her head, her eyes frightened. Koby, standing next to her, took the knife out of her hand. He had a slightly better angle and when I gave a nod, he tossed it across to me.

The knife made a nice arc in the air. All I needed to do

was catch it without attracting Jackie's attention. Mick had watched all of this, and I hoped he was prepared to create a distraction if things started to go bad. The throw was on the mark with the knife coming straight into the strike zone. I caught it, almost fumbled it, then managed to conceal it.

"This isn't right!" Jackie fumed, shaking the script. The shotgun was even less secure in her grip now.

I wasn't sure what my plan was, but I wanted as many players in motion as possible, so I cut the bindings on Cody's hands as carefully as I could while I pretended to give him more water. The knife sliced through the bindings, and I said a silent thank you to my grandfather, who had shown me how to use a whetstone and told me to always keep my pocketknife sharp.

Cody's eyes met mine with a mix of determination and anger. I shook my head back and forth, letting him know that he shouldn't take any action unless there was no other choice. I could see in his eyes that he didn't like me wanting him to literally sit on his hands.

Do nothing, I mouthed.

Tina, who was lying next to Cody, looked at me expectantly. There was no way I was cutting her free. We didn't need her going all loose cannon on us and sinking the ship.

I shook my head firmly, causing Tina to scowl at me behind her gag. I left the knife open and slipped it into my pocket.

"Trash!" Jackie tossed the script at a cowering Em. "Rewrite!" Her eyes were wild, and she was back to holding the shotgun in both hands. Had I lost my opportunity?

"Get away from him," Jackie scowled at me.

I was glad I hadn't cut the ties around my ankles. I stood up and hobbled back toward Mick.

"While we wait for—"

"What about Kayla?" Eli asked. I'd caught his eyes a couple of times, and I knew he was stepping in to distract Jackie.

"What about her?" Jackie swung around and faced Eli.

"Who's going to take care of her if you get yourself locked up or killed?"

"It's too late." Jackie waved the gun. I wondered what she meant. Was Kayla dead or did Jackie know that nothing could keep her from jail or the grave?

"I think you should forget this crazy idea of a movie and maybe film an explanation to Kayla instead," Eli told her.

"What do you care about her?"

"Have I ever come across as an asshole? I've got a daughter. What you said, about your daughter, about Scott and Kayla, I see that. I admit I didn't give Kayla the understanding I should have. But I see it now. And if this day ends…badly, don't you think it would be nice to leave her with an explanation? Tell her about your daughter and why you're doing this." Eli was good, leaning into his usual role on the show as the calm and rational one.

Jackie looked conflicted. She looked over at Em, who was shaking so badly that the pages of the yellow legal pad rattled.

"You're right," she told Eli. "But keep working on the rewrite!" she barked at Em.

"Jake will film it," Eli said, glancing over at Jake, who looked terrified. Jake shook his head and tried to move behind Dani. Eli pinned him down with his eyes. You could almost see the two warring factions inside Jake. I admit I was surprised when his better nature won out.

"Yeah, I can do that." Jake nodded slowly.

"Pick the shot," Jackie told him.

This seemed to help focus Jake, putting him on familiar ground.

"The barn. That side where the light's better." He pointed around the corner.

Jackie knew Jake was right. She looked back at everyone and waved the shotgun toward them.

"Move." Using the shotgun, she herded everyone around the corner. She looked at Tina and Cody and seemed satisfied to leave them on the ground. We all looked ridiculous, shuffling around the side of the barn like grownups imitating ducks.

"Not against the wall. Come on out ten feet," Jake told Jackie. She looked at us and waved the shotgun, indicating that she wanted all of us behind Jake and facing her.

This wasn't going to give me an opportunity to cut my feet free from the hobbles. I hoped that Jake or Eli could get her attention away from us.

"Make-up. Jackie, you need Gabby to clean you up some," Jake told her. He was right. She looked like the crazed fugitive she was.

Jackie looked over at Gabby.

"My box is in the barn," Gabby told her.

"Be quick." I didn't think it would be long before Jackie cracked completely.

I tried to calculate if I could drop down, cut the string from my feet and charge her all in a single action; or would I need to cut the string when I had the chance and then wait for another opportunity to charge her? It would all depend on how long she was distracted. If I miscalculated, someone could end up in bad shape. Maybe a lot of someones.

Gabby did her best to shuffle quickly into the barn to retrieve her make-up box. She stumbled a bit as she made her way back out of the barn with a box that must have weighed twenty pounds. She looked up and met my eyes for a second, causing my muscles to tense up.

I watched her as she approached the anxious Jackie, who was shifting the weight of the shotgun from arm to arm. I thought of the old saw about bringing a knife to a gunfight and knew that I had to get inside the end of the barrel of the gun before she could point it at me. What worried me the most was that, as I wrestled with the gun, she could pull the trigger and send lead in the direction of any one of the bystanders.

Jackie looked around and our eyes met. I could only hope that she didn't sense what I had planned. I gave a sidewise glance to Mick and could see that he had figured out what was about to go down. There was eagerness and resolve in his face. As soon as I saw that Jackie was looking elsewhere, I put my hand in my pocket and grasped the knife.

Six feet from Jackie, Gabby went down on her knees, half throwing the box of cosmetics toward Jackie's legs. Jackie looked down, startled. I didn't have time to think. I dropped down, sliced the thin hay string binding my feet, and lunged forward.

I kept my eyes on the shotgun as I came in close. My hand grabbed the back of Jackie's forearm and pushed it up sharply as I let my body collide with hers. I heard her give a loud grunt as we went to the ground.

I felt the shotgun come loose from her grasp as she rolled out from under me. She was quick and on her feet in a second. But she went down again when Mick, who was still hobbled, threw himself in her path. Tripping over him, she still managed to avoid his grasping hands and get back to her feet. She had gotten up twice in the time it took me to stand up with the shotgun in hand.

Jackie had passed the end of the barn and was sprinting toward the cars. I yelled for her to stop and saw no hesitation in her stride. I could have shot at her, but not knowing whether the gun as loaded with slugs, buckshot or birdshot, I lowered it instead. As I did, I became aware of two things.

Jake was on my right, camera in hand, still focused on Jackie. And Bigfoot had come from the side of the barn and was in hot pursuit of Jackie.

Cody Morgan was running on a diagonal course to intercept Jackie. Like a professional football tackle, he took his chance when he was close enough and threw himself at her. All of us watched in awe as he hit her midthigh, carrying her sidewise for five feet before they both came crashing to the ground.

"Toss me the knife!" Mick yelled at me as I started toward Bigfoot and Jackie. I underhanded it to him as I headed toward the two combatants rolling around on the ground.

Cody had hit Jackie hard enough that it had taken the wind out of her. She was moving but couldn't get to her feet. Cody didn't look much better. Both of them were still managing to pull and tug at each other.

Mick was at my side by the time I'd gotten Jackie in a hold I could keep her in.

"Check on Morgan and then go get some handcuffs out of the car," I told him.

Jackie lay with her face in the dirt, cursing and kicking while I held her down.

"Morgan's sore, but I think he's okay. I'll radio for an ambulance as well as backup," Mick said as he headed for my car.

I could hear some of the others helping Cody to his feet behind me as I continued to press Jackie down.

Ten minutes later, we had her handcuffed and were taking her over to my car.

"I should put you in the car and leave it out in the sun," I told her, remembering what she'd done to Tina. A fleeting voice in my head asked if anyone had checked on Tina. It was very fleeting.

"Nobody at the office was even worried about us." Mick frowned.

"I'd have thought Pete might have wondered where we were," I mused.

The handcuffing and the trip to the car were all overlayed with Jackie's extensive four-letter vocabulary. When we got her to the car, her mood shifted and she began to cry.

"I wish you'd killed me," she muttered through her tears. I got into the car and started the engine so I could run the air conditioner. I radioed in and asked Marti in dispatch to call Cara and tell her I'd lost my phone, was fine and would call her when I had the chance.

CHAPTER TWENTY-TWO

The next day, Mick and I were in Captain Grant's office, sitting across the desk from him.

"The prosecutor wants you to give him a comprehensive report within two days," he told us.

"We went over all the evidence with him," I said.

"And they have Jackie in jail for ten counts of false imprisonment and a dozen other charges. We have plenty of time to put together the murder cases against her," Mick added.

"The prosecutor's office kicked back your charges against Tina Knightly," Grant told us.

"Hey, those were legit charges," Mick argued.

"Everyone knows you're right about her egging Mendoza on and even paying him to break the law. Plus, she lied about it when you questioned her. The trouble is that it would look like payback on our part. On top of that, everyone in the prosecutor's office is terrified of Knightly."

I chuckled and the other two looked at me.

"At least that video has gone viral. She looks awful in it." I started to laugh out loud thinking about it.

Jake had caught *Bigfoot Captures Crazy Killer Woman* on video, and at the very end, after Bigfoot collided with Jackie,

Jake had panned the camera back to the barn and zoomed in on the tied-up, gagged and very dirty Tina Knightly. It would have been reasonable to assume that everyone would be sympathetic to this image of another victim of Jackie's rage, but whether it was because of Tina's reputation, or just because she appeared after the sidesplitting footage of Bigfoot tackling Jackie, the general consensus was that Tina looked laughable.

"Did you recover the other evidence?" Grant asked.

"Cody was able to show us where Jackie had buried the clothes she'd worn the night she killed Mendoza. While she was throwing bleach around, she'd gotten some on her pants and socks. At least half a dozen bleached-out spots were visible," Mick reported.

"Good job. Write it all up." He looked at Mick. "I want to have a word with Larry."

Grant looked at me after Mick had left.

"I want you to patch up the rift between you and the sheriff," he told me with a hard look.

"Now, you can't—" I started to say, but he interrupted me.

"Yes, I can. I can't tell the sheriff to fix it with you, but I certainly can tell you to make it right. This rift between the two of you is making it harder to get our work done. Besides, I'm sick of watching you two try and avoid each other in the halls."

"It's going to take both of us to fix it and I don't think he's feeling very forgiving." I bristled at Grant thinking he could order me to patch up my relationship with my father. This went beyond sheriff's-office business. Besides, Dad was the one being a hardass. I'd already admitted that I screwed up.

"I've told you what I expect from you." Grant waved me out of his office, and I left feeling irritated, which just pissed me off more because I should have felt great, having just overseen the arrest in a huge case.

I started to walk down the hall, then remembered that

Dad was in the building, and I didn't want to bump into him. I turned and went the longer way back to my office. After the conversation with Grant, though, a little voice inside my head was telling me that I should have just walked past Dad's office like normal. I told the little voice to shut up.

"What's he doing here?" I asked Pete when I saw Mauser lying down by my desk.

"He's just wandering the halls now that you and your dad are battling it out. I'm thinking of using him as a support dog when the doctors tell me I can start to wean myself off the crutches."

"You'll break your leg."

At that moment, Phil Eccles and Julio Ortiz walked up to my door. It was their first day back from vacation and they'd been laughing their heads off at all the drama I'd gone through with Tina.

"What's up?" I asked, not liking the grins that both of them wore.

"We just wanted to know what it was like to be stalked by Tina," Phil said.

"Lay off, guys. She's made more threats. She might just decide to do an exposé on you two. Hey, why didn't y'all come back from vacation early to help out?"

"We knew you could handle it." Phil smiled.

"I am kinda jealous that Mick got the big murder case and not me," Julio said, and I knew he was serious.

"All the excitement is over. We can get back to business as usual," I muttered.

"Which reminds me," Phil said, handing me a sheet of paper. "I already sat down with patrol, and here are your uniform responsibilities over the Fourth of July holiday."

Everyone in the department, whether they were assigned to patrol or had other permanent assignments, pitched in at holidays to cover all of the special duties. Those duties included increased sobriety road-checks, crowd and security for the parade, and handling all of the complaints about fireworks and bonfire parties.

"I wasn't sure if you're going to be riding in the parade this year," Phil said to me.

In past years, I'd ridden one of Dad's horses in the parade with the mounted posse. Dad hadn't said anything to me one way or the other about this year.

"I assume I'm not."

"That's what I figured."

An hour later, I was stewing in my office when I got a text from Jimmy. *Would you go fishing with me?*

There was an innocence about Jimmy that always brought out the best in me. *Sure. Where? When?* I replied.

Today. Dad says I can fish at the pond we're going to buy if someone is with me.

Dad and Genie had told Jimmy after they got married that he could call Dad whatever he wanted. The fact he'd decided on "dad" was fine by me. There was no way that I could be jealous of anyone as kind and good-hearted as Jimmy.

Sure. I've got a pole. Do you?

Sure.

I smiled. I didn't know he had ever been fishing.

Worms?

There was a long pause before he texted back. *I don't know where to get worms.*

I'll pick them up. I can meet you at four-thirty. That would be good since Dad would be going to the county commission meeting that night, so I wouldn't run into him.

The afternoon was hot, but a little less humidity and a nice breeze made it a perfect summer day that had me playing classic rock as I drove toward Dad's place. Jimmy was waiting in the driveway with his fishing pole in hand.

"You didn't have to wait out here," I told him.

"I didn't want to miss you." He smiled.

I held up the cup of worms I'd picked up from a bait shop that a local man had been running out of his garage for over thirty years.

"Yuck!" was Jimmy's pronouncement on worms.

We walked the same path I'd walked with Dad just a few days ago, out past the barn and down into the woods.

"Dad says I can ride Mac in the parade."

I felt a hint of irritation. Not that Jimmy would be taking my place, but that Dad hadn't bothered to talk to me about it.

"I think you and Mac will get along perfectly. You'll have a great time," I told Jimmy.

"But you always ride Mac in the parades."

"I don't mind you riding him. Anyone else, I'd be mad. But not my new brother." I gave him a big smile.

"I've been practicing on him. I think I can do it."

"Good. I'll probably see you there. They've got me working crowd-control. I'll make sure to wave to you."

"Will you wave to Dad?" His tone was serious.

"Sure."

"Even though you two are mad at each other?"

Hearing him say it made me feel a little silly about the whole thing.

"Yes," I promised him.

"Good. I don't like you two being mad with each other."

We entered the clearing and walked down to the bank of the pond. Jimmy wouldn't watch as I put the worms on our hooks. Both of our poles were old-fashioned reels, and we were using simple red-and-white bobbers. After our first cast, we sat down on the ground to wait for a bite.

I noticed that Jimmy seemed nervous and wasn't talking about his job as a bag boy at Publix, his friends or the upcoming holiday. I got a funny feeling that was confirmed when he turned and yelled, "Hi!"

I didn't have to look to know I'd been duped.

"Hey, Dad." Jimmy started to get up, but remembered his pole just in time to keep it from falling into the pond.

"Jimmy, you didn't tell me you'd invited Larry." Dad was trying to sound stern, but I knew that he was like me and couldn't be too hard on Jimmy.

"I thought we could all fish," Jimmy said in a way that let

us know he was aware he was pushing his luck. I glanced over my shoulder and saw that Dad was carrying his favorite pole, one that I could remember from the first time he'd taught me how to cast a line.

Neither Dad nor I said a word for a couple of minutes. I tried to relax, but we weren't exactly having an *Andy Griffith* moment.

Finally, Dad said, "Hand me a worm."

Jimmy smiled and handed the cup to Dad.

"I thought you would be at the county commission meeting," I said.

"I decided to let Captain Grant go. If he's going to be my new right-hand man, he's going to have to get used to the politics."

Ten minutes later, after a couple of nibbles on our lines and Dad and I trying to maintain the chilly atmosphere in the warm summer air, I said neutrally, "Jimmy says he's going to be riding Mac in the parade."

"Probably should have told you." Dad's tone was equally emotionless.

"I think it's a good idea," I said with a little less frost. "If you think he's ready."

Dad turned and looked at me.

"We've been going for regular rides. They're getting along well."

"Mac's a good boy."

"He and I get along great," Jimmy assured us.

"I'm sorry that I screw up sometimes," I told Dad.

"You don't screw up any more than I do. I just wish you'd let me help you avoid a few pratfalls."

We heard the sound of voices, and Dad and I turned to see Cara and Genie coming down the path.

"I think we've been had," I told Dad, and saw the big smile on Jimmy's face.

"They put me up to it!" Jimmy laughed uncontrollably in a way we all found infectious.

"If you think we were going to let you two keep up your

little grudge match, you have another thought coming," Genie said.

"I'm just along for the ride," Cara told me, but her bright smile belied her words.

"I bet." I smiled.

"Jimmy, I don't think we're the only ones fishing in this pond," Dad said, and nudged Jimmy's arm before pointing to a sixty-foot pine tree snag standing just inside the tree line on the other side of the pond. At the very top of the snag, looking majestic, was a bald eagle.

"Wow!" Jimmy said in a half whisper. "That's an eagle!" He got a serious look on his face. "He's fishing too."

"Maybe not right now, but I think that's why he's hanging out here," Dad told him. "Fish is one of their favorite foods."

"I like fish too." Jimmy smiled before he turned serious again. "What if we catch all the fish? What will he eat?"

"We'll leave him plenty of fish," Dad assured him with a hug.

"From the looks of things, y'all haven't managed to catch anything yet." Genie laughed and ruffled Jimmy's hair.

"This is going to be a great Fourth of July. Can we go see the fireworks after the parade?" Jimmy asked.

"I think we can do that," Dad said.

Cara leaned into me, and I held her close as I watched the eagle cock its head at us, then soar up into the clouds.

Larry Macklin returns in:

Labor Day's Revelations
A Larry Macklin Mystery–Book 21

ACKNOWLEDGMENTS

As always, thanks to my wife, Melanie, for her editing skills and support; to H. Y. Hanna for her inspiration, assistance and encouragement; and to all the fans of the series. Larry never would have come this far without all of you!

Original Cover Concept by H. Y. Hanna
Cover Design by Florida Girl Design, Inc.
www.gobookcoverdesign.com

ABOUT THE AUTHOR

A. E. Howe lives and writes on a farm in the wilds of North Florida with his wife, horses and more cats than he can count. He received a degree in English Education from the University of Georgia and is a produced screenwriter and playwright. His first published book was *Broken State*. The Larry Macklin Mysteries is his first series and he released the Baron Blasko Mysteries in summer 2018. His most recent series, the Mortician Murder Mysteries, was launched in 2022.

The first book in the Macklin series, *November's Past*, was awarded two silver medals in the 2017 President's Book Awards, presented by the Florida Authors & Publishers Association; the ninth book, *July's Trials*, was awarded two silver medals in 2018. Howe is a member of the Mystery Writers of America, and was co-host of the "Guns of Hollywood" podcast for four years on the Firearms Radio Network. When not writing, Howe enjoys riding, competitive shooting and working on the farm.